INDIGO

Also by Gina Linko
Flutter

INDIGO

GINA LINKO

RANDOM HOUSE 🏠 NEW YORK

Text copyright © 2013 by Gina Linko
Jacket art copyright © Rich Legg/Vetta/Getty Images

Visit us on the Web! randomhouse.com/teens

Educators and librarians, for a variety of teaching tools, visit us at RHTeachersLibrarians.com

Library of Congress Cataloging-in-Publication Data
Linko, G. J.
Indigo / Gina Linko. – First edition.
p. cm.
Summary: Seventeen-year-old Corrine's ability to read people's physio-electricity seems to
have brought about her sister's death, but a new friend, Rennick, thinks it might actually be a
sixth sense that can be controlled.
ISBN 978-0-449-81283-9 (trade) – ISBN 978-0-449-81284-6 (lib. bdg.) –
ISBN 978-0-449-81285-3 (ebook)
[1. Psychic ability–Fiction. 2. Grief–Fiction. 3. Sisters–Fiction. 4. Love–Fiction.
5. New Orleans (La.)–Fiction.] I. Title.
PZ7.L66288Ind 2013 [Fic]–dc23 2013002699

Printed in the United States of America

10 9 8 7 6 5 4 3 2 1

First Edition

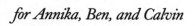

for Annika, Ben, and Calvin

INDIGO

My self-imposed silence was kind of half-assed. The no-touching rule, I followed that religiously. But I still talked, a little. The old me knew how to commit to things. But because the new me didn't, because I wasn't that brave now, my life kept hobbling along. I did keep to myself. Mom made me see therapists and psychologists. They talked a lot about post-traumatic stress disorder and obsessive-compulsive disorder. But I knew that was garbage. I knew I had to keep myself quarantined, distanced.

Once in a while, I could still feel it in me. Starting to heat up right there under my sternum, churning in my ribs, wanting to come out.

Mom and Dad never bought it. When we moved down to our summer home for good, Mom fell in with our old friends Sarah Rawlings and her daughter, Mia-Joy. I wanted to keep away from them, from everyone. But I learned pretty quickly that if I could put on the facade of normal—even the tiniest bit—with the Rawlingses, Mom would let up on the counselors and shrinks. And Mia-Joy didn't need to ask me a zillion nosy questions. She didn't mind that I didn't talk much, or that I never touched other people. In fact, Mia-Joy barely seemed to notice. It just gave her more time to talk, which is exactly what she'd been doing since I could remember.

But after Sophie, after everything, Mom felt a calling to come work with New Orleans Congregational, and Dad decided that post-Katrina New Orleans would be a boon for his construction company. The second big oil spill kept New Orleans in the news, and people wanted to rebuild the city even more, Dad said. People needed a new start here. Mom and Dad agreed; Dad would build their strip malls, and Mom would rebuild their shaken faith. So we left our old life in Chicago.

That's how they sold it to me. And Mom told me, in a hushed voice, her eyes crinkling in that worried way at the corners, that *we* would start over too. We needed to. Sophie was gone.

I just nodded.

I wasn't even doing that today while Mia-Joy went on talking at breakneck speed as we sat behind the counter, peeling shrimp in the twinkling-clean white-tiled kitchen of the Rawlings Crawdaddy Shack. Mia-Joy's mother stood at the large steel stovetop, her hair a mass of russet curls like

Mia-Joy's. She stirred the gumbo pots, the lunch rush less than an hour away. Mia-Joy's ancient-looking Granny Lucy sat in her rocking chair next to the screen door, chewing on her black licorice, eyes closed as always. But just when you had forgotten she was even around, she would jump into the conversation and remind us that she was still here and, yes, she did know everything. The late-July air hung hot and damp against my skin, and the kitchen smelled of sweet onions, red peppers, and fresh bread pudding.

"My daddy doesn't seem to want me to go, but Mama doesn't mind," Mia-Joy explained. The shrimp were slippery in my hands, and they made my mouth water. Seafood in the bayou was a different experience. The buttery crab legs. Red beans and rice with paprika shrimp. In Chicago, in my regular life, seafood had tasted more...Midwestern...stale... bland. It was out of its element.

Much like me.

But Mia-Joy was New Orleans in every sense of the word, even if she was itching to get out. French Creole, with a father who fished on a shrimp boat, a brother who headlined at a jazz club on Bourbon Street, and a granny who taught her the finer points of twenty-first-century voodoo. When Raymond Kanzler stood Mia-Joy up for the Turn-About last year, Granny Lucy had told her, "You give that boy a headache he ain't never gonna forget. Just turn his picture upside down. Keep it that way for a week." Mia-Joy did it too. But she was already on to another boy, another adventure. She was sparkling, alive, colorful, just like New Orleans itself.

"You mind your grades, Mia-Joy," her mama said, keeping her back toward us, her attention on her stove. "Then we'll talk about your summer in New York."

"What did I tell you?" Mia-Joy squealed at me, popping one of the boiled shrimp into her mouth. She would go to New York after our senior year. She would model. I didn't doubt that. I smiled back at her. Forte. Allegretto. These were my musical descriptors of Mia-Joy. Loud. Up-tempo.

I pictured a mash-up of my old life and my new one right then. Mia-Joy hanging out with Annaliese and Cody from back home. Mia-Joy cackling with laughter when we pulled pranks on the swim team. No, scratch that. Mia-Joy would never be able to keep any secrets, would never be able to keep a straight face. Mia-Joy was a lot of things, but subtle was not one of them.

"Corrine, you're scratching your palm, *chérie*," Granny Lucy called over.

I looked down and she was right. I wondered what she was going to tell me that meant: Was I going to kiss a fool? Inherit a windfall? But the old fishing lures hanging on the restaurant door clinked and clanked as it opened—G-sharp, E, C, E. I didn't catch what Granny Lucy said. Sounded something like "catching an old train."

A middle-aged couple walked in, heads together, laughing. He made me sweat just looking at him, a bushy beard and a sport jacket in this heat. She was a tiny woman, but her shoes made this great little *slap-clap* noise on the tile floor, and when I looked I saw that she had on ridiculously high heels, bright red. I caught a look at her face then—quickly, because I didn't like to make eye contact anymore—and I realized that it was Sylvia Smith, the professor from Tulane.

She had curly red hair, moved like a bird. You couldn't mistake her.

A flush crept up into my neck and ears. Mom had made me meet her during those first few weeks when I had been nothing more than a hot mess. Mom had probably envisioned things getting better, me eventually taking lessons again, needing a tutor here.

I slunk down into myself. But it didn't matter. Professor Smith would have no reason to remember me. I had refused to play the violin for her, refused to even speak. Mom had apologized like crazy, and we had never spoken of it since.

"Where y'at!" Mrs. Rawlings called, her voice booming throughout the little restaurant.

"Mornin'," Professor Smith answered. Mrs. Rawlings met her at the counter, and they began to small-talk. The bearded man chuckled and his ample belly jiggled. I couldn't tell if Mrs. Rawlings knew Professor Smith or if they were just doing that whole Southern-friendly thing. I still couldn't tell the difference.

"She stayed," Mia-Joy said, elbowing me in the ribs, nodding toward Professor Smith. "During Katrina. People say she saved like three different neighbors. Tracked down insulin for this one old lady who was in a wheelchair."

I nodded. This was how it was now. People in the French Quarter defined themselves by Katrina. I knew what that was like–to define yourself through some kind of catastrophe, through loss. I kept my eyes cast down, working at peeling shrimp, but my gaze kept wandering back to those red high heels. She had stayed here. Weathered the broken levees and destruction and somehow lived through it to wear red high heels again. That was something.

The door jangled, and I immediately felt weird. Bothered. I didn't really know why. The heat? Thinking of my violin?

I stole a look at the door. Beat-up old black Converse gym shoes and frayed, too-long jeans. I told myself not to even look up. No interaction.

But then I noticed rain clattering against the window. The sound. *Shoosh, whoosh, shoosh.* It wasn't just a midday summer drizzle but more like a sheet of slanting rain, right here in the middle of this sunny New Orleans afternoon. The sky was blue, the clouds cottony white, and yet it rained, beating a rhythm on the restaurant windows.

Something about that didn't sit right with me–the sunshine along with the rain. That should have been my first clue.

But I shrugged it off. That was just how New Orleans was–unpredictable in every way.

The new customer was still stomping his Converses on the welcome mat, and when I glanced at him I caught his silhouette. He shook his dark wet hair free of the rain, and I thought I was prepared. *Okay, tall, dark stranger. He'll be hot. Big deal.*

He squared his shoulders and looked at the menu board, up through his dark lashes, and I could *not* make myself look away. I always looked away. I tried to seem invisible to people. *Keep the circle small*, I told myself. Fewer people in the circle, fewer people to hurt, fewer people to hurt you.

But I was glued. He had a messy mop of dark hair, wavy and untamed, defying gravity as it swirled up and away from his forehead. As he spoke his hellos, he had that drawl, that deep Southern twang to his vowels that turned his speech into music to my Midwestern ears. "Good mawnin'," he said, and his voice was low, just above a mumble. Legato. Slow and smooth.

His eyes were the brightest blue, and his eyelashes were ridiculous, like fringe. They should've looked silly on a boy. But they didn't. They worked against the square, rugged cut of his cheekbones, his jaw. The corners of his mouth turned up in a friendly way, but when he spotted Mia-Joy and me staring up from our pot of shrimp, he truly smiled. Big shiny white teeth twinkling like the tiles of Mrs. Rawlings's kitchen.

His smile made him look younger. *Did he go to Liberty?*

I expected his eyes to be meeting Mia-Joy's beauty, taking in her long legs, her icy-green eyes, her caramel skin, but I was wrong. He looked straight at me, a half-smiling, half-startled expression, but only for a moment. Then his face changed, softened. He nodded a hello, like he knew me.

I felt a little fizzle at the base of my neck and all over my scalp then, like someone had touched me after rubbing socked feet over a shag carpet. Static electricity. The little hairs on my arms stood up, and a current vibrated right through me, settled in the back of my molars, like chewing on tinfoil. Yuck.

For a beat, I held his gaze. I held this note between us a tad too long, which was so much farther beyond my usual boundaries. I felt shaken and naked. I averted my eyes, caught my reflection in the window: my long dark hair, my pale skin. My swimmer's body had dwindled now into a ghost of its old self.

I turned away, and I lost hold of the big stainless-steel shrimp pot, dropping it clean out of my lap. The clank of the steel on the tile shocked me back into reality.

"Fluckity fluck," I swore under my breath, Mia-Joy's favorite faux curse. I bent down to pick up the shrimp. Mrs. Rawlings snapped my behind with a dish towel. "I am so sorry," I said, feeling the blush of the moment climb up my neck and onto my Irish-white face, my paler-than-pale cheeks and earlobes.

I heard the customer asking if he could help, but Mrs.

Rawlings refused, instead taking his order for crawfish jambalaya. I did not look back up. I cleaned my mess silently, cursing myself, throwing away the shrimp, costing the Rawlingses at least thirty dollars in product.

I made myself think of Sophie. A reminder. Because that's what I had to remember. That's who I was. And I had to interact as little as possible. Or else my bad luck, my mojo, whatever . . . it would creep out again. Get its roots in somewhere. Like kudzu, squashing the life out of everything beautiful around it.

When Mrs. Rawlings asked me to sit for a reading after the lunch rush, I shook my head as always. The Rawlings family was usually respectful of my limitations. But for some reason that day, when Mia-Joy begged, "Please, Corrine," I gave in. I said yes. I told myself it was the guilt of the lost shrimp. But there was something else going on, and I think at some level I already knew it. Something was coming. The air around us felt heavier, expectant.

I sat down at the counter, ignoring the looks passing between Mrs. Rawlings and Mia-Joy. The heat of the day was in full swing now, pressing down on us, closer, thicker. The air-conditioning in the restaurant worked—technically—or so Granny Lucy always reminded us, even though she sat by an open screen door all day long. The backs of my legs immediately stuck to the red vinyl of the stool. Mia-Joy plopped onto the stool next to me.

"Lawdy Jesus, you must've said the right thing today," Mia-Joy said to her mother. "Something changed her mind."

"Maybe a full moon," Granny Lucy called from her rocker near the back door, the runners of her chair crunching on the shells of the peanuts she was eating.

I forced myself not to roll my eyes.

"Put your hands on the table, honey. Flat, palms down. And Mia-Joy, shush, so as I can concentrate here."

Mia-Joy made a show of zipping her lips, bugging her eyes. I listened to Mrs. Rawlings, placed my hands on the table. I still had a callus on my left forefinger from the violin. It had been months since I had played, but I felt the callus there now, rubbed the pad of my thumb against the hardened skin. I missed the weight of the instrument in my hands, the smell of the wood when it was under my chin.

I knew from watching other readings that Mrs. Rawlings liked to hold the hands of a customer before she shuffled her tarot cards, get a feel for the person, but she was being respectful of me. And I was glad. But truthfully, my mind wasn't really there. I was already thinking about going home.

I watched Mrs. Rawlings shuffle her cards. The deck was larger than a regular one. The cards were old but well taken care of, only slightly tattered. On the back, the black-and-white design of an elaborate snake faded to yellow only at the edges, where I assumed the oil from several generations of Rawlings hands had accumulated from shuffling the cards.

Mia-Joy's mama placed them on the counter and then lit

a single candle. She was a big woman, built sturdy. Mezzo forte. Even louder than Mia-Joy. She looked fierce and powerful, with a broad face and a broader waist, but she had the same eyes as Mia-Joy, playful and sparkling, Crayola green, and when they fixed on you, you knew you were only going to hear the truth, plain and simple. She suffered no fools. I waited for her to deal her cards, but I didn't believe in this kind of stuff. My mom was a minister, for God's sake. I didn't believe in full moons or tarot cards or ...

As I sat there, I realized that maybe I should.

I looked down at the freckled, pale skin of my hands on the counter in front of me, and a thought hit me hard. If I truly believed that I had to keep the circle small—and I did, I believed it—then how could I so easily discount Mrs. Rawlings and her dilapidated old cards? Or the lady down at the 7-Eleven who reads fortunes from chicken bones?

I sighed, shoved the thought aside. *Two steps away from a straitjacket, Corrine.*

I heard Mrs. Rawlings finish shuffling and slap one card onto the counter. It didn't register with me, though. *Nearly six months. Since Sophie.*

I heard the slap of another card in front of me, and Mia-Joy clucked her tongue. I focused on the cards, swallowing hard against the dryness in my throat.

Mia-Joy pointed at the first one. "The Lovers," she said. The card had a stylized silhouette of two people in an embrace, the background full of red valentine hearts. "It can mean love in lots of ways: family, romance…Maybe just a hookup." Mia-Joy laughed loudly.

"You were scratching your palm, your left one," Granny Lucy called from her seat. "Means you is fixing to meet an old acquaintance, *ma chérie.*"

I shrugged. Mia-Joy pointed to the next card. It bore a shrouded figure against a dark background, a black face in the hood. "Death," Mia-Joy said. "Dum da dum dum." Mia-Joy's laugh sounded forced. My jaw tightened, and beads of sweat formed on my upper lip. *It means nothing.*

"Don't freak out, honey," Mrs. Rawlings said. "Everyone goes running at that card in the movies. But it doesn't mean death all literal-like. It can mean change. Transition. Opportunity."

The next card was a chalice, a fancy golden cup covered in jewels. I looked at Mrs. Rawlings, her broad face turned down to the cards, her eyes studying. It was quiet for a moment, and I heard a fly buzzing in the kitchen, the hum of the dishwasher.

Mrs. Rawlings looked up apologetically. She said, "Cups mean water."

"Water?" I said. I could stomach love and death. But love, death, and water? Was this my freaking résumé? I got up quickly from the stool and turned toward the door, watching the edges of my vision get all inky and swimmy. Sparks of liquid orange flickered at the dark edges of my sight. I reached a hand out, tried to find something on which to steady myself. My hand itself felt far away, detached from the rest of me. I heard Mia-Joy as if from a distance: "Corrine, it's good—"

I passed out flat on the white-and-black tiled floor of the Crawdaddy Shack, the fly buzzing at my ear as I lost consciousness.

I shoved the outdated tape into the ancient black cassette recorder. It was a crazy old machine, on its last legs and totally about to crap out on me. I had begged Mom to invest in some newer equipment. But she had insisted that she knew how to use this tape recorder, and if *she* was the one who had to use it, then *she* would choose to stick with it. I pushed the PLAY button, and Mr. Lazette's voice picked up right where he had left off—the story of the Madame Bridgit ghost on the hotel terrace on Dauphine Street.

I picked up my sketchpad, my favorite pencil, and my little pocketknife from Granddad. I sat cross-legged on my bed, scraping at my pencil, getting just the right point on it, listening to Mr. Lazette.

"I was only a chile, ya see. I recall I seen it twice the summer of the fire on Basin Street. Didn't know it was a ghost then. Saw her wandering on the roof of the Dauphine Hotel. Made me nervous to see—"

Mom knocked on the frame of my open door, and I stopped the tape. "Come in."

"You sure you're feeling okay, honey?" She carried in a

tray and set it on my overcrowded nightstand. I looked it over: a tuna fish sandwich, carrots, a glass of sweet tea.

"I'm fine."

"Sarah said you let her do the cards."

I nodded.

"Was it fun?" Mom's smile stretched tight across her face, wary. My mom, my middle C, my four-four time. My anchor.

"You're worried. I'm fine."

"It's just that when I hounded you to hang out more, to overstep your boundaries, I didn't mean you had to delve into voodoo." Mom said this last part with that jingle-bell laugh of hers, but I knew there was some worry there.

"It was stupid," I said. Now that I wasn't sitting there with all eyes on me, those hokey cards staring up at me, I knew it was dumb. "I just got overwhelmed, I think."

Mom sat down carefully on the edge of the bed. Her legs did not touch mine, didn't even graze my knee. I took a bite of the tuna fish sandwich, and we sat in silence.

I ate a few more bites and took a couple sips of the iced tea. It was cold going down my throat.

"I'm glad you're feeling okay." She looked like she wanted to do something—touch me, hug me, tuck my hair behind my ear. I wanted to let her, but I couldn't. I didn't dare touch her. I realized in that moment that I could feel something, a tiny something in my chest, churning, blossoming.

I swallowed hard, inched myself farther away from my

mother. I was too tired of asking how, why, what. The only thing I knew was that it was there. And I had to respect it.

"He looks a lot like that," Mom said, pointing to my sketch of Mr. Lazette. "Again." She shook her head and gave me a smile. Her eyes, the same blue eyes as mine, looked amazed and entertained, but hidden underneath sat some fear.

I felt it too. "His story is creepy. Good, though."

"I know. It's a regular ghost story," she said, rubbing the backs of her knuckles across her bottom lip like she did when she was thinking.

She first started interviewing the senior citizens up at Chartrain Hills because of a New Orleans history project I had to do at school. I couldn't do it. It was early in the semester, when we had just moved here. I hadn't said more than five words to anyone. She did the interviews for me, taped them.

Mrs. Janell Jackson. Her great-grandmother had traveled on the Underground Railroad, had been a contemporary of Harriet Tubman, and Mrs. Jackson could really tell a story. The truth was, Mom saw me enjoying something a little bit, putting that project together for history class, so she urged me to interview some of the old folks myself.

I couldn't. But she kept bringing me tapes. It just kind of happened. She said the old folks liked talking even more than I probably liked to listen.

"What should I do with these stories?" I had asked Mom after three or four of them.

"You'll think of something," she said.

And that's when I started sketching the tale-tellers. I had always loved to draw: pen and ink, charcoal, pastels. But after Sophie, after the move, it became the only thing I remembered how to enjoy, even just a little bit.

"When will Dad be back?" I asked, finishing off the iced tea. I had seen his handwritten note to Mom in the kitchen, on our chalkboard next to the phone.

"Next Thursday," Mom said, taking a carrot off my plate and getting up. Dad spent about half of his time back in Chicago, with Harlowe Construction booming at both ends of the Mississippi River.

I nodded, reached over to press PLAY on the tape recorder.

"Have you thought about letting me show these sketches to anyone?" Mom asked, leaning on the door frame.

"No," I answered simply. Mom nodded. She didn't push.

I didn't want anyone to see my drawings. It was only a hobby. I wasn't that good at it, not like the violin. But even more important, sharing my art would be a much too personal interaction now. These sketches of my tale-tellers. And I could never answer the questions that these sketches would bring. Especially the one.

The question that even made Mom nervous. Fearful.

How could I listen to the tapes of these people, listen to their tales—with Mom giving them the prompt "What's your story?"—and then sit down and sketch them, without ever having seen them in my life?

How could I do that? And how could I be uncannily correct each time? Right down to the placement of a mole, a chicken pox scar, or a set of wrinkles on the forehead?

I couldn't answer those questions.

But I could draw them, and I loved their faces, their histories, their connections.

I didn't let myself think about it too much. In Chicago, I would've laughed at the idea of drawing people from only their voices. I would've called it crazy. But so much had changed for me, in me, since Chicago. And plus, this place. New Orleans. It made certain things seem so much more possible than the Chicago suburbs ever did. When New Orleans was just our vacation spot, our summer house, that made sense. New Orleans was a getaway. But now it was supposed to be home, and so many things seemed cockeyed because of it.

Before, I had been a logical girl. A swimmer, a music lover. A math geek. I loved the way that math and music fit together, the numbers, the patterns. Things made sense with numbers and notes, with scales and time signatures, with equations and proofs. A equaled B. Logic ruled for me back in Chicago. Some things were possible, and some things were not. In Chicago, streets were parallel and perpendicular, named in order of the presidents of the United States. You could easily figure things out there. In Chicago, the seasons followed the rules. It didn't rain when the sun was out. People followed the rules in Chicago too. You buried people under the ground, in graves. You didn't have famous cities of the dead, with fancy aboveground mausoleums and crypts. You didn't have reputable people talking about seeing ghosts at every other hotel in the French Quarter. You didn't have labyrinthine mazes of back streets and alleyways. New Orleans was unpredictable, messy, and exciting.

Was it because New Orleans had so many mysteries? Ties to American voodoo? A link to the macabre?

Well, New Orleans felt different than Chicago. It felt *more*. Real. Not real. Crazy. Not crazy. Such a thin, thin line.

Sometimes when I would lie awake at night, watching the pear tree branch sway in the wind from my bedroom window, feeling the Gulf breeze on my skin, I felt so close, so very close to something. I felt open. That was the only way I could put it. *Open.*

I had never felt that way in Chicago. Well, maybe when I had played a certain piece of music and interpreted it in just the right way, I felt it. But it was rare. Here, though, I often felt *open*. Like I was very close to something. Had it right on the tip of my tongue. But what was it?

The telephone woke me late that night, but I didn't answer it. Instead I tiptoed to my doorway and listened to my mother's end of the conversation. The concern in her voice freaked me a little, but I reminded myself that she was a minister. She often got phone calls in the middle of the night. I stood in the doorway, watching the concern in the knit of my mother's brow.

"Oh, honey," Mom said to the person on the other end of the phone. Something in her voice struck me as more personal this time.

I waited until she hung up, then walked across the hall to her room. "Who is it?" I asked.

"Mia-Joy's grandmother."

"Granny Lucy?" I whispered.

She nodded, and my stomach dropped. I reminded myself that Granny Lucy was ninety years old. She was actually Mia-Joy's great-grandmother. She'd had a stroke last fall, and she had not been in the best health for months now. But Granny Lucy had just been in the kitchen with me today. With Mia-Joy and her mom. Today. *You're scratching your palm,* chérie.

Mom sat on her bed, already pulling on a pair of jeans. Her paperback was open on the quilt, a box of Triscuits and spray cheese on her nightstand, her bedroom TV muted on the home and garden channel. Mom always was a night owl, like me. Sophie had been too.

Mom sighed. "Sarah doesn't know where Mia-Joy is. And they really think this might be it for Granny Lucy." She shook her head.

I averted my eyes. It was Saturday night. I knew Mia-Joy was at the cemetary.

"You're going to Sarah's?" I asked.

Mom sat for a moment like she was in a trance, thinking. "I am," she said. She got up, quickly changed into a clean shirt. "You don't mind, do you, honey?"

I shook my head, watching her find her purse, locate one shoe under her bed, all the while trying to decide. *Should I tell her where Mia-Joy is?*

Mia-Joy will get in trouble. But she'll be so sad if she doesn't get to say goodbye. But she's prepared for this. She's known goodbye was coming. But I could give her this last chance.

I followed Mom downstairs and latched the dead bolt behind her, then sat down at the kitchen table, still waffling.

I got up and took my phone off the counter. I thought briefly of my other teenage life in Chicago, before everything, when I had carried my cell everywhere, texted constantly, a state of never-ending interaction.

I called Mia-Joy. This in itself was something I rarely did, but it seemed safer than going to get her myself.

"This is Mia-Joy. Leave me a message."

"Call me if you get this," I said, my voice shaking. I hung up, put the phone back on the counter. I stared at it, willing her to call me right back. I waited, listening to my own shallow breaths. It didn't buzz.

If I went for Mia-Joy, would it somehow circle back and harm her? Or someone else, because I got too involved?

Then something hit me. Granny Lucy had been there today in the Rawlingses' kitchen. Had she touched me when I passed out?

I ran my hands through my hair, feeling my breath catch in my throat. "Oh Jesus," I said under my breath. Had I done this? Had I caused this to happen to Granny Lucy? I tried to remember back to before I passed out, back to the tarot cards. Had I noticed it in my chest? Had it been there at that moment? Alive? Swirling?

I swallowed hard. I listened for the phone to buzz, for Mia-Joy to call me right back. But she didn't. I concentrated on the sound of my breathing in the still kitchen for what seemed like a long time, thinking of Granny Lucy, of Mia-Joy, their quick retorts to one another, their easy relationship.

I thought of the finality of death. How it snuck up on us, like we somehow believed that death and loss were things that *other* people had to deal with.

I thought of Sophie, of my guilt. I pictured Granny Lucy's hand on my shoulder or touching my cheek when I was passed out. Could she have possibly touched my hand? Held mine in hers, palm to palm?

Oh God. No, that couldn't be. No. But *maybe*. Just like Sophie.

Love. Death. Water.

I thought about Sophie, that gap between her teeth. She had begged me to take her to see that air show. I remembered exactly how the air smelled that morning on the shore of Lake Michigan, crisp and earthy. I didn't want to remember.

I pushed against it. I didn't want to go there. But the proverbial door had been opened, really, ever since Mrs. Rawlings had done my cards. I sank into my kitchen chair, my head in my hands.

Every moment, I spent so much energy pushing away the memory of that day.

But it was always there. Hovering. Owning me. Defining my every action and inaction.

Part of me felt like I was falling, plunging back into that memory.

It had been windy.

Sophie loved airplanes, and I smiled when I thought about her goggles. She had bought this old green-tinged pair of lab goggles at a garage sale. They were way too big for her, fastened onto her head with an old shoelace. She was trying to look like a pilot, I guessed. I pictured us that day, that final day, and I could see myself making peanut butter sandwiches at the counter to take with us for a picnic afterward, and she was bouncing around the kitchen wearing those goggles. They pushed her nose up in a funny way, made it look kind of piggish.

I laughed out loud, put my head in my hands, and then the first tears came. I rubbed them with the back of my hand, and I shook my head against them. I had to remember.

Sissy, she called me. "Sissy." I said it out loud, and my voice broke, and I sobbed. "Sissy," I said again, and it was like we were there, on the beach after the air show.

The wind blows through my hair, wraps it around my face, some goes in my mouth. She laughs that silly belly chuckle that she has when something is really tickling her funny bone. She crouches down, her feet in a tidal pool. She pokes at something with a stick, a reed she has found on our walk.

"This mudpuppy just cannot get up the side of this hole, no matter how many times it tries." She laughs some more and I watch her. I am not always the patient, indulgent big sister that can appreciate Sophie like this, but I can today. I do now.

Her goggles slip farther down her nose, but she doesn't notice. I see now that she has the salamander dangling from the stick. The sky darkens over and the wind picks up.

A storm is coming.

"Let's go see 'em, Corrine."

I lead the way to the rocky north shore, to the place I heard has all the good rocks, the Petoskey stones, fossilized coral that Sophie is dying to see. When we get there, I realize that the terrain of this beach will be hard for Sophie; it is tough even for me. The sky has blown into a pewter-gray cloud, and I consider telling Sophie we need to turn around.

I don't.

We hold hands for a while. I help her with her footing. The beach is at a steep angle, covered in sharp, jutting rocks. Large rocks. Each step is treacherous, a possible twisted ankle, skinned knee, but after ten minutes or so Sophie is confident. She lets go of my hand and begins to crouch down between rocks, moving on all fours.

We get near the shore, and the rocks are smaller here, more varied. Even I can see the riches in the surfaces that gleam up at us. "Agate!" she squeals, picking up a particularly sparkly one. She is amazed, mouth agape. She reaches out, touches another one, and I giggle. She is so happy. And I think, I love this kid. We are not perfect siblings. We are not always tethered so closely. I often complain about toting her to and from Girl Scouts, or babysitting on a Saturday night, or having to hear her and Mitchy Rogers make fart noises at the dinner table. But I think it right then: I love this kid.

The rain begins. Just a smattering of raindrops, but big fat ones. I don't think about how these raindrops will make the walk back to the sand beach more dangerous. It doesn't even occur to me. Oh, how I have second-guessed so many of these details.

24

Sophie spends a lot of time pocketing small stones near the shore. "I think this is a Petoskey!" she says, showing me a tiny stone with peach-colored spiraled ridges. I nod enthusiastically, but I can't tell what it is. The wind is pushing the waves higher onto the beach, so we have to leave via the large rocks just as we came, and when we start back, she leads. She stands erect, no crouching over. She knows the weather is turning, I'm sure, so she hurries.

I watch her slip like it is in slow motion. She's way ahead of me.

Mom's gonna kill me, *I think, picturing Sophie bloodying her knees. Maybe even stitches. But before that thought is even fully formed, I see that it is worse than this. She's going so fast across the rocks, and she hops—two-footed. She lands, slipping. She hops again, and one foot slips. She yelps. Her feet slip out from under her and her head falls backward. It is an awkward, painful-looking fall, with too much momentum, too much force slamming the back of her head onto the rocks.*

After the six or eight steps it takes me to get beside her, I see she is unconscious, and her body seizes, trembles, and jerks, the whites of her eyes showing, her limbs working so unnaturally.

The sight of Sophie, the blood on the rock under her head, the ugly movements of this seizure, it wrecks me. I panic.

"Oh God, oh God," I say, scanning my brain, trying to think but coming up with nothing. Something about her tongue. Where's my cell phone?

The wind blows hard then off the lake, and the air changes, a change in pressure, a change that registers on my skin. The hairs on my arms stand up and then . . .

Black. I don't remember anything that happens. I lose time.

But when I come to–later, much later–I am lying awkwardly on the rocks, Sophie nearly on top of me, both of my hands on her face, one on either cheek. It is raining hard now, thunder clapping and rolling right above us. The waves roll in, slapping us with cold lake water. It is later, much later, and I am dazed.

What happened?

We are both soaked to the bone, and it is cold. My teeth chatter, and I begin to cry when I see that Sophie's teeth are chattering too. She is okay! She opens her eyes, and they register me next to her. I'm so happy. I'm so relieved.

"Sissy," she whispers.

Sophie sits up. I sit up too, but my head feels woozy, too big, and the air around me gets that crackle in it again. My skin begins to feel heightened, stretched differently on my body.

A burning begins in my chest, an unnatural sensation. It's prickly and growing–electrical yet not really. I bring my hands to my chest and take a deep breath. Everything in my vision turns a little bit lighter, tinged with blue.

I turn to Sophie, ready to say something, ask her if she feels something. She is shaking. And I think: shock.

But I see her eyes roll back again. Another seizure?

Without thinking, I reach toward my baby sister and I place my hand on her cheek, a comforting gesture, a big-sisterly gesture, a loving gesture.

I see blue–that very specific indigo blue–all around me. All of a sudden, everything is bathed in it. Sophie's face, the rocks below us, the cloudy sky, my hands. And the current, the charge running through me, it surges. No, it explodes inside me, inside my chest, down and out each of my limbs, inside my head and out my eyes, through every cell.

Then the surge grows bigger even, louder. Crescendo. Everything vibrates around us. And I am blind.

Everything goes white. I can feel Sophie fall away from my hand. I worry about her head hitting the rocks again, but I can't see. I somehow grab her with both arms, and I get her, hold her. I feel her body shiver, shake, and then it goes limp. And I can't see her, and it's still surging through me, and I pass out.

I'm awoken by a paramedic in the back of an ambulance. I know before anyone even tells me. Sophie is dead. I feel it. I did it.

I shook my head and brought myself back to here, now. Back to my kitchen. And Mia-Joy's last chance to say goodbye to Granny Lucy. It took several deep breaths to uncurl my fists, to stop gritting my teeth.

I pushed away the thoughts that I had done the same to Granny Lucy as I had to Sophie. I shook my head against the idea. I hadn't felt it in the Rawlingses' kitchen, not before I passed out, not when I regained consciousness. I hadn't felt it stirring or churning in my chest.

Panic danced at the edges of my consciousness, for Mia-Joy, for her family. Because I knew what it was like not being able to say goodbye.

I had to go. I made my decision. *You cannot hug Mia-Joy,* *cannot touch her, even if she cries. Even if she reaches for you, des-* *perate in her time of need.*

I ran upstairs, pulled on some shorts and a T-shirt, threw my hair in a ponytail, and took off for the Lurie Cemetery.

It was a short walk of about ten minutes to Lurie. I had gone there tons of times, even once to do a séance with Mia-Joy when we were around twelve, but that had been during the daylight. It was dark tonight. The air, thick and muggy yet considerably cooler than earlier, held the now-familiar scents of magnolias and salt water. Once in a while, the breeze would bring a few sad notes from a saxophone playing at the Mint Julep, the only jazz club within walking distance of my house.

The streets in my neighborhood were not completely dead, just quiet, with occasional laughter floating from the restaurants near the cemetery. An old, wrinkled banjo player sat on a street corner, although at the moment, he wasn't playing anything except for the timely tune of his snoring, his head lolled against the nylon back of his old lawn chair, his banjo resting hopeful on his knee. A group of teenagers passed by him, laughing and talking, oblivious to him and me.

I walked by quietly, hoping not to wake him. I took these sites in around me with quick sideways glances, careful not to meet anyone's eyes. It was habit now. I didn't even have to think about it. It had required a lot of practice at the beginning, right after Sophie, because I had not come by it naturally.

At the corner of Manderly and Lurie, a young couple strolled arm in arm toward me from the bank of cafés across from the cemetery. I heard laughing and the clink of glasses coming from the veranda of the nearest bar.

I crossed the street, tried to look invisible, and stole around the side of the wrought-iron entryway to the cemetery. I eyed the mausoleums and monuments, the architecture of the white crypts, the gargoyle statuary, the intricate wrought-iron crosses.

Recently, I had been here to sketch, by myself, of course. But it wasn't much of a secret that Liberty kids would be here on a Saturday night in the summer. Even I had heard about it.

I opened the wrought-iron gate and it creaked only slightly, although I was aware of how much creepier the place seemed at night. A stone gargoyle startled me as I turned the first corner toward the crypt of Madame Vallion. I knew that's where they met. I knew there would be beer, probably the cheap kind in quart bottles, probably someone with a joint. Mia-Joy was, of course, in love. And Jules Jackson hung here, so Mia-Joy would be here, batting her eyelashes, trying to get his attention, and, of course, succeeding.

I got a little turned around near the stone crypt with the graffiti-style portrait of Jesus, but I figured it out pretty quickly. I was calming down now. I realized that I was much more comfortable with all these dead people, all these resting souls, than the idea of having to interact with real people, *alive* people.

I walked along quietly and heard the first murmurs and laughter in the distance. A firecracker shot off and nearly knocked me over with surprise, but once I realized what it was, I headed toward the low bass of party music, the people, specifically Mia-Joy.

And now that I was nearing her, I realized that I needed to figure out what to say. I knew that it wasn't an unexpected thing for a ninety-year-old woman to die, but I also knew what was about to happen for Mia-Joy. I was delivering that moment you forever divide your memories between—the before and the after.

I pictured Mia-Joy's face as I scuffed my feet against the gravel on the walkway. I thought of all the little ways she had helped me in the past year. At school, how she had let me eat at her lunch table without any of the pressure to talk or fit in. How she stuck up for me once in a while to keep the kids from really laying into me. I didn't often witness her doing it, but I knew she—my association as her friend—was what kept them at bay.

Back in Chicago, I'd sat at the cool table. I had the upperclassman boyfriend. The right kind of clothes. The newest cell phone. I would've probably teased the new me too. At the very least I wouldn't have stuck up for the new me, the damaged me. I didn't like that truth, but there it was.

I had learned so much since then. Or unlearned it.

Mia-Joy existed above all the high school bullshit. She sat at the cool table, yeah. She got the cutest guys. But she had friends, like Yo-Yo Craig and Ella Stanley and me, who maybe didn't fit the norm. Along with her lip gloss, her obsession with boys, and her too-short skirts, Mia-Joy had her own mind.

And her loyalty never wavered. That day on the quad when Chrissy Jones had brought the—

That's when I nearly bumped right into him. The stranger from the Crawdaddy Shack. I turned the corner at the Montaigne Mausoleum, the largest one, with the white gables and turrets. I turned it with my head down and my thoughts on Mia-Joy, and there he was, coming right at me. If he hadn't said hello, I would've smacked right into him.

I looked up, startled. The shadows of the cemetery kept me from seeing his face completely, but there was no mistaking that hair, his slim, broad-shouldered silhouette, the drawl in his greeting.

"Hi," I said, my voice surprising me.

A few yards down the path, I saw shadows move and separate. A group of kids turned toward us. Someone spotted me, and I heard the voices, the calls for Mia-Joy. The group parted, and I watched Mia-Joy come through it, walking toward me quickly.

The stranger stepped aside, and Mia-Joy picked up her pace. "Corrine?" And then she was there, right in front of me. "It's Granny?" she said. I nodded. She turned to a girl behind her, Mary Louise from physics. Mia-Joy said a few words to her, then began to walk, retracing the path I had just taken. "Is she gone?" she asked, turning, her stance rigid as I hurried to follow her. "Tell me I'm not too late. I never should have come out here tonight. I should've known better. Tell me she isn't gone yet, Corrine."

"Not yet," I said, picking up my pace to catch up with her.

"Thank you, God," Mia-Joy said under her breath, and started running. I let her go. I had done my part.

I stopped for a second before I realized that *he* was right behind me. The other kids, they had gone back, had lost interest. But this stranger, here he was, a few feet behind me.

When I turned around, I stole a quick glance at his face. We were under the far reaches of a nearby streetlight, so I could see the line of his jaw, the curve of his brow. But mostly I averted my eyes. Why I didn't just ignore him and keep on my way, I couldn't really say, but tonight had been full of firsts.

He reached out his hand then, like he wanted me to shake it, and I instinctively took a step back.

"I'm Rennick Lane," he said, and waited, but then he let his hand drop back to his side. When I didn't answer he said, "You're Corrine. Mia-Joy told me."

I nodded, stole another glance at his face. Big teeth, rabbity. But in a good way. "It's nice to meet you," I said, surprising myself once again.

"I think maybe it's you," he said.

"Me?" I said. He took a step closer to me, and I could smell cologne. No, deodorant maybe? Or laundry detergent, something fresh. And then it happened again, the hairs on the back of my neck prickled.

I backed away.

"Mia-Joy's pump. You're electrical."

"What are you talking about?" I said. I knew Mia-Joy had an insulin pump. But what did I have to do with that?

"I heard her telling that other girl. How it's messed up. Tell her to go back to shots. See if it fixes itself."

I studied him for a second. Those eyes. They were so direct and unflinching. "*You* tell her," I said, suddenly annoyed. I was leaving now.

That was enough. All I could take. I turned on my heel and walked away quickly, agitated. On the way home, I consoled myself with the thought that I had helped Mia-Joy. I had hopefully given her a few last moments with Granny Lucy.

I was *electrical*? I didn't know anything about Mia-Joy's pump. I pushed it from my mind. I had enough to think about, feel responsible for. *Could I possibly be the cause of–?*

No. I couldn't go there.

Granny Lucy had suffered a massive stroke. She was still alive that next morning. But it didn't look good. I heard Mozart in my mind again at this news. *Concerto No. 2.* The harps and flute joining in the first sonata. It had always sounded like hope to me.

"And Sarah's worried about Mia-Joy," Mom said as she clicked away on her laptop, trying to eat a bowl of cereal, answer her email, and talk to me, all before making it out the door before eight a.m. "She had another incident with her blood sugar."

I stood by the counter waiting for my toast to pop up. Frozen.

Although I told myself not to, I had spent most of the night dissecting Rennick's comment about Mia-Joy and her insulin pump.

Mom closed her laptop, put it into her bag, took her dish to the sink. "I really have to go." She stopped and looked at me, slowed herself down. "I love you, Corrine," she said, and blew me a kiss.

She turned and left out the back door.

My toast popped up, startling me. I left it in the toaster. *What am I doing here? Am I just going to wait around until I know for sure I hurt someone else?*

I tried to shake the thought out of my head. I sat down and took a few deep breaths, my pulse pounding in my temples. Had I caused this with Granny Lucy? Had she touched me?

Was I hurting Mia-Joy somehow? Her pump?

Or—and this thought hit me like a lightning bolt—did it work in other ways that I hadn't even let myself consider? Was it cumulative? Was I like some kind of radioactive bomb, and people around me only had a certain threshold?

My God. I couldn't even face this possibility head-on.

Or was it something else? Was it connection—emotional, mental, or something else entirely?

Electrical?

Did it come off of me in waves somehow?

And hadn't I slacked? Hadn't I let myself become intertwined with the Rawlingses in a way that I would never have considered six months ago?

I had been careful, so careful for months. Nearly six

months. Long enough for the shock of it to wear off a little bit, long enough to lull me into thinking that maybe I was just exaggerating this whole thing, or imagining it.

But here I was.

In that moment, I had no doubt that my interaction, my presence, had caused all of this somehow. A=B. Occam's razor, right? The simplest answer was the truth.

"No!" I said, looking around the kitchen for something to take my anger out on. I ripped the toaster cord from the wall, picked the whole thing up, and threw it at the fridge as hard as I could, giving a little shriek as I did it.

I picked up my phone, texted Mia-Joy quickly, trying not to think too much. Could Rennick be right? I couldn't risk it. *Your pump is messed up? Switch to shots.* I typed.

I ran upstairs, reached under my bed. I touched my violin case, felt the fine layer of dust on the top. Part of me needed to play right now. I sat back on my heels, considering, and let out a sigh. It had been so long. Would I be terrible? Would I even recognize myself in the music anymore? I thought inexplicably about the old yellow sponge.

When I had first started playing by ear, with the Suzuki method in first grade, Mrs. Smelzer had given us each a sponge to use as a shoulder rest. I had loved cutting that sponge into just the right shape, using a rubber band to hold it on to my oily, dilapidated rental violin. I thought of the shape of it under my chin, the tension of the strings under my fingers, the vibration of the bow against my hand, the smell of the rosin. *Why haven't I played since Sophie?* I wondered. Could I really answer that? *Because it seems selfish to feel happy without her.*

"Happy," I said out loud to my empty room, and my voice sounded brittle and alone. I grabbed my sketchpad off the bed and opened it to my most recent drawing. Mr. Lazette's nearly finished portrait stared up at me. Grizzled and round-faced, he looked a little bit like Santa Claus, but with a more serious mouth.

There was something final in his stare. I didn't like the way he looked, like he was saying goodbye. Was he next? Was he going to die?

Because of me? Some thin thread of connection?

I had to cut my strings. To absolutely everyone.

I plopped myself onto my bed, pictured myself leaving, running off to some remote place. There would always be people. But I had an iron will, didn't I? Hadn't Dad always teased me about that since I was a little girl? How I had sat at the dinner table with my mouth clamped shut well into the night, determined not to eat my peas. Dad had given in eventually, with me nodding off, sitting with my arms crossed, a determined scowl on my face. I didn't give in. Not me. Never me.

I felt a pang of guilt when I thought about the petty fights with Annaliese or Cody back in Chicago, the squabbles with Sophie over whose CDs were whose, over stupid things. I never caved. I was stubborn and childish.

I could keep people away from me. I could quarantine myself. If all it took was willpower I could do it.

I faked a stomachache that day and the next, and I holed up in my room. When Mom came in with the news of Granny Lucy's death, that finality, I took it like a punch in the gut.

I struggled for my breath for a few seconds, and Mom moved toward me like she was going to comfort me some-how. "No," I said forcefully. I sat up, scooted away from her. "No," I repeated ferociously. Logically I knew that Granny Lucy's death might have had nothing to do with me. I knew that. She was old and sick.

But . . . I wasn't sure. And what was I going to do? Just keep on going until I was sure I killed somebody off? Like Mia-Joy?

Mom left me alone. I had a stomachache, a real one, for the next two days. Again, I didn't leave my room.

"I'm not going," I said.

"You're going to Lucy's funeral," Dad answered back through gritted teeth. "This bullshit has gone on long enough."

I agree, I thought wearily. "I'm not going, Dad."

"And if I make you?"

Fear flashed across my face. Dad grabbing me, throwing me over his shoulder. There wasn't much that would scare me more than Mom or Dad deliberately grabbing my hand, forcing physical contact. Dad must've seen the fear.

"Corrine." Dad wavered. He was a big guy, a forceful-looking man with a square frame and a personality that got things done, but I knew he didn't want to scare me. It wasn't in his nature. "Corrine," he said again.

Mom spoke up, her calm demeanor breaking. "Corrine, you loved Lucy. This is just a . . . crime. Let her stay, Paul," she said to Dad.

"Leslie," he started, but Mom turned then, burying her face in his shoulder, and my stomach churned. Dad gave me a hard look. I thought of how the funeral itself would be a reminder of Sophie's, how Mom would have to relive it. And I gave in. I didn't want to be that bullheaded kid. I would do this for my parents, and then that was it.

"Okay, I'll go," I said. "Give me a minute."

In the end I went, but on my terms. I stood in the back of the church for the service, away from Mia-Joy and her family. Away from everyone. I watched my parents as they gave their condolences. I studied the curves of their backs, their downtrodden shoulders matching Mia-Joy's parents', and all I could think was, *At least they have each other.*

When I first spied the ornate cherrywood casket, a wave of guilt, slow and powerful, washed over me. I fought back the tears, and I dug my fingernails into my palms. This was why I was going to have to isolate myself. This was why I was not going to give in to my parents' demands anymore. I had to quarantine this, whatever it was, firing up and coming to life in my chest. And I knew the first glance of that beautiful coffin would be forever burned into my psyche. Just like so many memories of Sophie. This was the *why* of it.

When the service was over, the procession began, the New Orleans–style funeral, with Granny's casket being pulled by a horse-drawn carriage through the Quarter to her family crypt. We followed on foot through the streets, her family loaded down with flowers—calla lilies, her favorite—and Mia-Joy's brother's band played old, lilting hymns, with Stone on sax, accompanied by a tambourine, a snare drum, and a trio of gospel singers, call-and-answer style. There was an older gentleman with a bright white beard, a bald head, and the deepest bass voice, giving foundation to all the instruments. I watched him and tried to get lost in the music.

A hundred people, at least, walked in the procession, and I gladly hung back, with Mom giving me a few glances to make sure I was joining the group. I walked by myself, watching the old singer, trying not to let the guilt overpower me, trying to swallow back the urge to run away and hide.

When the parade strolled by the Union Passenger Terminal, it kicked on then, fiery and alive in my chest. I lost my footing for a second, and then I ducked into the station, deciding I couldn't go to the cemetery, couldn't do this anymore. Every cell in my body seemed to be alert, crackling with energy, as I hustled into the waiting area and collapsed in one of the sleek, wooden chairs. Could I possibly run? Just hop onto a train and get out of here?

I watched the seconds tick away on the large Art Deco clock above the ticket counter. Electrical?

I cracked my knuckles and read through the departure times. A ten-thirty train to Chicago was the first one going anywhere far. I could leave here. Although I wouldn't be looking up any old friends, maybe I could visit Sophie's grave before I decided where to go, what to do with myself—as if I could answer any of those questions. Ever.

It wouldn't solve it. I knew that. I couldn't run away from this.

I would just rest here for a minute and then walk home or catch a trolley, once I knew that the funeral procession had passed. I slunk inward and kept my eyes low, thinking. I thought about Annaliese and Cody back in Chicago. How easily Cody had let me shut him out after Sophie's funeral. How hard Annaliese had worked to help me. How I wouldn't let her.

I couldn't dwell on it. I had been right to push them away.

Brahms. The same four measures, over and over. The deep bass accompaniment. A minor. Guilt.

Solitary confinement. That was the only answer.

Because even though I was sure of my curse, of my power, I couldn't end it. I couldn't end *me*. There was still too much inside me, too much of my mother's daughter that could not contemplate that. I knew, deep down in that dark place of truth, that someday, maybe someday soon, I might be able to contemplate it, but not now. And for that I was grateful.

The air around me tightened and shifted in a tangible way, and I looked up, expecting something. I didn't know what.

"You've got to be kidding me," I said under my breath, but there he was, striding right toward me. Rennick. He had already spotted me, and he waved, walking all confident and breezy.

I didn't trust myself with any more interactions. When your own body betrays you in such a violent and deadly way, how can you trust anything about yourself? And that was me now, teetering, unsure, the rug forever pulled out from under me. A constant state of disorientation.

I had knocked my head pretty badly once on the diving board at Chaney Pool during swim practice and went under, and there had been a five-second span of time when I panicked. Couldn't tell up from down, front from back.

That was like my life now.

I hurried into the women's restroom. Was it a coincidence that Rennick was here? Or had he been looking for me? Had he been at the funeral?

I took my sweet time in the restroom—washed my hands, fiddled with my hair, read all the graffiti on the wall—hoping against hope that he would get the hint.

He didn't.

The train station had become bustling while I wasted time in the bathroom. Several groups of what looked like day-care children and their chaperones had entered the station, as well as a large knot of older kids, all wearing orange T-shirts, some kind of field trip.

I scanned the room and there he was. Standing right by my chair, arms crossed, waiting.

I tightened my posture, balled my hands at my sides, hunched my shoulders. It was crowded. Beyond crowded. And I couldn't touch anyone. I swore under my breath.

I had to get away. I skirted toward the nearest exit and found myself outside on the concrete sidewalk in front of the station. A small crowd stood in line near a hot dog vendor; a mom with a half-dozen kids walking in line with linked hands passed in front of me. I didn't want to cut through the children, so I moved laterally.

"Hey!" I heard from behind me. I knew it was him. I turned left, tried to pretend I didn't hear him.

I balled my fists a little bit tighter, and my nails burrowed into my palms. When I was finally clear of the children, I walked quickly toward the makeshift farmer's market set up on the large lawn in front of the station, hoping to get lost in the crowd.

I was in so much of a hurry, I narrowly missed running straight into an elderly man using a walker. As I worked my way more slowly through the throng of people, with my hands balled at my sides, close to my hips—my normal stance—someone grabbed my arm. Low, near the wrist.

I gasped, frozen. "Don't touch!"

It was Rennick, of course, and he looked at me peculiarly, but he didn't let go right away. Just for a moment, he held my wrist. Long enough to let me know that he was in charge. Then he dropped it, leaned in close to me.

"I'm not going to hurt you, Corrine. But you have to listen to me."

"No, you don't understand. You can't talk to me. I can't be the—"

"I see the blue—the indigo—when I look at you," he said, and then it was like the noise, the commotion, the world around us faded to gray. The bass of a nearby car radio, the couple speaking French beside us, the traffic sounds—they ceased to exist. It was just him and me standing there on the lawn, his eyes locked on me. I remembered the blue, the blinding indigo light on the rocks with Sophie. I had no doubt that this was what he was referring to.

My body slackened. I saw the edges of my vision get swimmy, begin to tunnel, but I pushed it back as quickly as it came.

"What do you know?" I said in a voice that I had intended to sound in charge but instead came out as nothing more than a squeak.

"Follow me."

"No," I answered, but then I was following him.

He led me farther into the farmers' market, through the aisles of stalls, each one spilling over with brightly colored merchandise. There were too many people, too close and too loud. Before I knew it, we were at a standstill in front of a quasi voodoo booth, bearing gifts of gris-gris and Mardi Gras beads, tourist junk.

He grabbed my arm again, low near the wrist. "Come here."

"No! Please!"

He gave me a look but didn't let go. I yanked my arm violently, but his grip didn't loosen.

"Please," I whispered, terrified, his hold so close to my hand. *My hand.* The source of it all.

His brow furrowed, and he shook his head at me. Whereas he had seemed so nonthreatening before, so laid-back and friendly, now he was serious, forceful. "I'm not going to hurt you, Corrine," he said again. "But you have to listen to me before you get on that train and I never see you again."

"No, you don't understand." I tried to get myself thinking straight, but the pressure of his hand on my wrist, that physical touch, felt like a bomb about to blow up. "I don't want to hurt you," I said, getting my wits back a little. There was no way this stranger could know about Sophie, about me. "You have to let me go. Please. It's dangerous for you. I'm not—"

"I see things," he said in a low, stern voice. He looked

at me for a second, that playful, lackadaisical smile of the Crawdaddy Shack now gone. His deep blue eyes bored into me. "I see things about people, Corrine."

I tried to yank my hand away, but he held it still, and I didn't know if it was just because I hadn't been touched in so many months, if it had always felt so hot, or if it was just his touch—*this* touch—but my skin under his hand was burning. It didn't hurt, not in a harmful way, but like the sun on your face in a swimming pool.

"Please," I begged. "Don't make me scream. Because I will. You seem nice enough." I was speaking quickly, trying desperately to ignore the unhinged note in my voice. "Just let me go before you regret this."

"Here, here we go," he said, pulling me across the aisle toward a fisherman's stand. He drew a five-dollar bill out of the back pocket of his jeans and laid it on the woman's metal table. "Do you have anything that's really fresh?"

The woman eyed his hand around my wrist just for the briefest of beats, but then she looked at me. I could've said something. I didn't. So the woman turned to Rennick, answered him. "Fresh and tasty, whatcha got a hankerin' for? Gator nuggets?"

"No." He shook his head, drew me closer to him, hid our hands behind him. "I need something that just came in, a fresh catch. Just been dead for minutes, maybe less than an hour."

She turned and took a few steps back toward some crates,

a great big tin wash bin. "Trust me," he said low. "You *can't* not know this, Corrine. It'll change everything."

"Crawdads came in just a few minutes ago, some of them still snapping they claws." She gestured toward the white bucket she held up.

"Two, please. Dead ones, okay?"

She took her time wrapping two crawdads in butcher paper. My abductor reached for them with his free hand. I yanked hard just as his attention waned, but he was too strong for me.

He pulled me back; it was no use. He moved us away from the stand.

"No!" I screamed at him, not caring who heard me. "No, please!" Tears were coming down my face now. I kicked him hard, once, twice, in the shin, but he didn't seem to notice. He pulled me through the crowd, toward an old stone bench in front of the train station. He sat down and sat me down too. He ripped open the butcher paper with his teeth and grabbed one of the crawdads in his hands.

He opened the palm of my hand that he had been holding, and I could feel my heart beating in my neck, in the thud of my eardrums. I wondered briefly, sadly, if the curse, the poison, the death of me had traveled into him already, had affected him. I wondered how he would die. Would it be soon? Would it take a long time? Would it be painful?

He placed one of the crawdads in my open palm and closed my other hand around it. I heard sobbing and was surprised when I realized that it was me. "What are you doing?"

"Just focus on your hand, Corrine. Think about it."

I thought about the dead crawdad. I thought about dead Sophie, Granny Lucy, Mia-Joy. I thought about this crazy stranger who thought maybe he could help this loony girl who everyone talked about. How he would soon be dead like this poor crawdad.

Why? I wanted to hit him. I was suddenly so intensely angry, furious at this kid. What gave him the right? "Asshole!" I yelped, and I tried to rip my hands away from his grip. But again, he just held on to me, a pained look on his face. Well, he would get his, I thought ruefully, but then I thought better of it. I didn't mean it. I didn't.

Here I sat, inexplicably, when I should've been in isolation. A crawdad in my hand instead. In my chest, under my ribs, a swirling heat came to life, and then my skin, every cell, awoke. The heat exploded, radiated from my middle to my limbs, my hands. Just like with Sophie.

My hands. I was powerless to stop it.

I opened my eyes when I felt it. It surged through me, out of me, around me. This coursing, burning current coming from my core, churning out into the rest of me. It was part of me, coming from me, but also alien and outside of me as well. It felt powerful and alive, but it was also unwieldy and reckless.

And there was the blue. Everything indigo. Rennick

stared at me, smiling, expectant, his eyes wide. The crawdad's antennae or claw or something tickled the inside of my
closed hands. I realized then that Rennick's hands were both
cupped around mine, and we slowly opened our hands up,
and the crawdad was moving, pinching. Alive.

I dropped it on the ground, watched it wriggle around.

"I knew it," he said, reaching down to pick it up. "That
is crazy! Holy shit!" He held the crawdad, looked at it in
amazement. "I'm sorry to force you, but you had to find out.
I knew someone else like you. Once. A long time ago. And I
heard that you–"

"It wasn't dead to begin with," I said, disbelieving, shaking my head, watching the blue leave my vision in swirling
inky puddles.

"It was."

"This is some kind of trick. Who put you up to this?"

He furrowed his brow, leaned in close to me, said quietly,
"You brought that thing back to life."

I stood up and shook my head. I stepped away from him,
pulled myself inward. This was some kind of joke. Some
kind of cruel joke. "You don't know anything."

He stood, took a step closer to me. "I heard about your
sister, Corrine. I Googled you and I–"

"You don't know anything."

He squinted at me. "I do," he challenged.

And it was the weight of everything on me at that
moment, the frustration, the guilt, the helplessness of not

being able to do anything about anything, not being able to pull my arm away from this guy. He deserved it. I brought my knee up hard, right into his groin. "That's for not letting me go."

He doubled over, surprised, out of breath, and inexplicably laughing.

"Jerk," I grumbled, and took off. I was hollowed out, unraveled.

I hailed a cab back to the Garden District. Rimsky-Korsakov's *Flight of the Bumblebee* played its frenzied measures inside my brain. Beating its wings, its rhythm against my temples. I was fourteen before I really mastered that piece. It was designed to sound like chaos. To play like it. But it wasn't.

He didn't follow me back to my house.

I dragged myself up to my room and fell into bed, exhausted. I closed my eyes and the room spun. The world spun out of control around me. I concentrated on my breathing, slow, steady. My body ached, my nerve endings frayed and raw. I stripped down to my bra and underwear and lay on top of my covers. I was hot, too hot. My mind wanted to puzzle through everything that had happened, but my body wouldn't let me. The exhaustion was ridiculous. My head felt heavy and fuzzy, full of cotton.

I fell asleep quickly. And I slept hard, dreaming of an indigo light, glowing, pulsating, coming for me in waves, each one getting closer. Ready to swallow me whole.

I woke sweaty and alarmed just as the indigo light reached me in my dream. I sat up with that airless feeling in my throat, as if I had just screamed. I took a few deep breaths and calmed myself down, noticing that the sun slanting into my room had the half-lit pink look of twilight. I watched the shadows of the pear tree dance on my bedroom ceiling. Their movements made me think of Gershwin and old Fred Astaire movies, the beautiful dancing sequences. Black and white. Rhythmic. Soothing. Mezzo piano. Quiet.

I pressed the palms of my hands together in front of my face as I sat there and tried to remember what it felt like to ·just touch someone that way, palm to palm. Did it always carry so much heat? Back in my before-life? When I gave high fives? When I held hands with Cody through the vintage horror movies on Friday nights at the Casablanca Theater? When I held on to Sophie so I wouldn't lose her at the mall?

That crawdad had to have been alive to start with, just unconscious, asleep, something. I was ninety-nine percent sure.

But I had felt something. I couldn't discount it. That same kind of current, that same kind of buzzing beneath my skin, around my skin, enveloping me when I held that crawdad.

Who was he? This Rennick Lane? What did he know? And was there any possible way that he was right? That I had this power to resuscitate something recently dead?

It was a ridiculous question. Sophie.

I hadn't resuscitated Sophie. I hadn't helped her. I hadn't done anything but ensure that she died, that she ceased to live. She would no longer thumb wrestle with my dad, plead for a dog, play video games with all the lights off, or beg me to read her the first Harry Potter one more time.

"But you have the best Hagrid voice!" she would tell me, giving me those puppy-dog eyes. And when that wouldn't work, she would whistle through her teeth for me, that lonely little gap in her front teeth. It always made me laugh.

I threw my legs over the side of the bed, pulled on some clothes. The twitching movement of the crawdad in my palm seemed too near, too recent and real. I needed a reality check–something I had avoided for too long.

I went into my parents' room and got out the album. When we moved here, Mom had set right to changing Sophie's room into her home office so we wouldn't have to be reminded by her favorite stuffed green lizard lying alone on her bedspread, her empty window seat, her glittery sunglasses sitting on her dresser. The room was empty of Sophie's stuff now; it held a computer, a really cool glass-topped desk. A treadmill. None of us ever went in there anyway.

But my parents did look at the Sophie album. It had all of our favorite pictures of her through the years, through her nine years. Only nine years.

I never looked at it.

But I had seen Mom looking at it. Lots of times. Just a few weeks ago, I heard a racket in her room, stuff being thrown around, a loud crash, and when I got to the door, the

Sophie album was open on her bed. Mom sat with her hands in her face, her sobs shaking her shoulders, Dad picking up the remains of an antique crystal candlestick off the floor. One of her favorite flea market finds.

The pain in my rib cage, the weight of the guilt I was carrying, was astonishing. As I pulled the maroon photo album off the bookshelf, it was like I couldn't get a big enough breath into my lungs, not enough air in there along with all the guilt. But I needed to see. I needed to remember, to know what my hands had done.

I knew there was never any intent. God no.

But it is what it is. That's what Granddad always used to say. I had spent the past six months of my life trying to swallow that bitter pill, and now this guy with the hair was going to come out of nowhere and—grab my hand, for God's sake! He deserved worse than what I gave him.

I sat on the floor cross-legged and opened the photo album. There she was. Her school photo from last year. The way her curls popped up in the back, that crazy cowlick. Oh God, how it hurt to look at her.

Handel's *Messiah*. I hummed the hallelujah chorus. She had loved for me to play it last Christmas on the piano.

I fought the tears. Her blue eyes, all hopeful and ready for the world. That short nose, the freckles. Her gap-toothed smile.

I turned the page. Sophie as a baby, sitting in the laundry

basket chewing on the rawhide that belonged to Granddad's dog. Sophie swinging in the baby swing. Sophie eating her first ice cream cone. Sophie on the Canal Street ferry.

And here we both were, arms around each other, Sharpie mustaches that we drew on our faces—I had been trying to cheer her up after she broke her wrist falling out of the Sandbergs' hayloft.

Jesus, it hurt to look at these. I closed the album, leaned my head back on the bed.

When I was finished, I put the album back and went to my room. I took out my sketchpad and found my pastels. I picked the indigo pastel. It was like new, unused. I never consciously decided not to use it, but now that I looked at it, it was the exact right shade of blue. Just this side of dark blue, with a hint of violet. Just the right deepness to it. Like the ocean on a postcard kind of day. Or the sky when there's a rainbow.

Or the color of the powerful, flashing, crackling force of light that surrounds both you and your baby sister on the beach when you try to save her life, and you tell her, "Sophie, I got you, I got you," and you hold her close, and you see the way her face relaxes, like she knows that you'll save her, that it is going to be okay.

And you assume that blue is there when you lose time right then. You don't know what happens. But you are sure that blue is there.

That same blue of the waves, lapping at you both on the shore when you come to, and she's next to you—is she breathing?

And you reach out with your hand—

No. I shook my head, bumping it against the mattress behind me. *I am not thinking about this again.*

I was suddenly enraged, furious with Rennick "Mr. Crawdad Magic Trick" Lane. Did he think that he could gain some friends by telling them crazy stories about me? Was he trying to impress some voodoo-happy pals of his? Had he done that to me on some dare? Trying to get me to wig out so that he and his friends could laugh about it with some quart beers down at the cemetery later on?

I knew that I would go find Rennick tomorrow morning. I knew that I was going to give him a piece of my mind. I also knew that, no matter how mad I was, I didn't want to entangle him in my curse. But who knew what he might do next time?

I was going to put him in his place. Then maybe I'd just keep going and leave here.

I shook my head. No. I knew I couldn't run. It wouldn't do any good. I couldn't get away from this. I couldn't get away from *me*. I would just end up hurting other people. Someone else's loved ones. Someone else's Sophie.

5

I stayed in my room. Isolation.

But I also Googled things. Weird things like physio-electricity. Reanimation of crustaceans. I didn't believe Rennick. But part of me wanted to.

I didn't find any answers. Not even any leads. But he had me thinking.

It was late, and I sat on my bed eating cucumbers and ketchup—Sophie's favorite.

I had absentmindedly sketched several pictures of Mia-Joy while I sat on my bed watching TV. But I hadn't gotten her eyes exactly right. They flitted from one thing to another so quickly. She lived her life in eighth notes, bouncing here and there, staccato. And I hadn't captured it.

I heard a *click-clack* then. I cocked my head, tried to figure out where it had come from.

Click.

I stared at the window. It sounded like it came from there. *Click-clack.* There it was. Someone had thrown something at my bedroom window. I froze for a second. What? I didn't know if I should go see who it was or just ignore it.

Maybe because I had just been looking at her picture, I thought of Mia-Joy. Maybe she needed me. Was there something I could do for her—from a distance? I hesitated. I felt guilty that I hadn't talked to her since Granny Lucy's death.

Another rock. *Click-clack.*

I walked over to the window, peered into my backyard, which was bathed in only a small triangle of light from the nearby streetlamp. I saw a figure there. It looked larger than Mia-Joy. I squinted.

The figure waved, then beckoned. Before I realized who it was, I had this sense that I was watching one of the old black-and-white movies I loved. The streetlamp, the swoop of his gravity-defying hair, the line of his profile. He was the hero, the suave leading man. Lithe and broad-shouldered. Moving with confidence. Fred Astaire. I blinked and brought myself back to where I was, to who really stood down there in my yard.

It was him. Rennick. I stepped back and sat on my bed.

Son of a gun, I thought. *Did he come for another kick in the nuts?*

I wanted to be mad at him. I wanted to think he had pulled some big prank on me. But really, I was hoping there was some truth to what he had told me. Shown me.

But maybe his buddies were waiting in the bushes, ready to scare the shit out of the freaky Corrine Harlowe, who couldn't shake anyone's hand or give a high five. Or usually meet anyone's eye. I knew about the snickers, the theories all the kids at school had about me. Germophobe. OCD. Schizo. *Rennick.*

But there was a part of me that was curious. Could he know something? It was just so hard to trust myself, my judgments, anything.

I stopped still on my bed for a moment, reaching for my blue nail polish. What if I could control it somehow? Tame it. Not just be at its mercy. It was a singular thought. And because everything always seemed so out of my control, so beyond me, I hadn't ever *seriously* considered it. Until that moment.

What if I learned to control it? What if the crawdad was not a fluke? Was that plausible? What if I could *own* this thing?

I thought of Mom's quivering chin when she had broken the news about Granny Lucy's death. The way she had come into my room later that night and asked if I thought I needed to see Dr. Claude again. "Because, Corrine," she had said, "he can go through the medical reports again. Explain how Sophie died from cardiac arrest, likely brought on by the head injury. I mean, I thought we were getting somewhere." She had waited for me to respond. I was surprised that I was so transparent, that she knew what I was thinking, but then again, that was Mom.

My silence answered her. *She* liked to believe we were getting somewhere.

"You didn't have anything to do with Lucy," she had said. "Corrine, I lost Sophie, and ever since, I lose you a little bit more every day. Your father and I can't watch you do this!" Her voice had broken, and she had reached for me, without thinking, I'm sure.

I had recoiled, but I added, "I'll see Dr. Claude." I would do anything to keep that hopeless look off of her face.

Maybe even see what this Rennick knew.

In my before-life, before Sophie died, I had loved goals, challenges, winning. I tackled Beethoven's Ninth for contests when everyone said it was suicide. I chose Faulkner off the English list when everyone else veered toward Stephen King or Joyce Carol Oates. When Coach told me I had a better chance to go to state in the free or even the medley, I chose the butterfly. It was the hardest for me as a swimmer. I came in second. I did get a first at contest for Beethoven that year, though. But I never did understand Faulkner. I traded him in halfway through the semester for Stephen King and read six of his books over spring break last year.

Tame it. Control it. It sounded impossible. But didn't all of this?

I held the bottle of nail polish in my hand, frozen on my bed with this newfound possibility. I felt lighter as I painted my nails and listened to Rennick's pebbles bounce off my window. The guy did not give up easily.

I tiptoed out of my room, unsure whether I was going out there to ask him some questions or to yell at him to just leave me alone. But either way, I was going out there. My mother's bedroom door sat open. She lay sprawled on her bed, asleep, papers on her chest, her reading glasses still on. Dad slept next to her, snoring loudly.

I slipped down the stairs and through the kitchen, to the back door. The front door often creaked, and I was glad that I had remembered.

I unlocked the dead bolt, so quietly, remembering last year with Cody. When Annaliese and I had snuck out of my old house, toilet-papered Cody's whole front yard on his eighteenth birthday.

I froze when the screen door opened with the requisite snap. But I didn't hear anything from above. I turned the knob and walked out. I let my breath out on the back stoop as I closed the door behind me.

I turned around, and sure enough I heard a footstep near the brush that lined the back of our property, by the garden Mom had planted in Sophie's memory. I waited. Closer footsteps, the silhouette of someone near the lilacs.

The air took on an expectant, loaded quality, and I knew he was there. I felt it. And in that moment, I doubted my reasons for coming out here altogether. Did he know anything? Had it all been just a prank? I wavered, unsure. My feelings were so untrustworthy these days.

He appeared out of the shadows. "Hey," he said.

"You can't be around me," I said.

"Listen," he said, "I know you don't want to talk to me. I know you're mad at me. And I shouldn't have done that with the crawdad. It probably just scared you even more, shell-shocked as you are. But you have got to listen to me before–"

"Just tell me what you want to tell me," I said, and I tried to ignore it, but it was there, inside, deep inside like a pilot light switching on, heating up.

He started to say something, then stopped himself, rubbed at his chin, raked his hand through his hair in a funny motion. My eyes adjusted to the dark now, and I noticed his teeth, how they overlapped a little in the front. An imperfection.

"Two minutes," I said impatiently, feeling the heat swirl and grow.

"You listen to me," he said gruffly, pointing at me. "I'm going to knock on that door and wake up your parents, tell them I found you ready to hop a train, if you don't give me a few minutes here." He looked at me hard, threatening me, although I could see the apology in the shake of his head. But it was what it was.

I knew he would knock on the door, so I just gritted my teeth. "Tell me what you know."

I met his eyes briefly. The moon was low in the sky, a tiny crescent, a thumbnail, as Sophie used to say. It was an inky night, with very little light, especially in the back of my house, next to the hydrangeas and the electric meter. And, of course, right beneath the window of my parents' bedroom.

I listened to the hum of the crickets and toads as Rennick gathered himself. He rubbed his hand across his forehead nervously, and he started to say something twice but stopped himself again. I softened toward him for a second when I realized exactly why he seemed so different from anyone else in New Orleans. It was because he treated me normally. Like people did back in Chicago, back before everything. Easy. Normal. Everyday.

Here in New Orleans, I was not a real person. I was a freak, a weirdo. No one treated me like Corrine. I was a story. The sideways glances. The whispers. I deserved it.

Finally, Rennick pulled a couple of rolled-up papers from his back pocket and handed them to me. I took them reluctantly, carefully.

"Just read them," he said. "I looked into a few things. It's hard to know where to start, Corrine." He looked at me for a moment; the headlights from a passing car flashed in his eyes, and I could see concern there, tenderness.

It hit me, deep under my ribs in a weird way, and my breath caught in my throat. I shook my head. In that moment, in that flash of human interaction, all that I had been missing in the months of my emotional and near-physical quarantine hit me out of the blue. Why he—this near stranger—would wait out here for me, or why he cared, I had no idea. But it was odd and disconcerting how much it meant to me, here in my darkest hour.

"I'm sorry," I told him. "You shouldn't be around me." The skin on my scalp tightened, itched. The hairs on my arms stood up. The air around us thickened, and the buzz in my molars came back. My hand went to my jaw, and I pressed my fingers against it.

He hadn't seemed to notice. "Just promise me you'll read this, and know that—"

A spark jumped then from the electric meter, scaring us both.

"That's part of it," Rennick said, excited, pointing toward the meter. "Corrine, you—"

I held my hand up to quiet him. I heard something. Footfalls in the long, dew-wet grass. The swish of Mom's robe against it.

Mom appeared around the corner of the house, coming out from the front. Mom. In her blue polka-dot pajamas, her white terry-cloth robe.

She cleared her throat. "Corrine?" she said, low, questioning.

"Mom, I just came out—"

Her mouth was a grim line. She looked worried. Did she think maybe I was leaving? Running away?

"Is this the boy who was throwing rocks earlier?" Her voice sounded flat, unimpressed.

"I'm sorry, ma'am. I apologize." He looked at me hard. "Corrine..." I waited for him to say more, but he didn't.

"Mom, I'll be in in a minute," I said. She nodded, gave us our privacy.

"I never meant to scare you off," Rennick said. "I'm sorry about before."

"I'm sorry about the knee," I said.

He gave me a quick nod and was already through the lilac hedge when I called out to him. "Thanks."

I spread out the four crinkled pages in front of me on my bedspread. The first two sheets were filled with chicken-scratch handwriting, I assumed his.

The realization that he treated me like a normal person softened me toward him, enough to give him some kind of credibility. But still, that made it even harder to entangle him in my curse. I didn't want to hurt him.

But I had to know what he knew.

The notes were difficult to decipher at first glance. There was a lot of talk of auras, of certain colors, how to interpret them. This color equals this certain trait. There were Web addresses, article titles, references to all kinds of incidents. Articles on electricity—something called dirty electricity. And another term: atmospheric electricity. A new idea that scientists were testing now—that electricity could be gleaned from the air, harnessed, and used, not unlike solar power. I looked up some of it on my iPad. It was all very interesting stuff. But the last two pages really grabbed my attention.

They contained a xeroxed article from the *Sutton County Herald*. The headline read, "Child Saves Life, Credits Blue Light." The tune I had been humming in my head suddenly switched keys, went lower, C minor, with an eerie, spooky tone to it. My heart sped up and I read the article with interest once, then again more slowly, taking in the details. I noted the date at the top: September 28, 2002.

A seven-year-old boy found his father after he had fallen off of a ladder in the garage. His father was unconscious, and the boy knew enough to check his breathing. There was none. The boy called 911, but living out in the country, he knew he couldn't wait. And that's when it got really interesting.

The description of the blue light, the words he used, the feeling he described, matched exactly the way I experienced the blue light with Sophie.

In fact, it was the clearest part of that day. The most vivid memory. The boy, Jurgen Jameson was his name, said that the blue light "had some green and purple in it too, and it wasn't like a haze but more like a lens." This struck me.

It was exactly as I had experienced it. And then he described the feeling of the blue light "as if it started in my chest and throat and crawled out to my hands, into my daddy."

I dropped the paper back onto my bed and stared into space. "Holy fluck."

6

L ater that night, I lay on my bed, sharpening my sketching pencil. I thought of Mia-Joy. I glanced at my phone on the nightstand. I knew I should call her. A memory hit me, clear as day. Sixth-grade summer. Mia-Joy had been all limbs and teeth, so skinny. Bossy and loud, with frizzy hair. But then something had happened the year of seventh grade, because when I came back that next summer, Mia-Joy had blossomed, grown into herself. She'd become a swan. So then she was tall, thin, striking. Bossy and loud. Still herself. But what I most admired, and didn't realize until later, was that she hadn't really changed. Not inside. She had become the most beautiful teenager, the most beautiful girl most of us had ever seen in real life, and she didn't change.

She was obsessed with modeling, sure. She forced me to make audition tapes of her for every last reality TV modeling show in the world. But she still laughed that same loud bark of a laugh. She still kept the same friends.

At that moment, I looked up from my pencil and sighed. I realized how much I liked and admired Mia-Joy. How much I missed her. She never shut up. She watched only reality TV. She talked more and louder than anyone. She read only fashion magazines and apologized for nothing. God, she was fun.

She reminded me of Annaliese. Just a more brash, real version of Annaliese, without the ridiculous collection of cowboy boots and love of all things country-western. I had a sudden flash of Annaliese and me doing the line dance at the sophomore spring fling. She had worn that belt buckle with the bull horns. Oh God. I smiled and flopped back onto my pillow. It made my throat tighten a little bit. I thought of the old comics that Annaliese and I had been drawing right before the day with Sophie. Thinly veiled comics about our teachers at school. Poking fun at Mr. Vergara with his skinny jeans. Mrs. Temperance and her '80s perm. I laughed out loud.

It sounded so sad as it echoed off the walls of my room.

It hurt to remember how easy things used to be. I had been on a trajectory. My life was going in the right direction. It was clean and uncomplicated. How I missed it. How much I had taken for granted.

I flashed back to the memory of Cody telling me how my hair was the exact shade of a Hershey's Kiss. I used to love that. I would tell people that story. I thought it was so cute. Now, when I thought of that, of Cody and me together, I wanted to punch him. Just punch him right in the jaw. I knew it wasn't fair. But it all just seemed so... innocent, so self-indulgent. Our stupid surface romance. I wanted to scream at my former self: *You don't even know what's important! You have no handle on things! Wake up!* I cringed when I thought of how our biggest fight had been over how he hadn't texted me when he told me he would one night. Not over anything actually important, like when he became frustrated with me when I tried to talk to him about music, about deeper things, about dreams and the future, about life and what it meant to me.

I thought of the concert when I had first played *Requiem*. It was my debut with the Chicago Junior Symphony. When I got offstage, Cody had met me with one red rose, and he looked all handsome and preppy in his khakis and collared shirt. "What did you think?" I asked, still a little out of breath and existing on that other plane, the one where I didn't just play music, I played emotion, life, possibility.

"Great," he said, kissing me on the cheek. He bounced on his heels. He checked his cell phone. I still had goose bumps, feeling the magic of the music, right there, coursing under my skin. "We can still meet up with everybody downtown if we hurry." He yanked on my elbow.

"Oh," I said, "yeah." I forced a smile and hurried out with my friends.

Because I knew he was just being Cody. He was popular

and hot. A good prank partner. For his senior prom, we won king and queen, and we went up to the podium wearing those goofy glasses with the big noses and mustaches. We dressed up as Fred and Daphne from *Scooby-Doo* for Halloween. We sailed on the weekends on Lake Michigan with his parents. We went to all the fun parties. He made me cooler, more popular, and, fluck, he was fun.

But he didn't *get* me. I knew that even then, and it made me feel shallow.

I shook the memories away. Annaliese had tried after Sophie. She had tried. Cody had given up easily. And I had not been surprised. I had pushed them both away. I had pushed everyone away.

I grabbed my phone, finally working up the courage to call Mia-Joy. When she answered, I broke down. "I'm so sorry, Mia-Joy."

"I know, Corrine. It's okay."

"I'm sorry I couldn't speak to you at the funeral or that I–"

"Really. It's okay." And Mia-Joy sounded so fine. She sounded honest and forgiving. She always was.

"At the cemetery, we shared stories about her. Celebrated her life," Mia-Joy said. "I missed you there. You would've liked it, I think."

"Celebrated her life," I repeated. And I tried to hold on to that phrase.

Mia-Joy told me some of the funny stories that people shared about Granny Lucy when she was younger, teaching high school typing, how she used to slap kids' knuckles with a ruler if they weren't paying attention. How she used to wear her hair in cornrows, enough beads at the ends of them to make music every time she turned her head. I laughed with Mia-Joy and let her talk. She went on and on, and I listened, glad that I could at least do that for her.

"I should go," she said after a long while, sighing into the phone. "It's super late."

But I had one more thing I wanted to ask. "Mia-Joy, tell me what you know about Rennick Lane. Are you guys friends?"

"Why?"

"He knows things about me," I said.

"Corrine, he's Ren from the Pen. From school."

I backtracked in my mind a little bit. Liberty was a big place, and it was true that I had gotten in the habit of purposely not looking into people's faces, but I *heard* things. Rennick Lane was Ren from the Pen? The kid that everyone talked about last fall when he came to our school? That seemed crazy.

"Penton Charter?" I asked.

"Got kicked out. Had to go to public school. It's no big secret."

"And what was it for?" I had heard things. And I could conjure the memory of Rennick's silhouette now. Always alone, that movie-star rebel look about him. Leather jacket in the winter. Jeans and a T-shirt. Too cool.

"I don't know. Nobody really does, Corrine. Fighting, I heard. But he doesn't really seem the type, does he?"

"I don't know," I answered.

"He seems like he knows you. Acts like it. I thought you knew him."

"I thought *you* knew him."

"I'll tell you what. I watched him stick up for that boy with Down syndrome, Jarvis, you know who I'm talking about?"

"I do."

"Kids were being awful to him in the cafeteria. That one greasy kid, Pollack? He actually shoved pudding in Jarvis's face. It was ugly. Rennick took that douchebag by the collar and made him apologize to Jarvis. It was something."

"Yeah?" I said, feeling something for Rennick now. Pride?

"He eats with Jarvis once in a while now. He seems nice enough. I don't like to believe the gossip."

"Me either," I said, thinking of what kids probably said about me, what I *knew* they said about me. "Thanks."

"Corrine?"

"What?"

"No one, and I mean *no one,* thinks that the death of a ninety-year-old lady is your fault."

I swallowed hard. "Thanks," I said, and hung up quickly before Mia-Joy could hear the tears in my voice.

7

I woke up and my hands were itchy in that way they sometimes got. They couldn't sit still, tapping out invisible
rhythms on my palms or air-playing some invisible fiddle.
Normally, I could practice the nerves out of my hands. I
would grab my violin, and within the first few minutes I
would just settle in, become completely still, aside from the
motion of my bow on the strings and the flutter of my fingers
from one string to another. In those moments, I felt so bold
and sure about my place in the world.

I missed the violin. I missed feeling good about myself.

I didn't even get out of my pajamas, just clicked in the
next tape from Mom. My hands needed something to do.

This was a new lady. Room 232, the tape said. Lila Twopenny. Her voice shook, like older people's sometimes do,
but I could quickly tell that although Mrs. Twopenny was
at the end of her days, she still had her mind. She spoke

articulately about dancing in a ballet company, working as a bit actress in seven films. And as she got going, her voice trilled like a songbird.

She talked about her husband, Dodge, and her children, all girls. One named Nancy who died as an infant. Two other girls, Clara and Ruth. Twins.

I drew the delicate line of her nose, the upturn at the end, the high-arched eyebrows.

"Ruth had the touch," Mrs. Twopenny said. My ears perked up, as well as the hairs on the back of my neck.

I held my pencil still, very still. And then I hit REWIND, listened to that line one more time. "Ruth had the touch."

"Yes?" This was my mom's voice on the tape, interviewing. Soothing, a little bit sleepy.

"She had what they said was a healer's hand. That's what we called it back then. We didn't have any science to explain it away. Plus it made it easier for us all to believe in miracles like that."

Mom had perked up now. "What miracles, Lila? Can you tell me?"

Mrs. Twopenny cleared her throat, and I heard objects scuffling around on a table—getting a drink of water maybe? "I reckon Ruth knew at a young age. It hit her around twelve, I would say. She would heal right quick when she got scratched climbing the old oak down by the pond. But the first time I really stopped and paid attention was when Clara broke her wrist falling off of Dodge's old white mare, Lucky.

I pressed them bones in my own hand, could darn near feel the separation of the big bone in her wrist." Mrs. Twopenny paused here, and I could picture her showing my mother where on the arm it occurred. I realized I was clamping down on my own wrist, feeling the bones, guessing whether it was the one near the thumb or the pinky.

"We lived in Georgia at the time and rode all the way into Macon to get that bone set by a doctor who knew what he was doing. At the time, I thought it just so sweet that Ruth held Clara's hand, her wrist, with this serious-type expression on her face the whole way. It was right bumpy. A long ride in the back of our truck. Anyways, we got to the hospital and Clara's wrist was completely healed. Those medical doctors done looked at me and Dodge like we was crazy."

"Huh," Mom said. No one spoke for a long moment. Finally, Mom asked what I was thinking. "Were there other times?" Her voice was respectful, not necessarily believing.

"Oh sure," Mrs. Twopenny said. I was thinking of the crawdad. Of Rennick. "Ruth couldn't always fix things. Didn't know exactly how it all worked, could only do it when she saw blue, never did quite know what that meant but..." Mrs. Twopenny's voice got very small now.

My mouth fell open. I dropped the pencil. *She saw blue.*

"Our old reverend called her a witch," she whispered.

Mom said something. Something about how God works in mysterious ways, but I didn't hear it.

I rewound the tape, listened to it again, and then I let it

play out. Mrs. Twopenny talked at length about her daughters, her life, and it was interesting, but no more talk of the touch. I couldn't believe what I was hearing. Saw blue. The touch.

And then, near the end of the tape, she talked about her grandsons. Two of them.

Cale and Rennick.

It was easier to track him down than I thought it would be.

Holly, one of Mom's favorite nurses, answered the phone at Chartrain. "Does Mrs. Twopenny have a grandson that's my age?"

"Yes. Rennick. He lives with his grandfather, Mrs. Twopenny's husband. Why?" Holly sounded like she had maybe said too much. I knew there was always the patient confidentiality stuff.

"Nothing, Holly. Thanks."

I used Mom's laptop, found the Twopenny house.

And even though I knew that it would be easier to call him, I didn't want to. I had to do this in person. This was too huge. He knew stuff. Major amounts of stuff. I was convinced of that now. His mother had the touch, or whatever you wanted to call my curse.

I started up my mom's minivan, glancing behind me at the empty seat that Sophie used to ride in. She used to love to sing in the backseat of the car. Mom and Sophie had had this ridiculous fascination with all things Elvis. I could picture Sophie singing along with him in her car seat—her high little voice teetering over the lyrics of "Jailhouse Rock." I sighed and typed Rennick's address into Mom's GPS.

I found the Twopenny house easily. It was out in the country, past the Garden District, near the Audubon Zoo in the woodsy part near Lake Calhoun. The road had ancient live oaks lining each side of it, bending toward each other in a canopy of kudzu. The street turned from pavement, to gravel, to really just a worn path, and then I could see a cluster of four houses ahead at the end of the lonely cul-de-sac. The Twopenny house was small, painted an obnoxious yellow, but it looked well maintained, happy, if that's possible. And it was nestled right at the edge of the lake.

I walked up the white-painted porch steps and knocked three times on the door. No answer. I hadn't been counting on this. I took a deep breath and knocked again. Nothing.

But I knew that I couldn't just leave. I would lose my nerve, and he *knew* things. I had too much to talk to him about. Too much to ask. Too much that mattered.

I sat down on the porch steps and decided to wait. It was hot and clammy out, but the porch offered a little bit of protection from the sun. I cracked my knuckles and waited, making a mental list of what I had to ask him.

Your mother had the touch?

How can I control it?

What is it?

Who else do you know who has the touch?

How do you know it's electrical?

I got up, brushed off the seat of my shorts, and walked along the side of the house, peered into the backyard. The far side of the property backed right up to the lake, with a small patch of woods to the west. A gorgeous little arbor sat down near the lake, with an old-fashioned swing hanging from it, magnolias creeping up on all sides. A chipmunk stopped in its path near a live oak, standing up on its hind legs to inspect me.

"Hi," I said, and it scampered off. I walked into the backyard, eyeing the large vegetable garden, and noticed that even though the gardens seemed overgrown in general, they were all blooming and thriving like crazy, overtaking every possible walking surface–the sidewalk, the modest lawn, the small fountain near the shed.

I heard a voice then, and splashing. My first instinct was to turn around, go back to my car. But then I saw a figure, large and brown, toward the edge of the lake. My first thought was, *How did a* bear *get down here in Louisiana?*

But a tennis ball came flying past me into the yard and the bear followed it, and by then I had put together that this was no bear, but just a behemoth of a dog. It was taller than my waist, its width ridiculous. Paws the size of oven mitts. It ran right past me, chased down the tennis ball. Then it stopped and shook itself, covering me in lake water.

"Sorry!" a voice called, and I put my hand to my eyes,

shielding them from the sun. I could see it was Rennick. A shirtless, soaking-wet Rennick.

I gulped hard, telling myself not to stare. "I'm sorry," I began. "I just had to come. I want to talk."

"Yeah, I'm glad," he said. He stopped to shake himself too, not unlike the dog. I couldn't help but notice that he was thin, yes, but wiry, built. Defined. And when he reached me in the yard, I tried to keep the blush from climbing into my neck, my cheeks, but I knew it was useless.

The dog joined us, tennis ball in mouth, as if awaiting an introduction. I was so glad to have something else to look at, something that wouldn't turn me into a slack-jawed moron.

"This is Bouncer," Rennick said, taking the ball from the dog's mouth, throwing it farther than I could see in the sun. The dog took off. "Want something to drink? I have some stuff in the garage," he said.

I nodded, trying to smooth down my ignored and frizzled hair. I wondered how he could seem so easy, so confident.

I followed him toward the small garage, stealing glances at his tanned shoulders, the way his hair curled up at the nape of his neck. I stopped abruptly when I got inside the door of what I first had thought was just a junky shed. I guess I expected lawn equipment, maybe a rusted-out Chevrolet, an old boat, something that screamed Louisiana hillbilly, but this was altogether different, although the old country honky-tonk music played softly from a radio on the counter.

The garage was a large, bare space, with a high ceiling

and exposed rafters. There were red-painted cabinets along the nearest wall, along with a sink and a mini fridge. In the middle of the room sat a long wooden table, just plywood on sawhorses. On it was a bunch of equipment, electrical cables, batteries, wires, things I couldn't name. Books were everywhere. Piled in corners, stacks as tall as me. Books open on the table. Books on the floor, near the worn black leather couch in the back. But what really got me was the far wall. It was covered, absolutely covered, all the way up to the rafters, in canvases, papers, and tackboard. Painting after painting after painting. At first look, they seemed to be put up haphazardly, but if you studied them, they weren't. Each one added to the ones near it. They built on each other. Some kind of messy, intricate design. They were all the same kind of painting, but each one was unique, just a study in color, in shading, in tone, in complements. They weren't rainbowish, no. More like . . . descriptions.

Before I knew it, I had walked past the lab table and was standing right in front of the color wall studying the canvases up close, their brushstrokes, the technique. "They're beautiful," I said.

Rennick just laughed a little under his breath, but I heard it there, the twinge of nervousness behind his cool demeanor.

But for a second, it's like I forgot why I was there. I forgot myself in those paintings. They weren't rainbows, they weren't color wheels, not haphazard combinations or streaks of colors, but rather descriptions of things. Things that defied words and description, things that didn't really have names or titles. They were something akin to feelings. Truths. Shown through patterns and movement, through the slightest variations of blues. Shown through the arch of a slow gradation from yellow to orange, through the fierce growth from white to red to purple.

I saw...friendship? Patience? Pride? No, those words only hinted at what was in these paintings. It was indescribable. Like the feeling you get when you're eight years old and you wake up on Christmas morning, everything in front of you. Or how it feels to look into someone's eyes and know that they just really *get* you.

Or how it feels to do something right, something selfless—that floaty feeling underneath your ribs. This was here, spelled out in his paintings.

I was mesmerized.

But then it kicked on. Inside me. That roiling flame in my chest, and I was right back inside myself. Right back to the same old problem. I cleared my throat and turned around, embarrassed by how caught up I had gotten in the paintings.

"They're auras," he said. He had found a T-shirt now and handed me a bottle of water from the fridge. He looked less sure of himself.

And I was aware of how these paintings, this place as a whole, was private to him.

"Your grandmother is Lila Twopenny?" I said. I fingered the top on the water bottle.

"Yes, and my mother had what you have."

A beat passed until I realized I was staring at him, his dark blue eyes, the fringe of eyelashes. "How do you know about me? I'm sorry I've been . . . weird." I blushed, not knowing where to look.

"I scared you. I didn't mean to."

"This is all just . . . kinda . . . an ocean of crazy for me. I think that I—"

"I heard what people said about you at school. I read some things. I kind of study this stuff." He gestured toward his lab table.

"You think I'm electric?"

"It's what we tap into, I think. All of us who are *extra* somehow. Physio-electricity. You're a conduit." He motioned around in the air. "It's out here, you conduct it, and you turn it into something."

"But how?"

"Now you're asking questions I can't answer . . . yet." He smiled, back to his easy self.

"Have you seen your mom do these things?"

"No, she died when I was a baby."

"I'm sorry," I said. I waited for a second, took a drink of the water. "Could I ask your grandmother? I mean . . ."

"Sure. But it's all magic to her."

"It's not to you?"

"No." I liked his certainty.

"Do you know anyone else who can—"

"I did, years ago, when I was a kid."

I let out a sigh. I so wanted to be able to have someone who had all the answers. A guru of physio-electricity. But I figured that would be too easy.

"So what is this?" I asked, motioning to the stuff on the table, the equipment.

"Experiments."

"I see. . . . What are you testing?"

"Electricity. Life." He laughed. It was a good sound. "I just started copying the masters."

I raised my eyebrow.

"You know. Early electricity. Leclanché. Franklin. Faraday."

"In the hopes of . . ."

He smiled. Seemed amused. "In the hopes of . . . everything. I mean, why not? Seemed like a good place to start. I mean . . ." He paused and motioned to a contraption on his table. A silver ball, about the size of a soccer ball, hooked up to some wires. "It's a Van de Graaff generator." I shrugged at this. He flipped a switch and a barely audible hum filled the garage. The atmosphere shifted a tiny bit, and he motioned me over toward him. "When the masters first learned how to harness this, grab some of the static electricity out of the air, they were wild at what that could mean. The possibilities, ya know?" Rennick reached out for my hand. I shook my head. "Just put your palm on here." He motioned with his own. I shook my head again. "It's not going to electrocute you."

"You take your hand away. Then I'll try," I said, giving him a look. I waited, and when he did, I placed mine on the ball. It felt alive, in a very microscopic, tiny way. An electrical hum on the inside of my palm. Just as the ends of my hair began to lift up around me, I realized that I had seen this experiment in a video in science class. "The static electricity makes your hair stand on end," I said, remembering. Rennick chuckled, and I caught a glimpse of myself in the window reflection, the top layer of my hair standing out in straight lines from my head. I took my hand away. "So what's this got to do with me?" My hair floated back down. I smoothed it with my palms.

He nodded, sort of pushed his lips out, and I knew watching him that this must be his thinking face, his look of concentration. He switched off the silver ball, shook his head. "Maybe there's more to electricity. A whole new layer, just out there, waiting for us to tap into." He looked up then, gave a funny little laugh. "Or maybe some of us have already tapped in."

"But I want to know what this all means to *me*. To the touch." I didn't want to sound impatient, but there it was.

He got excited then, held his finger up in a *just wait* gesture. He grabbed a couple of wires with metal clamps at the end, then pulled a bucket out from underneath the table. He pried the lid off, and the garage filled with an acrid smell. Formaldehyde or a preservative of some kind. And instantly Rennick was transformed, a crease in his brow, his whole body full of tension, questions, but he looked strangely comfortable. This was a new confidence, a real one, not a facade. Rennick plunged his hand into the bucket and brought out a frog. A dead one, dripping clear liquid. He placed it on the table, and before I knew what he was doing, he had picked up a scalpel and slit its underside near the legs.

"Whoa . . . what are you—"

"Just hold on a minute. I mean, I could hook these up to dead frog legs, right? Make the muscles jump. Reanimate them?"

"Okaaay?" I answered.

As I watched, Rennick did just that. He secured the tiny silver clamps to the leg muscles inside the body of the frog, although I tried not to see exactly how, to keep my eyes away from the grayish-white frog innards and the bulging, glassy eyes.

Rennick pressed two live wires together and there was a spark. The legs of the frog twitched. He did it again, and I watched more closely this time. "It reanimates the frog. The legs move. Jump. But it doesn't bring the frog back to *life*. It doesn't restore that." He looked at me hard. "Just mimics it."

I thought for a second. "Do you think *the touch* mimics life?"

He shook his head, never taking his eyes from me.

"You think the touch *restores* life."

"Yes."

"So, how? That's a pretty big difference."

He just shrugged. "I agree." We stared at each other in silence. "There's a lot of things like that, a thin line between what we think we know and what we don't, really. Especially with electricity."

"I read about dirty electricity. Atmospheric too."

"Exactly. I mean, you put your finger in a socket, that electric current is going straight through you, quickest route it can find. But lightning doesn't do that. It kind of picks and chooses its route. Random. It can go in, wipe out the systems, organs, and leave not so much as a burn."

"So you think what I have is like lightning?"

"No, not at all," Rennick said. "I'm sorry. I got carried away. I just think there's a lot we don't know about tons of things, especially electricity. That's all." He gave me a sideways look. Plopped the frog back into its bucket, threw the wires on the table. "I just don't think we should be scared of what we don't know."

He held my gaze then. I saw myself in the reflection of his eyes. I was wide-eyed. Deer in headlights.

"You know what happened to my sister?" I whispered finally. "What I did?"

He nodded, wiped his hands on a rag. Our eyes never left each other's. We just held that gaze for a few beats. "I think you're wrong about that whole thing," he said.

It swirled too high then, the heat in my chest. It began to feel like hot coals beneath my ribs. "I have to go," I said, the clear, sharpened edge of truth coming alive inside me.

"But I think I—"

"Thanks," I said.

"Corrine, I'm glad you came," he said.

I walked briskly back to my mom's minivan, equal parts glad I came, scared by the connection I had made, and more confused than ever.

Mom asked me to go along with her to Chartrain the next morning. She had to visit a patient and said she could use the company.

I thought of her chin quivering. I thought of her at Lucy's funeral, knowing what memories it had brought to the surface for her, of Sophie. So I agreed. And there was also part of me that knew I agreed to go with Mom because this was me trying. This was me wanting to take a step.

Of course, once we got to Chartrain, Mom told me *who* she had to visit. Lila Twopenny. Of course. Her hospice patient.

Random? No.

The idea of coincidence didn't even seem to cover this.

I watched my mom carefully to see how she behaved. Did she know about Rennick? Had she been talking to Mia-Joy? As we entered Chartrain and Mom chirped hello to the staff and signed us in, I watched her face and it was mostly a study of worry—a furrowed brow, gray circles under the eyes. I knew I had caused them, and it didn't seem like she was in cahoots with Rennick.

Mom seemed surprised when I told her I would like to go in with her to see Mrs. Twopenny. "I just listened to her story," I explained. Mom gave me a look, but she didn't push it.

The room was decorated in bright yellows and reds, a loud flowered wallpaper pattern, lacy white curtains on the window. Someone cared about Mrs. Twopenny. Someone helped her room feel more like home.

"Good morning, Lila," Mom said.

"A visitor! Hello there, Leslie!" I recognized her voice and her face from my sketch. A burst of singsong laughter emitted from this tiny woman lying in the bed. "Introduce me!"

Mom smiled. "This is my daughter, Corrine."

I wanted to ask questions but didn't know how to begin. Could I possibly have some kind of curse that I could turn into a blessing?

Did the blue light similarity mean anything? Would my mom be seriously pissed if I started to interrogate this old lady? Should I have told my mom first?

"Say hello," Mom said to me, a stern look on her face. Obviously, Mrs. Twopenny was a woman not long for this world, and Mom wasn't going to bear me not saying hello.

I stood there dumbstruck, trying to figure out the best line of questioning. I ignored my silence rule. I didn't even consider it, actually. "Hello, ma'am," I said. "Nice to meet you." I took one more step closer to her, and when I did it was like I hit a wall of *feeling*. Energy.

It surprised me, and it froze me, so I didn't see—didn't really register—when Mrs. Twopenny's long thin arm reached from her side toward me. Before I knew what was happening, Mrs. Twopenny's frail-looking, age-spotted hand clasped onto mine. I stared at it for a moment before I could believe it.

I pulled back. My hand slipped from hers, but she grabbed my other one with both of hers. Tight, strong. She had sat up now. And that's when the lens of blue shifted in front of my eyes, coloring everything indigo, but not just coloring it, making it glow too, my mom's face, the flowered wallpaper, the now-blue lace curtains. The energy opened like a flower in my chest, pulsating and pushing through my extremities. I closed my eyes against it, the power of it, the surge. And I tried once more to loosen my hand from Mrs. Twopenny's. The woman was strong. But it was more than that. I was leaden in my position, a conduit. Frozen.

I let the indigo current—not unpleasant, but definitely singular in itself—flush through me, out the tips of my fingers, through the soles of my feet, my eyelids, out of my open mouth. Time stopped around me, and I sank into the blue, felt and saw nothing but this power, this surge inside me, throughout me, around me. Into Lila Twopenny. C-sharp major. It felt like C-sharp major. My favorite key. Anything was possible in that key. I could always make music in that key.

When I opened my eyes, I saw Mrs. Twopenny first.

Her hand had dropped from mine, and her eyes had closed. Monitors beeped and blipped; an alarm went off. The lights flickered, once, twice, then went out. I turned to Mom. Her mouth was agape, and she pulled me to her, held me close. I didn't think to push her away.

I took a deep breath, aware now that I had been holding it. The exhaustion in my limbs and spine weighed me down. I leaned against my mother, hollowed out.

The air settled in the room, the charge dissipating. Two nurses dressed in peach scrubs flew into the room, bringing us back to reality. They spoke in serious, professional voices.

"Check her BP," the blond one said. "Check it manually. This machine is not working."

"Everything's shot in here," the male nurse said, pushing buttons on the IV.

"Breathing is shallow." The blond one turned to Mom. "Would you mind stepping out?"

Mom pulled me by the hand. When we reached the waiting room across the hall, we watched two more nurses pushing new equipment into the room, and next came a doctor, running, the soles of his gym shoes squeaking on the floor.

This didn't look good.

I got my bearings, snapped back to reality. "I'm sorry," I said, briskly pulling my hand from my mother's.

I walked toward the nearest exit. My knees knocked and the edges of my vision blackened. I took a deep breath and steadied myself at the nurses' station. Mom caught up with me there.

She turned me around by the shoulders. "You listen to me, Corrine. I don't know what happened in there, but this is ridiculous. This isn't . . . you. You didn't . . . She was a *hospice* patient, Corrine." She said this last part softly but firmly. I knew she was trying to convince herself, probably even more than me.

"Now you know exactly how Sophie died," I said. I spit it out, trying to hurt her, trying to hurt myself.

I just left. She didn't follow me. I heard her sob once, but I didn't look back. I walked out the twin glass doors of the Chartrain Hills Nursing Home.

I killed her. This sentence ran through my mind on a loop.

I turned on my heel to go west toward home, but my knees wobbled, my lungs burned, and I heard a voice. "Hey!"

"Corrine!"

My knees gave. Someone caught me, and I was out.

8

I dreamt of my mother. She crept through St. Louis No. 1 cemetery, dwarfed by the aboveground tombs and crumbling mausoleums. She seemed to be looking for someone. The gravel on the pathway crunched beneath her feet as she slipped between two crypts. When I looked, though, the ground wasn't covered in gravel. Instead there were thousands of honey-gold chips of rosin. It smelled like orchestra practice back in junior high. I watched my mother, who was now crying, as she crunched the rosin beneath her feet, looking all around, calling my name. I tried to answer her, but no words came. I sat high on my perch at the top of a granite mausoleum, and when I couldn't take the sound of her voice anymore, the sound of her desperation when she called my name, I flapped my wings and flew away, realizing only then that I was a nameless, voiceless blackbird.

I awoke in the darkness, in my own room, under my own covers. I sensed someone in the chair next to me, a hand stroking my hair, and the touch was comforting, so comforting. But then, like being sucked into a tunnel, I remembered it all. Who I was. What had happened. Who I killed.

I felt instantly gutted. Hollowed out. What kind of monster was I?

I looked up at Dad.

He wasn't even angry, just relieved to see me awake. A tender smile, and this hurt more. I sat up in my bed, scooted out of his reach, hung my head.

"I killed her," I said.

"Sweetheart," he said. And he waited for me to look up. I didn't. I couldn't.

His voice was soft and patient. And I thought of him picking me up from canoe camp. I had let Annaliese talk me into going when we were eleven. But I had been homesick and called for my parents to pick me up on the second night there. Dad hadn't been mad. He hadn't scolded me for the wasted money. When I had apologized, all he had said was, "Your mom and I are always here."

Now he put his hand under my chin, tilted my face up to his, and I let him. I blinked back the tears, held myself together.

"Sweetheart, Mrs. Twopenny is fine," he said. "She's asking for you."

For a minute, I couldn't process what he was saying. "I was there. I saw . . ."

He shook his head. "Corrine, I swear on your granddad's name. She just passed out is all, and all the contraptions had some kind of electrical surge, went haywire, and . . . well, you thought . . . Hell, Mom thought so too. But she's fine."

"Dad, I don't know if I can believe you."

He looked at me like I had slapped him in the face. "Honey, have I *ever* lied to you?"

"She's really okay?" I said. I tried to consider what this might mean for me, for everything. I had not killed Mrs. Twopenny. She had survived the blue light. She had survived me. And in that moment, I knew I had to go back. I had to ask more questions. I had to find out more about Ruth, what Mrs. Twopenny could tell me.

"Do you want to go see her?" Dad asked.

"I do," I said.

And then Dad put his hands on my shoulders and said, "That's my girl." And for some reason, that just did it, it broke the dam. I collapsed into Dad then. He hugged me close, hard. And I let him, leaned into him, let him share my weight. I had missed him.

"Dad, thank you for catching me. Why were you there? At Chartrain?"

I looked up at him, and he looked at me, confused for a second. "That wasn't me, hon. That was that friend of yours. Rennick. Mrs. Twopenny's grandson."

And for the first time in a long time, there was a lightness inside my chest, inside my heart. The possibility that all was not lost. That I was not doomed. What was this kernel of feeling? Could it be hope?

We arrived back at Chartrain late in the night, the wee hours of the morning actually. Mrs. Twopenny lay sleeping in her room, a daffodil night-light giving off gold light next to her bed. The nurses asked me not to disturb her, and I didn't. But she was indeed alive. I watched the rise and fall of her breathing, and I marveled at it. Four-four time. Repeat.

An old man with shaggy salt-and-pepper hair and an even shaggier beard slept in the recliner.

I turned to Mom and gave her a hug. Although I wasn't near ready to leave behind everything about my self-imposed quarantine, I knew I had to break the rules, figure some things out, because now there was hope that maybe I could control it. Master it? I owed it to Mom, to Dad. It was odd to hug Mom and not pull away, yet somehow easy. I relished the smell of her shampoo while I held her tight. Coconut. My eyes stung, but I blinked back the tears. I had missed this, hugging my mother. I had missed normal life.

And even in the awkwardness of initiating the first hug in a long time, I thought of how easy it would be to return to a normal life of casual conversations and everyday physical interaction. In that moment, my mother holding on to me, me hugging her back and watching Mrs. Twopenny there with a little more color in her ancient cheeks than earlier, I felt like it all actually might be possible.

And there was a part of me—probably a large part—that knew I was being foolish and naive to let this one moment, this one victory, symbolize a new start for me. I tried to temper my hope, to reel myself back in.

I knew I had to. So when I went home that night, I did not sit and talk it all out with Mom and Dad. I didn't share the roast beef sandwiches at the kitchen table with them. I took my food upstairs instead, feeling their shared glances behind me.

I took the photo album off Mom's shelf and made myself look at Sophie's gap-toothed smile, made myself remember that although today had gone well—today had hopefully been some kind of game changer—nothing could bring Sophie back.

I took out her rocks. From that night on the beach: the Petoskey, the agate, two other rocks that I couldn't name. Sophie would've known what they were. I had shoved these in my sock drawer in a ziplock baggie so long ago, when Mom had given them to me after the funeral. I hadn't even wanted to look at them then. Or ever. But now it seemed so important. My last link to her. I rolled them around in my hand, wondered at their histories, their origins. Sophie's last rocks.

Who was to say that the next time I felt that surge of energy, saw blue, it would turn out like Sophie or Lucy and *not* like Lila Twopenny? Or who was to say it wouldn't be something else completely unexpected?

As I stared into Sophie's nine-year-old Girl Scout portrait, the rocks still in my hand, I knew that I understood nothing more than I had yesterday about this "touch," as Lila Twopenny had called it. Nothing except that I now had reason to stay and dig out some more information, some knowledge.

I knew I would have to talk to not only Lila but also Rennick.

As I bit into the hearty roast beef sandwich, I savored the salty taste. I hadn't enjoyed food—or anything—for so long. It tasted good.

And when the telephone rang, near dawn, not an uncommon thing to happen in a minister's household, I didn't pay it any mind. But then I heard Mom's footsteps coming up the stairs. I braced myself. Bad news? Mrs. Twopenny? Had it just been delayed for a few hours?

Mom knocked on the door frame. I sat up, bracing myself.

"Mrs. Twopenny's not in hospice anymore."

"She died?" I croaked.

"No, sweetie!" Mom said, sweeping into my room and throwing her arms around me. "They can't find the spots on her lungs in the MRI. Not on her liver. Not on her spleen."

Mom released me, stood there, waiting for a reaction, something.

"Holy shit," I said, not meaning to swear but not quite able to absorb her words.

Mom laughed, this loud, jingle-bell laugh, and hugged me again. Dad joined us, and there we stood, all three hugging, the photo album open on my bed to Sophie's smiling portrait.

9

Chartrain had a cat, a little tiger-striped cat with an attitude. It roamed freely, and when I got to Mrs. Twopenny's room the following day, the cat was curled into a ball at the foot of her bed. Mrs. Twopenny was snoring lightly.

I had heard of animals, even animals that lived in old folks' homes like this, that could sense death and would often sit or keep company with a patient for hours or even days before the medical staff knew that death was imminent. So the sight of the cat kind of creeped me out. Maybe Mrs. Twopenny was still going to die from my handshake of doom.

The cat woke up lazily and saw me standing in Mrs. Twopenny's room, gave me half a glance, and jumped off the bed, sauntering slowly out to the hallway. A nurse came in and checked a few things on Mrs. Twopenny's monitor. "You're kind of famous around here," he said.

"Yeah," I answered, feeling a blush creep up my neck. I averted my eyes. I could sense him watching me as he wrote some abbreviated nurse's code on the whiteboard. And I had this weird feeling then, a twist in my gut. Because what had happened yesterday was crazy and miraculous. But it was mine. Even though I didn't feel like I had control of it. It was on my shoulders—for better or for worse. For the moment it was a good thing.

But already, even though I hardly believed in my ability, there was a part of my mathlete brain worrying about malpractice insurance, trying to figure out how exactly I was going to live with this gift. Like, should I save all sick kids first, and old people last? Like some kind of supersensory triage? And how would I make those decisions? Fluck. Already I was wearing myself out with the logistics. Would I stay in New Orleans, or would I take my act on the road? I was already picturing circus sideshow banners with a caricature of me and my pointy chin smiling out at the customers. Or maybe I should just keep it all secretive so I wouldn't get too famous. Work out of Mia-Joy's basement or something. This was how a logical girl's brain worked in a very illogical situation. Not exactly A=B, but A=I'm screwed.

Although much less screwed than if I were the angel of death.

Mom came in then with her cup of coffee and traded hellos with the nurse, and Mrs. Twopenny was startled by the voices. She bolted upright in bed. It made me nervous.

But she greeted me—and my mom—with such exuber-
ance, I put my nerves about everything in the back of my
mind. Mrs. Twopenny swung her legs over the side of the
bed completely unassisted. She got up and hugged both of
us, squeezing me tight with those same frail-looking arms
and petite hands. She had color high in her wrinkled cheeks,
her hair pulled back in a silver chignon at her neck.

I let her hug me, but I pulled back quickly. No field of
energy drew us together today, but I was alert around her,
my senses heightened a bit.

"Lordy! You *are* like my daughter Ruthie! I already called
my Clara. She is coming down from Atlanta. She is going to
want to meet y'all."

She beamed at us, and although I had relaxed my silence
rule and bent my touching rules, I wasn't sure what to say
now. I was unable to take credit here, unable to explain it,
and frankly I couldn't really swallow it. The whole healer
thing.

"Miss Corrine, you realize you done fixed me?" Mrs.
Twopenny said.

I looked at Mom.

"It's a miracle," Mom said, putting her arm around my
shoulders slowly, as if asking permission. I let her and she
pulled me close. *Do I know this is safe now?* I told myself it
was. I wasn't feeling any of the warning signs.

"It is a miracle!" Mrs. Twopenny said, sitting daintily on
the edge of her bed, her hands clasped under her chin like

a child. "That's exactly what Clara said." She turned to me then.

I didn't know how to start. I had a lot of questions. First and foremost, could I ever expect to *control* this?

"What about your daughter Ruth?" Mom asked, sitting down in a visitor's chair and pointing toward the rocker for me. I took a seat and listened.

"Ruthie, she's gone." Mrs. Twopenny did not look up.

"She passed away?" I asked, but I knew this from Rennick.

"And she was the one with the touch?" Mom asked.

Mrs. Twopenny nodded.

"Mrs. Twopenny," I started hesitantly, "can you tell me how your daughter dealt with this? I mean, how did she control it?"

Mrs. Twopenny nodded again, brought her finger to her temple in a gesture that said she was thinking. "Couldn't always bring it around. Ruthie would sometimes get so frustrated. It wouldn't always come. And even if it did, it sometimes wouldn't work. *Too far gone,* Ruthie would say. *Too much for me.* But we kept it a quiet secret. It didn't set easily with some folks, you know." Mrs. Twopenny lowered her voice. "Ruthie tried. She really tried. Until the end."

Mom and I just nodded. It seemed both too much information and nothing at all. I wanted to ask how Ruth had died, but it seemed too private a moment for Mrs. Twopenny, who had yet to look back up at us.

"Does Clara also have the touch?" I asked.

"No, she does not, but she has her own gift. They tell me that is how it is with twins a lot of the time, with this super-sensory business." Mrs. Twopenny had finally looked back up at us, now that the topic had turned away from Ruth.

Mrs. Twopenny rang the nurse's button on her bed rail, and Mom and I looked at each other. "Are you worn out, Lila?" Mom asked. "We can leave."

Mrs. Twopenny shook her head. A nurse's voice broke over the intercom. "Lila, can we help you?"

"Yes," she answered, looking at us pointedly. "My grandson is wandering around out there by the vending machines. Can you send him in?"

"Certainly." The intercom clicked, and Mrs. Twopenny leaned toward us conspiratorially.

"Rennick has the same gift as Clara. I reckon it is hard to describe to y'all, but he'll do a fine job."

Mom gave me a look then. Of the *why-haven't-you-told-me-this* variety.

Rennick came in and nodded hello, stood near Mrs. Twopenny, wearing his uniform of jeans and a T-shirt. The atmosphere in the room changed. It became thicker, closer.

Mrs. Twopenny noticed it and looked from Rennick to me as she introduced everyone.

"We know each other," Rennick said to her.

Mom smiled. "Yes, pebbles at the window."

"I was hoping, Renny, that you could explain the colors."

"Well," he said, eyeing me with a sheepish grin.

"They were asking about your Aunt Clara, and it sounds a tad loony coming from an old lady who happened to just cheat death." Mrs. Twopenny giggled.

And it was contagious. I chuckled too, and Mom joined in. Rennick watched me closely, a smile on his face. But his eyes were serious.

He answered Mrs. Twopenny's question. "I see auras around people."

I glanced away from his gaze; so this explained the wall in the garage. I caught Mom nodding. She had taken in a lot in the past twenty-four hours. We all had. And if we were going to open the door to one miracle, could we shut it on another? Laugh at it? Discredit it? No, we were all joining the crazy party here.

I looked back at Rennick and nodded, hoping he'd go on.

"Specific colors mean specific things on people. Emotions. Character traits. Physical characteristics. There's a lot of science to it. I've read a lot about it, studied. But it's also an art...." He became suddenly self-conscious, rubbing his palm across his jawline, giving an apologetic smile.

"What does blue mean?" I asked him, wondering why he had told me he saw the blue and whether it linked to the indigo lens in my episodes.

"Depends." He gave me a look, considered.

"Rennick believes there's a magic in electricity we are only learning about now." Mrs. Twopenny's eyes twinkled, and I saw in that look how much she admired him. Rennick cleared his throat, looked away nervously.

At that moment, we heard voices in the hallway, great, boisterous exclamations, and like a whirlwind a dark-haired, very pretty older woman blew into the room, along with a camera crew, a guy holding one of those boom mikes, and two other people, who both carried clipboards and looked somewhat official.

The dark-haired woman had already perched herself on the bed with Mrs. Twopenny and started talking a mile a minute. "Well, good day. Mrs. Twopenny, yes?" the woman said, but didn't allow Mrs. Twopenny to answer. "They told me it was a ninety-year-old woman I'd be interviewing, but my goodness, do you look young." Mrs. Twopenny clearly fell for the flattery, raising her hand to her cheek in mock humility. "Would you mind being on camera? *Channel Thirteen News?*"

The woman paused now, and I put it together just as Mrs. Twopenny gasped. "You are Myrna Sawyer!"

More fake humility. "That I am!"

"My Clara is on TV too," Mrs. Twopenny explained.

There were too many people vying for too little space in the room now. The boom mike poked me right in the face, so I took a step toward Rennick, hoping to slip out the door. Mom eyed me over the head of the red-haired assistant with the cell phone to her ear. There were too many people here, and the other assistant's clipboard hit me on the arm. Although my rules were relaxing, and I knew I was going to be starting a new kind of normal, this was too much.

My skin tightened and the hairs on my neck prickled. I couldn't breathe. I needed room to breathe.

Myrna Sawyer popped off the bed as she spied me maneuvering past Rennick toward the door. "You, young lady," she said, jumping in front of the door before I could get there. "Are you the young lady? Are you the *one?*"

I couldn't breathe right, my temples thumped with each beat of my pulse. "I need to–" I tried to look over the head of the cameraman, who now had his camera pointed in my face. I tried to signal my mother.

I shook my head, reached for the doorknob. Then Myrna Sawyer reached out, grabbing my forearm. I supposed she wanted to guide me back into the room. But I got a shock when she touched me. Maybe it was just a regular, everyday, static-electric shock, but it scared me.

I jumped away from her like a startled animal. Myrna reared back, offended.

"She doesn't want to talk," Rennick said, just this side of polite. He stepped in front of me, opened the door for me. He followed me out.

I stalked into the waiting area, my arms crossed against my chest, my shoulders hunched. "I'm scared," I said

"I know," Rennick said. "It gets better."

"Yeah?"

Mom came out of the room now, and a man in a suit met her just outside the door. They stood talking, their faces serious. We were out of earshot. "Who is that?" I asked Rennick. Mom took out her cell phone and looked at it.

"I don't know." We watched their conversation and waited.

Mom was shaking her head as she came toward us. "I guess this place is swarming with news reporters. That was a bigwig here at the nursing home. And Dad just texted me. There are reporters at the house too." Mom rubbed her knuckles across her lip.

"Corrine's a real hero, front-page news," Rennick said. But none of us smiled.

"I can't talk about this yet," I said. Mom nodded.

Rennick rubbed his jaw. "I can help," he said.

"What are you thinking?" Mom asked.

"Corrine could come to my house for the day. There won't be any paparazzi there." He seemed a bit bashful, looking up through his eyelashes. And although I had been wondering about his motives, it came to me in a flash. I mean, why did he want to help me? But it just hit me—could Rennick Lane possibly *like* me? Was it that simple?

It was a comforting thought. So very normal. So very high school. So much like my old life. But no, I knew that Rennick had his own reasons. Totally.

I smiled as he explained to Mom where he lived. Forty-eight hours ago, I wouldn't have dreamed of going to Rennick

Lane's house for the day. But today was a new day in many ways. And it was tempting to think he could give me more insight into what I was going through.

I pushed away the idea that this was Ren from the Pen. The things I had heard at school, they didn't jell with the boy in front of me here.

Mom turned toward me. "What do you think, Corrine? It's up to you. We could just hole up at home. Dad could make sure the reporters let us in the door at least."

"I want to go with Rennick," I said. "I think we have a lot to talk about." This was me jumping in, giving it my whole self. Swimming the butterfly. I wanted to figure this thing out. And I felt myself slide back a little, back to my old self. Back into that comfortable place where I knew right from wrong, where I followed my instincts, where I acted with certainty and confidence. What was that word? Mrs. Smelser had taught me all about it when I had been learning that last piece by Chopin. A continuous, unbroken slide from one note to another. Glissando.

My decision.

Mom nodded. "I'm sure that's true." She gave me a look, eyebrows raised.

"Really, I want to go," I reassured her. Mom blew me a kiss then, and I surprised her by grabbing her hand and squeezing it. I think I surprised myself too.

"You better hurry," she said, glancing toward the door of Mrs. Twopenny's room. "And Mr. Huskins said to use the cafeteria kitchen door." I was kind of shocked that Mom was letting me go with Rennick, not really knowing him. It seemed out of character, but as I turned to follow Rennick toward the elevator, Mom called, "Tell your grandfather I'll bring those seeds I promised him next week."

And then it all came together for me. Duh. Mom knew his family. Figured. And this made me feel a little better too.

We walked toward the front entrance of Chartrain, and I kept looking over my shoulder, expecting a camera flash or something. I took account of my body, the way my skin felt, the normal, everyday feeling in my chest. It seemed almost difficult to recall the faraway feeling of the indigo flame under my ribs.

We neared the front desk, avoiding Holly, who was on today, and I peeked out the front window. Sure enough, there were two news vans, and at least a dozen people in front on the sidewalk.

We turned, facing each other for a second in an odd, what-do-we-do-now kind of way, and Rennick just laughed, easy and low. "Let's go through the back," he said. He stuck out his elbow for me to lock my arm through.

I hesitated just for a second and was actually about to loop my arm through his when he thought better of it. "Oh, sorry," he said, dropping his arm.

We walked side by side toward the cafeteria. I lengthened my steps to keep up with him. "I'm parked in the back lot, so that works," he said.

"Why do you care about me? Why did you try so hard to help me?" The words came falling out of me just as we hit the cafeteria.

I stopped, waited for him to answer. He looked back, a serious expression on his face, but one corner of his mouth rose into the slightest of smiles. "Your aura."

I waited, but he didn't say anything else.

"What about my aura?"

He smiled fully then, a little bit embarrassed–flirting? Was he flirting? I smiled too, and my stomach did this flip-flop. God, he was hot. That tousled hair. And he liked my aura.

"I can tell a lot about people from the colors, and I'm usually–no, *always*–right."

I told myself to settle down. How could I go from so abnormal right back to total high school girl in the amount of time it took to notice the ridiculous length of his eyelashes, the deep indigo of his eyes? I swallowed hard, rolled my eyes at myself. I started walking toward the kitchen again, and he fell in step beside me.

"I have a lot of questions," I said.

We reached the kitchen, where Rennick said hello to a few people. Then he pushed the back door open, toward the alley. We stepped outside and looked at each other.

"I really should say thank you. I mean, I don't know what is going on exactly, but the possibility that I am not the Grim Reaper herself is pretty explosive. I can't thank you enough for trying to help me."

"Of course I had to help you, Corrine. You saved my grandmother," he said, shielding his eyes from the sun. He pointed toward the gravel lot on the left. "And you've got this inexplicable power, this sixth sense going on. We extra-sensory loners gotta somehow look out for each other."

Oh, so that was it. I was part of some sliver of society with this gift or something. Of course that was it. Weird kinship. He had a duty to reach out a helping hand. I shook my head a little as I followed him to the car. Of course. I was silly for thinking it was something else. Something more personal.

As Rennick chivalrously opened the passenger door for me, I actually swallowed a laugh. I wasn't twenty-four hours back into the regular world. Not twenty-four hours back into interaction, talking, relating with others, and already I had fallen into the worst trap for a seventeen-year-old girl: a cute guy with a killer smile.

10

He drove like a grandpa, five miles under the speed limit, and he never took his eyes off the road. It made me want to make a joke about it. I almost did, but he was so earnest, sitting at the wheel of his dirty, beat-up Jeep, old country music playing on the radio.

"You know Mia-Joy?" I had nearly forgotten how to make conversation.

"Some," he said. "Interesting aura."

I wondered at this. But I plunged into a different subject. "You go to Liberty."

He nodded. Nothing else. I rubbed my knuckles on my lip, thought about all that had happened, where I was, who I was with. "You went to Penton Charter."

"I had to leave and come live with my grandfather. Help him out."

"That's nice of you."

His expression changed a little, darkened. "Plus, I needed a change."

I could tell he didn't want to talk about it. There was something behind his face I couldn't quite read. I let it go. I looked out the window, leaned my forehead on the cool glass. It felt too weird to talk, to let myself look at him, to not temper all of my movements and interactions. I couldn't exactly remember how to be normal. How did I used to hold my hands before? How did I tilt my head? Was I staring too much?

"We've lived like bachelors for a while," he said as he pulled into the driveway, as if this explained many things: the house, the boat propped up on his porch, him. He stopped the car.

"We're here." He got out of the Jeep, and Bouncer came bounding out from the nearby tree line. His front paws were on Rennick's shoulders in a heartbeat, and then he put his chin to the ground, looking up at me with those big brown eyes.

"He wants you to pet him," Rennick said.

I bent down next to the dog. His tail beat harder against the ground. His eyes were so humanlike. I reached out my hand. My *hand*. Was I really going back to a normal life? Was what happened with Lila Twopenny enough to prove anything?

I reached my hand out and placed it on Bouncer's forehead.

I was going to try.

His fur was smooth and glossy. I scratched his ears, his neck, and Bouncer rolled over on his back, put his paws in the air.

"Oh, you've made a friend," Rennick said, and I rubbed the dog's belly.

"You sure he's not a bear?" I said. "He's totally big enough."

"And he's just a pup."

"Really?" Bouncer was following us up the porch now.

"Yeah." Rennick laughed, his eyes crinkling into half-moons. "Dodge found him out near the gravel quarry. Someone had neglected him, hit him, I think. He was mean, snarling, if you can imagine it. Bit my grandfather on the hand. Bit me too. More than once."

"Jeez," I said. "Is that where you got that scar, the one on your elbow?" I had seen it when he was driving, a messy white zigzag of flesh from elbow to wrist.

"Yeah," he answered. "And this one." He pointed to his eyebrow, and I could see small, jagged lines.

"Were you scared of him?"

Rennick shook his head, put his key in the front door. "He just needed to learn kindness from someone."

I followed after Rennick and Bouncer, turning that phrase over in my mind, loving the frank way Rennick had said it. As if it had been so obvious. Kindness. The answer.

We walked immediately into a family room with polished wood floors and an old woodstove. The walls were cluttered with maps, some framed, some held up with thumbtacks; some were recent aerial images with crisp colors, others black-and-white, smudged, older than old. I walked directly toward a plain wood frame holding a dog-eared, yellowed, gorgeous map.

When I got closer, I could see that it was topographical, mapping the land, the rivers, the streams, and the swamp areas of this little wedge of the Gulf Coast. It was hand-drawn, intricate, handsome. And it inexplicably reminded me of Rennick himself.

"It's from the eighteen hundreds."

"Yeah?" I asked.

"Not too long after the Louisiana Purchase and everything. It's French."

I noticed then that the key and the compass rose were in French, which made the map seem all the more elegant. I found the French Quarter; it was marked, and there were several named parishes, all written in a romantic curlicue script.

I followed Rennick into the kitchen and sat down at the farmhouse table. The kitchen had white cabinets, white everything, very homey but spare and simple. There was no microwave, no dishwasher.

"We kind of live like pioneers," he said, chuckling. "Been just me and Dodge for a while. But Lila'll soon . . ." His voice trailed off.

I chewed on my thumbnail, didn't meet his eyes. I didn't want to take credit. It didn't seem real.

"You must be hungry," he said finally. He pulled out an old iron skillet.

I suddenly realized I was. "Starving, actually."

"Omelet or grilled cheese? That's about all there is on the menu del Rennick." He cast a smile over his shoulder at me, and I thought I saw his hand shaking a little when he placed the frying pan on the stove.

"Grilled cheese, and thank you," I said.

"I'm hungry too. I just figured–"

"No, I mean, thank you for getting me out of Chartrain today. For trying so hard to help me the other day. For–"

He stopped what he was doing, turned and looked at me. "You don't have to thank me, Corrine."

I shook my head. I got up, leaned on the counter. "Rennick," I said, and saw the left corner of his mouth go up in a nearly imperceptible grin when I said his name. "Why, though? Why did you try so hard to help me when I was nothing but a bitch to you? I mean, did you just know I could help your grandmother or–"

"No, I didn't even think of that." He didn't look at me. He stared down at the floor between us, scuffed the heel of his shoe back and forth for a second. And it hit me at that second how much Rennick reminded me of this shy kid Lester Meechum that I went to grade school with. I wondered at that. Could Rennick Lane be nothing more than the shy, smart, nerdy kid in the class, stuck in the body of a rebel with the hair of some kind of emo lead singer? This idea seemed right. And I was beginning to realize that Rennick didn't even know how he came off. Did he still see himself as that nerdy kid? A boy with a microscope and test tubes in his bedroom?

"Why did you help me?" I repeated.

"Can't a guy just like your aura?" He didn't look at me, but he smiled. My mouth turned up as well. The air between us prickled again, and the tension against my skin changed, the air against me . . . tightened. Rennick's head snapped up.

"Do you feel that?" I said. Bold. More like the old Corrine than ever.

Rennick nodded.

"What is it?"

"A charge. Electric. Physio-electric."

"I only feel that with some people. Between me and certain people. Or only before . . . before an event like Mrs. Twopenny." I was really putting my cards on the table. For just a moment, I realized that I was here in this backwoods house with some guy I hardly knew, telling him my darkest, deepest secrets and doubts. I tried not to stand outside of myself and see it like that. Because it seemed like the first time in a long, long time that I might be getting back to some kind of normal, and I didn't want that to end.

Rennick went to the fridge and took out bread, cheese, and butter. "I feel it too, sometimes. I know what you mean. I think . . . I think it ties into body chemistry, electrical impulses in the body. That's how a lot of what you do and what I see works. I think that's how it all works. Proving it is another story."

He turned toward the stove. I sat at the table again, and when he passed by the sink window with the sun streaming through, the light hit him; for a split second I saw a rainbow of colors around him, enveloping him, lots of reds and oranges. It left as soon as I noticed it. I blinked a few times and rubbed my eyes. I almost said something. I started to, but I stopped myself. Had I just seen his aura?

No. I dismissed it. A trick of the light.

"Rennick, I have a zillion questions."

"Well, that's a relief. Just ask. I want you to." He flipped the toasted bread with a spatula. "I just don't know how to get started. I don't want to scare you away." And although he wasn't turned completely toward me, I could see in his face that he meant it. His brow was furrowed, his jaw tight. He was nervous.

I sighed. "Tell me exactly what you see."

"Colors. Halos of color. Sometimes colors that seem like they are radiating off of people's skin, their whole bodies, like an outline."

"So what exactly is interesting about Mia-Joy's?" I asked.

"Jagged, ripped hole in her aura."

I watched him finish toasting the sandwiches. Had I been in Chicago, I would've laughed right here. Thrown my head back and laughed at the whole situation. But I was not in Chicago.

Rennick went to the fridge, got a jar of pickles, a pitcher of tea. He put the grilled cheese on plates, scooped out a couple of pickles from the jar, and brought the food to the table. "Grilled cheese and pickles. Gotta love 'em."

"So, a hole in an aura, does that usually mean . . . what?"

"There is no manual," he said, taking a seat next to me, handing me a glass of ice-cold tea. "But I've seen similar things with some people. It usually isn't good." He looked at me hard.

I swallowed. "Her diabetes? She's okay, though. Her mother said that it smoothed out since she switched to shots."

He nodded.

"You're not telling me the whole thing here."

"I think she's not okay. Mia-Joy will have a setback, if I'm right. And then we'll have to, you know, figure out a way for you to . . ." He let his voice trail off, and I realized then what he meant. He looked at me like maybe he had said too much.

"So you're sure that I'm a healer?" I said, taking a bite of my sandwich.

"Aren't you?"

I shrugged.

"My grandmother'll tell you stories about my mom, about the people she healed, the lives she saved. But she'll tell you too that Mom only really remembered the few that she couldn't help, the ones she couldn't heal."

I sat silently looking out the window at the garage. Thinking of the beauty it held. Thinking of Sophie.

"Your sister," he said, setting down his sandwich. "I know what you're carrying around."

We sat in silence, and I heard the clock above the kitchen sink ticking quietly. Bouncer came and rested his head on Rennick's lap. Rennick gave him a pickle. "The monster eats pickles, for God's sake." He shook his head and laughed like it was the funniest thing he'd ever heard. The timbre of his laugh. It was a beautiful note, G-sharp, then F-sharp.

"Go lie down," he told the dog, and the dog did.

I swallowed hard. "Sophie...It was the same as with Mrs. Two–I mean, your grandmother, the whole thing. It just didn't end up the same, you know? How can I ever...I mean, who knows if I might save somebody or kill them?" I shook my head, put my hand out for Bouncer, clicked my tongue. He came over and let me scratch him behind the ears. I needed something else to do, to look at, besides the well of concern in Rennick's eyes.

Rennick shook his head. "I don't think–"

I couldn't hear his excuses right then. I didn't want to. I changed the subject. "Tell me about your mother. Her power."

He didn't like this, and there was something there, in the way he held his jaw, guarded. "She could only summon it about half the time she wanted, Grandma said."

At that moment, the front door opened. An older man with a shaggy beard and salt-and-pepper hair came in. When I saw his hat, I realized it was the man who had been sleeping in the recliner in Mrs. Twopenny's room. Of course. Dodge.

"Hey-o," he called. He walked into the kitchen with heavy footfalls, whistling loudly.

"Dodge," Rennick said, standing up from the table. "This is Corrine."

Dodge stood up straighter, put a hand to his old fishing hat in greeting. He looked kind of like a quarter note standing there. "The famous Corrine. How can I ever..." His voice trailed off. He held his hands to his heart in a gesture that was at once so genuine and so heartbreaking, I had to look away. "Thank you, my dear." He walked toward me, put out his hand. I considered it. Then I offered my own. He held it between both of his for a beat, then kissed the back of it. He looked at Rennick, winked as he let go of my hand. "Prettier than you even said."

"Dodge," Rennick admonished him.

I tried not to blush, however impossible that was. Dodge's eyes held mine, and I saw a bit of Rennick in his grizzled gray face. The same dark blue eyes. I smiled. How could I possibly be standing in this man's house? A man whose wife I had just saved from imminent death? A man who accepted that fact with no question?

I didn't know which seemed more impossible.

"You want a sandwich?" Rennick asked, gesturing toward the stove.

"No sirree," Dodge said, pulling out my chair for me at the table. Rennick would not meet my gaze, and I saw the little boy inside him again. He didn't blush, but he laughed to himself, head down.

Dodge crouched down to nuzzle Bouncer. "Got myself some pickled herring."

"Fabulous," Rennick said, wrinkling his nose.

"Son, just go on out to the lake, sit on the swing if you can't handle the smell of it. Take the rest of your lunches. You can have some privacy."

"You mind, Dodge?"

Dodge shook his head.

Rennick grabbed his plate and motioned to me. He avoided my eyes, held the back door open for me. "This okay, Corrine?"

I nodded. "Nice to meet you," I told Dodge, grabbing my food.

"My pleasure," Dodge said, giving me a wink. Bouncer stayed with Rennick's grandfather, and we went out the back door toward the lake. It was gorgeous back there. I hadn't fully appreciated the wildflowers when I had been there yesterday. The scents. The scenery.

I took in the big vegetable garden too. I spied ripe purple eggplant. The frilly edges of coriander. No wonder Mr. Twopenny and my mother knew each other. Mom would love these gardens.

Rennick and I sat down on the big old swing that hung

from the magnolia-covered arbor. It faced the lake, which was murky and swampy, yet serene and beautiful in its own way. The muddy green tones of the water reflected in the way the sun played on the waves, the grasses and bulrushes swaying in the breeze on the water's edge, the throaty, buzzing croaks of the locusts and frogs echoing in the distance.

"So how long have you lived here with your grandfather?"

I picked the crust off my sandwich, pushed my feet on the ground to move the swing a bit. Rennick smelled like his clothes had been dried on a line outside on the first day of spring. And the shape of his jaw just kept drawing my eyes. Chiseled, that was a good word for it.

"I moved here last summer." He looked at me from the corner of his eye and added, "I didn't get kicked out of Penton." He wolfed down the last half of his sandwich. I did the same and became very interested in my iced tea, trying not to ask but hoping he would elaborate.

He didn't. I held my tongue for a quarter rest, tried to wait out a whole note. I wanted to hear more. A crow swooped down and cawed near the water's edge, picked up something in its mouth. I had to fill the silence.

"Do you think the newspapers, the reporters, will give up after today?" I asked.

"No."

I hadn't expected this answer. Rennick turned to me. "Things have been going on in New Orleans."

"What do you mean?"

"More people like us." I gave him a look. "People with extrasensory powers. Sixth sense of some kind. Clusters of us."

Bouncer came storming out of the back door, Dodge following. He walked hurriedly, a hitch in his step, and spoke in a low whisper. "Some reporters at the door a minute ago. Told 'em you weren't here."

"Should we take a walk?" Rennick looked at me seriously.

"Maybe if I just answer a few questions," I offered.

"No," Rennick said. "Bad idea."

"Take a walk," Dodge whispered, grabbing Rennick by the shoulder for a moment in such a serious way that it unnerved me. I wondered again how Ruth had died. And how she had lived too, with this secret, with people's judgments. With all her own doubts?

I followed Rennick, and I got that feeling again that I could see myself from the outside, going off into the woods with someone I hardly knew.

But Rennick motioned for me to follow him, and I felt that tenuous string between us. Some kind of real connection. I wasn't ready to break it. I wasn't sure I totally trusted him and everything he said, but he hadn't steered me wrong yet.

I went with my gut instinct. My heart knew this guy in some weird and cosmic sense.

I went with Rennick, not deep into the woods, just along the edge, and I was a little bit scared about everything. A little bit chilly in the shadowy canopy of the trees. A little bit excited about how every few steps Rennick would turn around and check on me with an easy smile.

My senses came alive as we hiked through the little patch of forest that backed up to Rennick's grandfather's property, the sprawling live oaks, the pungent pine trees, the swampy masses of kudzu. It felt good to hike, to walk and feel my body move and not to hold it in, not to cross my arms and hold my limbs close. I found a sliver of freedom out there in the shade of the forest, and I felt the blood pumping through my veins, my heart working. And I liked it.

We quickly came to a little shack, really only three ram-shackle walls with a slanted aluminum roof. Rennick said it was a hunting blind, his grandfather's, although I had never even heard of one before.

"Dodge and I camp out here and hunt for deer and turkey."

I tried to picture Rennick as a hunter. It didn't seem to work. But I reminded myself that I didn't really know this guy. At all. He sat down on the floor of the hunting blind, rested his back on the inside wall, and patted the ground next to him. "We only shoot what we can eat. Nothing more," he said, as if he had been reading my mind.

"Before, you said that you knew someone like me, long ago. Were you speaking of your mother? Or–"

"Someone else too. Dell was his name."

"Dell." I sat down next to him, my shoulder grazing his.

"Could he just heal anyone? Anything? Did he ever *hurt* when he didn't mean to?"

"We were kids, Corrine. I think Dell didn't quite know what he had. It's only looking back that I sort of put the pieces together."

"Could I talk to him?"

Rennick shook his head, his eyes dark. "You don't remember me, do you?" he asked, looking up at me through his lashes. He looked almost apologetic.

"Should I remember you?"

"We met once a long time ago." He didn't look at me now but instead drew in the dirt with a stick—his initials, a compass rose, squiggles.

I thought hard. Rennick Lane? Wouldn't I have remembered meeting this guy? This part nerd/part dreamboat/ part meddlesome *Scooby-Doo* kid who showed up right in the middle of trouble? "I don't remember. Where? When?"

"Summer. We were probably nine or ten. Lake Pontchartrain."

It hit me then. "You were the boy with the sparklers?" I looked at him wide-eyed, my jaw dropped. He nodded, didn't quite meet my eye. I couldn't believe it. I remembered that night. Of course I remembered that night.

I tried to reconcile this cool, easy young man with the awkward kid I had met on that Fourth of July.

He had worn thick black-rimmed glasses and had the kind of hair that lots of ten-year-old boys have: unwashed, untamed, too long in parts, too short in others. His ears stuck out from his head, and he was all hands and feet and teeth. Gangly. He had been an absolute nerd, no question.

So, I had been right about that. And for some reason, I liked that.

My family and I–Sophie had been just three or four years old then–were having a campfire on the shore with a big gang of my parents' friends and their kids. It was a Fourth of July tradition. Rennick–or the kid I knew now as Rennick–sort of hung around the outside of our little group, on the fringe, for a long time that night. He was digging a lot near the waves, near the rocks, I remembered that.

An older boy, Rory Kelleher, started picking on Rennick. Calling him names. Looking back, I think that Rory kid was trying to impress these two blond girls in bikini tops and cutoff jeans.

The whole thing went on through the evening, with Rennick moving along the shore, digging with a stick, Mia-Joy and I playing kick the can with some friends, and the older group of kids and Rory doing nothing, like only fourteen-year-olds can. And this Rory kid kept yelling over to Rennick once in a while. Calling him a nerd and a dork.

It wasn't anything too horrible, but even at nine I knew what a moron that Rory kid was. I remembered clearly that I was building a hill of sand for the tin can to sit on, and I was going over the circle of sharps in my head as I did it. And I saw Rory filling up a water balloon from a canteen. He called over to the nerdy boy, to Rennick, "Hey, kid! Come show me what you found down there digging!"

Rennick looked up all eager, glasses cocked at a ridiculous angle. The girls around Rory giggled with delight, and I just couldn't stomach it. I stood up and shouted real loud, "Rory Kelleher, would you just shut up, you fat bully? Go bust that water balloon on your own head!"

I got busy playing kick the can then, but I could feel Rory's stare on me, the whispers of those older girls. I also heard a few snickers from some of my playmates. But what really made me smile was the sound of the little boy's laugh. Just one yelp, one guffaw, right from the belly, had gotten out too quickly for him to edit.

The timbre of that laugh. It hadn't grown to G-sharp yet, but in my memory I could hear the hint of it.

That had been Rennick.

And it had been Rennick who had stood rapt, twenty, maybe thirty feet away, still and at attention when I played the violin around the campfire that night. I had been impressed with that. Because so many people didn't care, so many of the kids ran around, screaming, playing, ignoring me. And that was fine. But that kid—Rennick—he listened intently. And when I chose my second song to play, I picked *Canon in D*. For him. I thought he would like it. A lot of action.

When it was dark and the teenagers had found better things to do down the beach at their own fire, my mom began making s'mores for us, and she told me to politely go offer that left-out kid one of them. That's what she said, I remembered that: "that left-out kid."

"He seems like he wants to join you guys," Mom had told me. "Invite him to play with you."

So I did. He waved over his brother, an older, tough-looking kid with the shaggiest dishwater-blond hair. They both had dirt on their faces, and I had no idea where their parents were, but these kids were more than happy to join us in a game of flashlight tag. I remembered that Rennick came walking up, and he didn't look at me but said, "It's so true when you play your violin."

I always remembered that, till this day. I knew what he meant.

But what happened after that game of tag was what he probably remembered most. Rennick brought out some sparklers. My dad's friend Mr. Parker lit a few with his cigarette lighter, and the rest of us kids lit our sparklers off each other's. Well, Rennick's brother's hair caught a spark. The wind had been just right. I was spinning in circles with my sparkler, my feet squishing against the now-cool sand, and I was watching my sparkler leave a trail of rainbow lights. And then from the corner of my eye, I saw his hair just light up, a big poof of a flame, yellow and orange and bright and fast.

His hands went to his head, but it was like he didn't quite know what was happening. I acted fast. I dropped my sparkler, ran the few feet to him, and tackled him onto the sand, rolled his head in it.

When I was sure the flames were out, I got up. By now, he was crying, shaking, his long hair singed on the right side. Our parents had formed a circle, someone called 911. The rest of the memory was a blur.

I shook my head, brought myself back to reality. I saw the grown-up Rennick doodling in the dirt. He had written his brother's name in it, Cale. I remembered it now. I had thought it seemed like such a funny name back then. I didn't think I had even learned Rennick's name that night, but he had thanked me over and over, his father too.

"Your dad was an Army guy," I said, remembering his stern manner, a close-cropped crew cut.

Rennick stopped drawing, looking at me very seriously. "You saved Cale."

"I can't believe that was you," I said, but even as I said it, I could see the familiar hints of that boy in this young man: the way he held his brow, kind of led with his eyes—the curiosity there, a sort of indifference toward the periphery.

"How is your brother? Your dad? Where are they?"

"Dad is in the Air Force. Cale joined the Army right after school. Last year."

"He graduated from Penton?"

He gave me a funny look then, incredulous. "Cale didn't get kicked out of Penton either," he said.

I gave him a hard look. "So why are there all these rumors about you?" I said, knowing I was walking the line.

"Well, rumors are not truth." His voice was tinged with hurt.

And now I was backpedaling. "Rennick, I—"

"People talk. Don't believe everything you hear, Corrine. I'm just different. People like to . . . I don't know."

"No, tell me." I knew I was on shaky ground here. But I had to ask. I had to know. I had been through too much bullshit to just talk around everything forever and ever.

Rennick rubbed at his chin, and he looked up at me through his lashes. He laughed, not a funny laugh, but an I-can't-believe-I'm-going-to-tell-her-this laugh. "You know," he said, giving me a smile, "you aren't the only one who knows how to keep people at arm's length. I have a little practice in the self-preservation mode myself."

"So tell me why." I was pressing, I knew it. But what else could I do?

"Let's turn the tables, Corrine Harlowe. Why should I trust you with my secrets?"

"You sought me out. This is on you."

"True enough," he said, smiling. "But what if I like this dangerous, handsome-rebel approach? Why should I get rid of that so soon?" He arched his eyebrow and my stomach flip-flopped.

"It seems to work for you at school. But (a), you aren't a stranger because we met on that beach. And (b), no one said anything about handsome." I raised my eyebrow right back.

The laugh. Golden. Ringing through the trees. "You are a tough one." He considered for a moment. "I didn't really know my mom. She died when I was a baby." He looked at me like he didn't know if he was going to go on.

"I'm sorry," I said.

"I was stillborn. Born dead. She saved me, though, with the touch."

"You're kidding. Whoa." It was all I could say. I marveled at this nugget of information. One little sentence. But so much history. He must've been able to see it on my face, the gravity of his revelation.

"I know," he said, nodding.

The wind blew through the trees around us, and I tried to think about what it would be like to be him, to know so much but really so little about this thing around us. To be surrounded by it, defined by it.

I cleared my throat. "So how does it relate to school? Not that it isn't noteworthy or–"

"Let's just say that Cale never forgave me for her death."

"Why? But that doesn't make sense."

"Neither does blaming yourself for Lucy Rawlings's death. Or Sophie's." He wasn't joking with me now. There was no harshness or sarcasm. Just a tender, soft note in his voice.

"It's not the same. It's not that simple."

"I know. It never is."

Off in the distance, I heard a three-note whistle, and Rennick got up from the ground, dusting off the seat of his jeans. "It's Dodge's whistle. They must be gone now."

He held out his hand to help me up, which I took, but when my hand touched his, my scalp tingled, itched. Again my skin tightened, the air around us charged, and I quickly drew my hand away, got up from the ground on my own.

I followed him silently. I wanted to ask more questions, but I felt it there, heating up and coming to life behind my sternum. So I hung back, walked behind him, tried to digest all that I had learned. I did know Rennick Lane, my heart did know him.

We walked slowly back toward his house, silent. If the walk out into the woods had been filled with a sense of beauty and freedom, the walk back for me was a blur. All I could see were my feet. My flip-flops, one in front of the other.

About halfway to the house, Bouncer met us in the woods, tail wagging and tongue lolling. He passed Rennick right up and came and nuzzled my leg. I chose a perfectly sized stick from the underbrush and we played fetch all the way home.

When we were in clear view of the house, I could see the new smoky pink and purple formations of sunset light refracting off of the lake. I stopped in my tracks, scratching a panting Bouncer under his muzzle. "It's beautiful here."

"Promise me you'll be careful, Corrine," Rennick said.

He stood in front of me, did not turn around, but I could see this line to his shoulders, the fear, the resolve in it, and it made me wonder about his story a little more.

"How should I be careful?" I said, my voice barely above a whisper.

"Just be careful. Keep yourself safe. And don't worry too much about what they print in the papers about you."

"Okay," I said. He had me worried. I was still coming to terms with the idea of this power itself; now to have to top that off with fear that my power might not be looked on favorably . . . I didn't know what to think. My head was spinning. My insides felt oddly hollow and brittle, like I could snap.

"Let's get out of here, do something fun," he said, finally turning around.

"Okay," I said. Rennick opened the back door. He ushered Bouncer into the house and called out to Dodge to let him know we were leaving.

"Doesn't it seem a little unreal to you that we met all that time ago?" I still couldn't believe the coincidence.

"It doesn't seem so crazy." Rennick led us toward his Jeep.

"Why not?"

"Your aura is pulling me in."

"Oh, really?" I smiled in spite of myself.

"Your aura loves me already," he said, opening the passenger door, and he gave me a smile, his one-dimpled smile, and winked.

I let out a laugh as I took my seat, and I tried to ignore the way my stomach flip-flopped at his words. Rennick got in beside me and started the Jeep. "Where are we going?" I asked, glad to be anywhere but home. I needed something to do while my mind worked on everything. Could this all be real? Me? My powers? Rennick? I couldn't take it all in, and I caught myself thinking about Chicago. If I had been in Chicago, if I had been swimming laps at Chaney Pool, walking home from there at dusk, on our Midwestern streets, under our Midwestern streetlights, I would've laughed at all this stuff. Sixth sense. We Midwesterners were too practical for that.

"You'll see," Rennick answered. "It's why I moved here. With Dodge."

He drove us into the city, through the French Quarter and out toward the wharf. And I had to admit to myself that everything, the touch, all of it seemed more plausible here. This city of ghost stories, birthplace of American voodoo. Even the way the air felt on your skin in the Crescent City. It was all a little bit left of center. Things felt different here, with just a hint of the mystical, the magical, the impossible.

"You know, I thought about you for a long time after that night, after that July Fourth," Rennick said. Goose bumps trailed up and down my arms.

"You did?"

"I saw your aura even then. It was unmistakable. I mean, I didn't know what I was looking at exactly. I know more now."

"What do you know about me?" I said, my voice quiet, waiting.

He held the steering wheel tight, looking straight ahead. I saw him draw in a deep breath. "I know you're brave. I know you're generous and kind. You saved a young kid's life that night on the beach. You're whip-smart and stubborn. Decisive. And I remember you have a laugh like a sleigh bell."

I thought of my mom. I always thought her laugh sounded like a jingle bell. "Haven't I laughed since you re-met me?"

"Not truly."

Well, considering the string of events since I had re-encountered Rennick Lane, that was understandable.

"Do you still play the violin?"

"Yes. No. I did."

He nodded. "Corrine," he said, and there was a serious-ness to his face now. "Thank you. For saving Lila. You'll never know what that does for Dodge."

And there it was, this tangible thing between us, this knowledge and certainty that I had brought his grandmother virtually back to life.

I saved Lila Twopenny. I said that sentence to myself. But who I saw in my mind was Sophie. Beautiful Sophie.

Rennick pulled us into a small marina. Three boats—two large bay boats and one small motorboat—were docked, and there was a small storefront, with hand-printed signs for bait and ice. A larger sign, weatherworn and charming, declared in bold blue and yellow letters: CRESCENT CHARTERS.

"This is Dodge's outfit. Been running it for sixty years. Dad was going to make him shut it down. He couldn't keep up with stuff. The hard labor end of things."

"Does he fish for shrimp or something, sell them in town?"

"No, it's a charter company. He takes people out who want the real N'awlins Angling Experience, ya know?" Rennick put on his best drawl when he said this and I nodded a little. "You'd be surprised. Businesses, vacationers, Northerners, they come down here, and they want the experience of fishing in the marshes. They've heard the stories about how big the redfish can get. They want to see alligators. So they rent out a little slice of bayou life."

"They pay Dodge to take them out on his boat?"

"Yeah, and they can drink beer, enjoy themselves, fish with someone who knows what they're doing, who does all the real work of it. It's a real load of shit. Hell, I even gut and clean their catch for them at the end for a fee. You'd be surprised how much people will pay when they don't want to deal with a little mess."

"So you came to help out Dodge? That's awfully nice of you."

Rennick got an embarrassed look on his face, his eyes cast down. "That's not entirely true. I mean, yes, Dodge had a heart attack last spring, then Lila went into the home. It got real bad, real quick, but when Dad said that Dodge couldn't keep the charter going, it was just going to kill him. I could see it. I mean, I'm not exaggerating. It would do him in. So I volunteered."

I quelled the urge to reach out and grab Rennick's hand as we walked across the gravel parking lot. We were nearly to the bait shack. "You showed him kindness," I said, almost in a whisper.

Rennick stopped, turned toward me. "Corrine, it makes me sound like a saint. But the truth is, Dodge gets me. I needed a change. It worked both ways. My father and I don't *relate*." He didn't continue.

I didn't know what to say, so I didn't say anything.

"The stories at school make me sound better, cooler. Sorry to disappoint." He said this with a laugh, but I could hear a bit of a real question in there.

"Don't say that. Don't even think that," I said. "Bad boys are highly overrated." Even as I said it, I realized that this hinted at something between us. Was I overstepping the boundaries?

At first, Rennick didn't seem to notice. He only took keys out of his pocket and laughed. But I saw something lighten in the way he held his shoulders, no longer in defense. And then the soft upturn at the corners of his mouth. He liked that I had said it. Had he been hiding behind this bad-boy story?

The pieces of his real story. His reasons for coming here. I wanted to know the whole story, but I didn't want to pry. I could tell the feelings here, they ran deep. This meant a lot to him, and my reaction did too. While I watched Rennick fumble for the right key to the bait shop, I realized this was a moment I would revisit many, many times. An important moment. Something very much at the core of Rennick had just been approached. And I wanted to do right by that, to hold it with me, keep it in my heart. Even more than the pictures on the wall of his garage, this was him.

My heart knows him. The words hit me out of nowhere again when Rennick opened the bait shop door. I pushed them away. But they stayed there, on the outskirts of my thoughts. Where was that phrase from, anyway?

Rennick flipped on the lights. "Why don't you fill up a cooler?" he said. "Grab a few Cokes and stuff. I'll get the rods and night crawlers."

"We're going fishing?"

He turned around then, caught me with a dazzling smile. "Nobody will be looking for you out on the water." I must've looked unsure. "Is that okay, Corrine?"

I nodded. I was so grateful for the distraction. For everything. And for the chance to be completely alone with Rennick for a few more hours. But was it a sin in a port city like this to admit that you'd never been fishing before?

We took the small motorboat a few miles down the coastline to a marshy inlet where Rennick said we could catch redfish or just sit and be. I liked the way he tilted his face up to the sky when he said that. I liked the intimacy it insinuated.

The sun was at its fiery noon peak in the sky. So I wore a sloppy white old-man fishing hat from the bait shop to protect my pale skin, and I was happy for the cover it gave me. I could glance out from under it and watch Rennick as he steered the boat, and then as he set up our gear. He moved deftly. Confidently. He felt at home here.

When he killed the motor, he sat still for a long time, and then he pointed out an egret on the shore. It was a beautiful white bird, tall and fragile-looking.

"Dodge swears that an egret once flew down and stole the hat right off his head while he was fishing. He swears it was because he can sit still and be more patient than any other fisherman in the world. I think he was asleep." Rennick laughed, his eyes crinkling up in that adorable way, and the sound of it echoed in the mangrove trees around us. The egret stretched its wings into a broad expanse, and once again settled into position.

Rennick reached for the fishing poles. He handed me one, made of some sort of extremely light metal with a large shiny reel on the end. I wasn't a moron, I could figure out what was supposed to be done here. But how exactly did one get the line out into the water?

Now Rennick was opening up his own little cooler, much like the one I had packed full of Cokes and water. "Dug these up myself in the backyard with Bouncer." He opened up a little Styrofoam container that was packed full of black dirt and fat writhing worms.

Not wanting to look like an amateur, I picked one right up, let it slide around in my hand for a moment, dangled it in front of my face, watching it squirm, trying not to worry about the worm, trying not to think of the crawdad, everything.

"I need to put a hook on the end of your line first," Rennick said. He bent down to his tackle box, rocking the boat a little bit, and looked up at me from under the fringe of his lashes. "You ever been fishing, Corrine?"

"In theory."

It was a stupid answer, I realized this immediately. I just meant that I had seen people do it. But Rennick began to howl with laughter. "In theory?" He held on to his stomach, and he laughed, and the boat rocked on the water in time with his guffaws. I threw my worm at him, and it hit him right on the cheek and then dropped to the bottom of the boat. Rennick swatted at it, then laughed some more. I wanted to dissolve into a puddle of liquid dorkiness right there.

When I couldn't help it anymore, I began to laugh with him, and that's when I reached over the edge of the boat and splashed him, just a friendly little splash. And then he did the same to me.

The water felt cool and clean on this hot day. After a few rounds of splashing, Rennick stood up in the rocking boat and secured our fishing poles. He pulled his shirt above his head, still laughing. I tried not to gawk. I tried. But oh, his torso, it was beautiful. Thin and ropy. Defined muscles. His abs tanned and golden from the sun. "Stand up," he told me.

"No way," I told him.

"Don't make me carry you," he threatened. "You started this." He pointed at me, smiling. And that's when he flipped his sandals off and just jumped in. I stood up and watched him over the side, the boat rolling with the motion of his jump.

"It feels so good," he said, surfacing, shaking his hair. "Here, give me a hand up."

I didn't even hesitate. I offered him my hand to help him into the boat, and just as it was sinking in that I had offered my *hand,* I realized that Rennick had me. He didn't want into the boat.

And he pulled me in. I laughed just as I realized how gullible I was, and then I was tumbling headfirst into the water.

It slid over my skin, crisp and cold, and it was clean, practically clear blue. I stayed under longer than I needed to, just to feel it against me, and opened my eyes. I could see him across from me, and his eyes were open too. I smiled. He smiled.

And that's when it clicked on.

It scared me, startled me. So when Rennick reached for my hand again, I didn't grab on. I shook my head and swam away, feeling the water move around me, feeling each one of my old swimmer's strokes cutting into the force of the water.

He caught up to me quickly, and when I stopped swimming we broke the surface. I treaded water, and I could see we were a good distance from the boat. "Let's race," I told him.

It had been months since I'd trained, but I told myself it was like riding a bike. He squinted in a challenge, and then we both dove under. But I was off like a shot. I had always been good right out of the gate. Always took my lead that way.

When I slapped the bow of the boat with my hand, Rennick was right on my heels, but I had beat him. Fair and square.

I gave him my best triumphant smile.

"I am not slow," he said, disbelieving, shaking the water from his hair.

"I'm just faster," I told him, gloating.

"You are full of surprises," he said. He had a bead of water right at the tip of his nose, and I wanted so badly to touch it, wipe it away. But I didn't.

Rennick pulled himself up onto the rope ladder ahead of me, and when he offered me his hand, I didn't take it. Just a quick shake of my head. If he noticed, he didn't say anything.

We spent the rest of the afternoon and into the twilight with Rennick teaching me how to cast the line, how to bait with ballyhoo, how to take a hook out of a caught fish. It was all exciting and fun, and quite high up there on my list of favorite distractions. My favorite being Rennick with his shirt off. Second being his eyelashes.

I loved watching him cast the line, maneuvering the pole just so as he reeled in a catch. The muscles in his arms flexed, and he held his mouth in this perfect pout of concentration. It was obviously all so second nature to him. He threw back all of the fish we caught, dismissing them as not big enough. He got a little self-conscious while he was throwing back the last one, a pretty large sunfish. He glanced at me out of the corner of his eye.

What was it that he thought he was apologizing for? Could he really feel as though I would judge him for not being macho enough or something? I tried to picture what kind of home life could have nurtured that in him. I pictured a young Rennick, my Fourth of July Rennick, and my heart hurt for him. And I was just so thankful for Dodge. For what he meant to Rennick.

I caught my first fish, a catfish the size of a snow boot. "This is the ugliest thing I've ever seen!" I said, staring at the nasty thing, its glassy eyes staring right back at me. It was slippery and wet, with thick, slimy whiskers. It bucked in my hands, still moving its mouth, looking for water.

Rennick took it from me, unhooked it, held it in both of his hands, and, of course, shoved it close to my face, making smooching noises. "He just wants one kiss, Corrine." The catfish whiskers tickled my cheek, and I laughed, pushing it away. Rennick tossed it back in the water with a laugh.

As the afternoon wore on and the sun became too much, Rennick turned the motor on and steered us into a thick shady patch near the shore. We sat in the quiet little hideout of kudzu and mangrove trees, eating weird little snacks that Rennick had packed, like corn nuts and celery stalks that had seen better days.

It was a fun afternoon. A beautiful day of distraction. Even when the motor wouldn't start when we were ready to call it a day, Rennick just grabbed the two oars from the cargo space and started to row. I offered over and over to help him, but he wouldn't hear of it. And I tried not to wallow in the romance of the gesture—but I did. I stared at Rennick's silhouette against the pink sunset on the water. I watched him through the haze of twilight, with the heady, sleepy feeling of a long day in the sun.

But really, in the forefront of my mind all day was the big question: Was I going to trust that my hands carried the power to heal rather than the power to kill? Did I really believe it?

And that question had been there when Rennick's hands held on to my fishing pole, showing me how to keep just the right tension, how to slowly reel in my line. His hands were close to mine, only a sliver away, a breath. But he didn't touch me. Didn't push. Didn't ask. Not yet.

In my heart, I thanked him for not bringing it up yet. He knew it was there. Between us. Around us. But I had to ignore it for a while. I had to. Because these were questions that just had to simmer.

My phone buzzed in my pocket as we walked back to the Jeep. "It's my mom," I told him.

"I can take you back," he said, but then shot me a look, raised his eyebrows. "But I'm good to stay out."

"Yeah?" I said. Were we feeling each other out?

"Yeah," he said, smiling as he opened the passenger door for me.

"I'm hungry," I said.

"Where would you like to go?"

"Anywhere with air-conditioning."

The restaurant looked a little questionable from the outside, a bit tattered, weather-beaten, but when we got inside, it was charming, with candlelit tables and quiet music, not fancy, just nice. Clammy Joe's, the place was called. Rennick filled in for people here once in a while, when he wasn't busy with Dodge. The staff greeted him by name, and the pretty blond hostess gave me a smile when she showed us to our booth.

The place smelled of seafood–fresh and succulent seafood, like the Rawlingses' place. My stomach growled. We sat in a corner booth. A cup of crayons was on the table so you could draw on the brown paper tablecloth. In the middle of the paper, a circle was cut out, exposing a hole in the table about six inches wide. Rennick saw me eyeing it.

"It's the garbage can," he explained. I gave him a funny look. "For all the shells. You really are from Chicago," he joked. He smiled warmly at me, and I settled in. The place gave off a homey vibe. I couldn't really explain it, but in that second, when I looked up at Rennick again, I saw his aura in the dim light—that's what it had to be—and I saw the reds, the oranges, and purple, a thick wavy line of purple, especially near his head.

"What is it?" he asked, looking up from his menu. "You look like you've seen a ghost."

"Nothing," I said, checking out the menu. "What does purple mean in an aura?"

"Feeling. Connection. Love, maybe. Why?"

"No reason," I said, and blushed. The heat rose in my neck, into my earlobes. Rennick. Purple. I tried not to think about what he was seeing in my aura. "So how long've you been helping out here?"

"A year or so. Since I moved in with Dodge." He paused. "Thanks for spending the day with me."

I nodded, smiled. "Thank *you*." He watched me as we talked, his eyes never looking away from me. He studied me and it made me feel self-conscious and pained but also wonderful and worthy. I realized this was why I hadn't known who Rennick was at the Shack that first day he looked at me;

it was because he never looked at anyone. Never *really* looked. Not at school. Not here in the restaurant. No one. His focus was only on what was in front of him, and at school that was usually the worn paperback in his hand or the sketchpad on his lap. He never looked at people. Except for me.

I held on to this truth, and I watched it. The pretty hostess with fresh silverware. No eye contact. The people laughing one booth over. Nothing.

But here he was just staring at me. I realized I was mimicking his body language. My elbows were on the table, me leaning toward him over the hole in the middle.

I watched the way his mouth moved, always with a curve up at the ends. The shadows from the lone candle on the table played on his face and lit his deep blue eyes. He was an optimist, the swift, purposeful way he talked with his hands. His demeanor, it gave him away. And I could see that in how he moved, how he dealt with people, his easy nature.

"It must be easy to make friends, to see people for what they really are. The auras." It came out sounding flippant.

He recoiled a little, sat back in his seat. "I bet it's harder because of the auras."

"Really?" I couldn't figure that one out. "How can that be?"

He shook his head, leaned in toward me. "I don't want to sound . . .". He searched for the right word, rubbed his palm across his jaw. "I don't want to sound judgmental, but there are very few people who seem . . . interesting."

"Is that so? What's wrong with most people?" I leaned in even closer.

"There are lots of problems," Rennick started, ticking them off on one hand. "Green. Lots of green. Jealousy. Self-involvement. And yellow. Things. Too much worry about things, material stuff, wealth. Half the time all I see is a bunch of green and yellow. And then there's the other problem."

"What's that?" I said, mesmerized by the way he spoke, the lines of his face, the slope of his nose, the shadow of a beard on his jawline.

"The absence of aura."

"Why? How?"

"My theory is, because too many people live on the surface, never delve in deep. I think it goes along with yellow. The yellow fades to nothing. Materials matter and then . . . people aren't really living anymore. No aura."

He sat up straight then, looked the tiniest bit embarrassed. I noticed that Beethoven's *Moonlight Sonata,* or at least a Muzak version of it, was playing over the restaurant speakers. I had always loved this song. It sounded so difficult, so bitter, with the notes trying to eke out just a little hope.

I took all this in as our waiter came up. "Good evening, miss," he said. "Rennick, the usual?"

"Nah, I'll have the crab legs, Tim," Rennick told him. "Caesar salad."

"Scallops," I said. I wanted to order the crab legs too, but

I had a feeling Rennick was going to want to pay, and they were expensive.

"And to drink?" the waiter asked.

"I'll have a Coke," I answered. I had missed this. Being out. Living. The thrill of a date. I had missed all of these normal things, although tonight didn't feel completely normal. I had never, ever known—or even really dreamed about—the instant attraction toward another person, both physically and emotionally, like I felt with Rennick. He was the bass to my treble clef, and even as I thought of that stupid, cheesy analogy, part of me wanted to poke myself in the eye with my fork—but I liked it anyway. It made sense.

"Root beer," Rennick answered.

When the waiter left, I said, "I could stay here all night." I hadn't even meant to say it, but it was true. And I smiled then, deciding to be brave. "So what colors are in my aura? What made it interesting to you?"

Rennick squinted, leaned away from me. "I'll sound like a stalker."

"I'm glad you stalked me," I said.

"Your aura is really beautiful. I mean..." He rubbed at his jaw. "Sometimes it's more about the intensity than the specific colors. Yours is just powerful." I rolled my eyes. "No," he insisted, "that's the truth. For a long time, I stopped... expecting more. Kinda was losing hope in people, I had lost it in myself." His voice was serious, his face gone dark.

"Tell me."

He waved the moment away, laughed nervously. "I watched you, in school. Around."

"Around?" I said. "So tell me. How do you explain our supersenses?"

"The pineal gland," he said.

"What's that?" I hadn't been expecting a real answer.

"A tiny section of our brains, shaped like a pinecone, deep in the brain stem. Controls all kinds of stuff, but there's evidence cited in a few scientific journals the past few years that a large percentage of people experiencing extrasensory phenomena have a more advanced, larger pineal gland."

"Really?" I said. I didn't know how this made me feel. To think it was magic was one thing. To hear a scientific explanation of sorts hit me another way. Scarier? Was it really part of me?

"The pineal gland kind of links the right and left sides of the brain more than in normal brains, gives us more cohesion between the hemispheres."

"I'm both-handed," I said, kind of shocked, thinking of when I broke my wrist in third grade and could write with my left hand nearly as easily. Until then I hadn't realized it was something most people couldn't do.

"Some scientists call the pineal gland the third eye because it gives us another sense," Rennick said. "I like to think of it as us being Leyden jars. The pineal gland makes us more in tune, helps us hold on to the energy around us. But why specifically in New Orleans, I don't know."

Leyden jar? Where had I heard that before? "So there are more of us here? Different senses."

Rennick nodded. "Yeah, a few. Seers. Psychics. All over it's happening, but there are clusters in a few places. Here is the biggest, I think."

"Clusters," I said, trying to fit together a few puzzle pieces. "Like cancer clusters?"

His eyebrows shot up. "Maybe. Something in the environment like that. Or maybe we're all just evolving." He got self-conscious then. "I don't know. I just have theories. I don't mean to sound nuts. Or like a know-it-all."

"But why New Orleans specifically?" This part bothered me.

The waiter reappeared, placed our dishes in front of us. The scallops were humongous and looked delicious, but Rennick's crab legs looked even better. He caught me looking at them. "Let's halve it," he said, picking up four or five of his crab legs to put on my plate.

"No, no," I said, shaking my head. "Thank you, though. Let's back up. Keep going with what you were saying before. After you stalked me at school. *Around.*" I could tell I was embarrassing him, but I loved it.

"I kind of asked around, got your story—"

"Googled me."

"Yes," he said, "I Googled you." And I saw the color rise in his cheeks for the first time, just for a moment.

He cracked open a crab leg, dipped it into the butter, and held it out to me on his fork. "Haven't you ever just given into something, just known that it seemed right?"

I leaned forward then, listened to the crescendo of the piano in Beethoven's sonata. I let Rennick feed me. The crab was decadent, so buttery. I savored the taste, savored this moment here with him, this new beginning for me. "Yes," I said. "Sometimes things just feel right."

For a moment, I thought he was going to kiss me, and I both wanted him to and was extremely scared. But then he looked away and the moment was gone.

We continued to eat, and he grabbed a crayon, the blue one, and wrote on my side of the tablecloth.

What is wrong?

I read this and considered, popping another scallop into my mouth. I picked up the red crayon. I didn't know exactly why this seemed safer than talking, but it did.

I still don't believe it all.

It was kind of hard to write upside down, but I didn't want to stop.

You are so pretty, Corrine. This one caught me off guard. I couldn't help but smile.

I bet you say that to every aura.

He laughed at that. I took a drink of my Coke. I watched him patiently, traced the planes of his handsome face with my eyes.

Tell me, he wrote.

I smiled to myself and pressed the red crayon to the paper, but before I had formed a thought, he wrote again.

Why don't you believe in yourself?

What a loaded question, I thought. I sighed, took a sip of my Coke, and realized that we were both leaning toward each other again, the laundry-fresh smell of Rennick filling me up.

I'm afraid of things. I'm only one for two in the lifesaving department.

Rennick dropped his crayon then, looked up at me with such empathy. This leveled me. That he cared so much. I stabbed a scallop, dipped it in his butter.

When I looked back up, when I had quelled the urge to cry embarrassing tears, I saw that he was still watching me. Same look. Same eyes.

"Corrine, you didn't kill your sister." He reached across the table for my hand. I pulled back, sucked air through my teeth, immediately afraid. He sat back instantly, stricken, but recovered quickly.

"I'm trying," I said, but I sounded pathetic, and I hated myself for the whine in my voice.

"I have theories," he said matter-of-factly. Obviously switching topics for my sake. "About auras. They're like magnetic fields of energy, attracting and repelling forces in the universe."

I nodded. He was telling me about himself. The tenor of

his voice told me that he was letting me in. I had the sense that he was going to bare himself for me, show me what no one else got to see, so to speak. I leaned closer, listened intently. What was it that made this guy tick? Because there was just something about him. I felt like maybe if I could get to the bottom of him, if I could see how he operated on a philosophical level, then maybe... maybe I could figure myself out too. There wasn't really a lot of logic to that feeling, but I held on to it. With a choke hold. Because really, what else did I have?

"Growing up, Cale hated me a lot of the time. We were brothers. I'm sure lots of brothers torture each other in creative and sadistic ways. We did." He rubbed his chin, squinted. "I've never talked about this with anyone."

"Tell me," I whispered.

He considered and waited for a long moment, fiddling with the empty crab shells on his plate. I didn't know if he was going to continue. Finally he did, but in a different direction. Hopefully, obliquely getting back to himself. Underneath it all.

"Cale blamed me for Mom's death. And for a long time—"

"Why?" I asked, but he just waved my question away.

"Dad and Cale are cut from the same cloth. They're harder. Tougher than me. Not worse. Not better. Just different. It got harder in high school. I didn't meet the old man's expectations."

"Go on," I urged.

"It's not a new story, or even really interesting. I wasn't the son that he thought I should be. That was Cale. Football player. Tough kid. Went straight into the Army."

Rennick shook his head. "Me, I was a nerd. Art classes. Science garbage all over my room. It's not like it was my dad's fault. It's not like it was Cale's, but I could feel myself rebelling against Dad. Little ways. He got his back up. Bottom line, after Dodge's heart attack, Dad was going to make him close up the charter business. And then Lila had to be put in the home, and I could really see it all killing Dodge. So I chose—I offered—to come live here. It was good for Dodge, and good for me too. Just healthier for me."

I played with the straw in my now-empty Coke can. "Dodge *gets* you," I said. And Rennick nodded. I tried to read the emotions on his face. I mean, what was it? Was he embarrassed that he was not the tough-guy persona that everyone at Liberty had made up for him? Did he think he was soft or somehow *less* for not being the typical guy, if there was such a thing? And what kind of father couldn't see the beauty and greatness in this guy?

"So the rumors? Ren from the Pen?" I asked.

Rennick smiled. "Things aren't always what they seem, Corrine." He stared at me hard.

"I hardly think that that applies to me and Sophie." It sounded harsher than I had meant. Rennick just nodded and signaled to the waiter for the check.

"I should've known you weren't a brawler," I said, looking

at his hands drumming on top of the papered table. His long, brown-from-the-sun fingers, the absence of scars on his knuckles. They were gorgeous hands, really, thin but strong-looking, like him.

"Why's that?"

"Your hands are way too pretty. They're an artist's hands."

"Speaking of pretty," he said, with this gorgeous, flirty smirk. But he didn't get to finish. The waiter chose that moment to place the bill on the table and ask us if we needed anything else.

Rennick took out his wallet.

"Thank you," I said, "but I really can pay for myself."

"No," he said, leaving some bills on the table. "I mean, it's a date, isn't it?"

He stood up then, and I couldn't help but smile. "A date. Sure." And I noticed that he definitely watched for my reaction.

Rennick drove us home like a bifocals-wearing grandpa. As we got nearer to the house and turned down Manderly, I saw that the reporters and their interest in me had not waned at all. If anything, the news vans had multiplied. I had Rennick pass my house and take a roundabout way to the back alley. The narrow gravel pathway was just wide enough for a vehicle. Rennick pulled up to the back of the garage and hid the Jeep from view.

The sky rumbled and a handful of thick raindrops

plopped on us when we got out. We ducked behind the lilac bushes. "You are awfully popular."

"Just stay down." We crouched low and, thanks to the banana trees and the lilac hedge, were pretty hidden as we ran up the back steps. Loud thunder boomed through the air, the rain coming down in a sheet of cool water. I put my key in the door. "We made it!"

"Excuse me, Miss Harlowe?" A reporter came from around the front of the house, but I turned the key in the lock and threw the door open.

Rennick stepped in behind me, and my flip-flops squeaked on the kitchen floor. He shook his gorgeous hair, and I heard voices. I had figured that Mom would still be home, but that was it. Rennick shot me a look, and I shrugged.

I stuck my head into the family room.

"Honey?" Mom's eyes apologized to me even as she beckoned for me to come. I did so hesitantly. Rennick followed close behind.

Dad stood up from the couch and offered his hand to Rennick. I heard Mom introducing them, but my eyes were glued to the couch. There sat a hollow-eyed young couple and a gangly kid of maybe ten or eleven years old. His face was swollen and sad, his head cancer-bald, with a violent red and purple scar from his left temple to the top of his head.

"I'm Seth Krane?" His voice was so small, so high.

"I know," I said, and then I placed him. Declan Krane worked for my dad. This was his son and he had cancer, something rare, in his blood, I thought. There were little cans with his picture on them collecting donations all over the Garden District, at the Starbucks, at the Circle K. "It's nice to meet you."

Seth's mother cleared her throat and got up from the couch, offering me her hand.

"I can't," I said, shaking my head. I backed up a step and bumped right into Rennick. He pressed a palm flat on my back, between my shoulder blades. A gesture in support, I thought.

"We are so sorry to bother you, Corrine," Seth's mother said, her words tumbling out fast and desperate. "We have no other hope. It's critical, they say. Just keeping him comfortable."

Her words were atrocious and difficult to hear, but inside I was freaking out. Was this what it meant to have the touch? What if I killed that little kid instead of helped him? My brain kind of shut off. My mother's voice was audible, but it sounded far away from me. She was explaining what had happened to Sophie, how uncertain I was. But all I could really focus on was the pressure of that hand on my back. I took several deep breaths and refocused my eyes.

I studied Seth's face, the hazel eyes buried deep under his hairless brow, the crooked teeth answering my gaze with a smile. A smile for me, with empathy and understanding, as if *I* was truly the one in the most messed up of situations. My mind reeled. What did it feel like to know you were at the end? How could he have such a look of peacefulness on his face? Acceptance?

I opened my mouth to explain myself, to politely decline. And that's when Seth's father stood up. Balding and slight, he spoke quietly in a low baritone. "Miss Harlowe, we know we have no right to ask what we are asking. But we... Seth wants you to try. And we understand there are no guarantees."

I listened, and as I watched the father look down at his fragile little son, I saw how he gazed at him, that loving, adoring hand stroking the boy's face as if it were the most beautiful thing in the world. And the father bent down then and gave Seth's ragged scar an absentminded kiss. And the look on his face, it was pure and gorgeous and familiar.

This was how my parents had looked at Sophie.

And the dark hollows around Seth's mother's eyes, these were my own mother's eyes not so long ago. The look of grief and loss. Unspeakable loss. The worst loss.

The pendulum had been swinging for me. But right now, for this moment, it stopped. It was decided.

And then I found myself speaking before I had even decided to. I sat down in the old rocker across from the couch. "I can try, but even I don't quite understand it."

"Thank you, God!" the mother gasped, and clutched at the little boy, pulling him to her bosom.

"We appreciate this, Miss Harlowe," the father said, looking right into my eyes. "No matter what the outcome."

The man turned and spoke to my father in low tones, and my dad clasped his shoulder. When I caught Dad's eye, he nodded at me slightly.

I knelt in front of the seated boy on the couch. I held both my hands out, and I asked him to place his hands in mine. I stole a look at Rennick, who was watching from behind me. I didn't know what to expect. I didn't know what to do.

Hadn't Rennick said that his own mother had only been able to summon it about half the time?

I closed my eyes and focused on Seth. I thought about him, what was going on with his own body turning traitor on him. I focused on myself, my insides, yearning for that small, indescribable spark to generate inside my ribs. I focused on the indigo light, on the feeling and sensation of being a conduit.

I held this pose, kneeling in front of Seth, reaching within myself to find the start of it all. But nothing.

"Your hands are sweaty," Seth whispered.

"They are," I laughed. I opened my eyes, but I didn't let go of his hands.

I tried to remember the feeling of it, right there, under my sternum, the wispy flutter of the first few sparks, and then the full burst of flames. But nothing happened.

I tried for a long while, but in the end, nothing.

"I'm sorry," I said.

The mother wiped tears from her eyes. "Don't apologize," she said. "You tried."

"It's okay," Seth said, and he placed a small hand on my cheek. Inside, I broke. Just a cleaving away from all that made sense. At that moment, I believed. I knew I had the power to help this boy, to save lives. I had this.

I just didn't know how to control it. Yet.

"We very much appreciate it," the father said.

"I don't know how to start it," I said. "It's—"

"It's okay." This was my mother's voice.

"I think I can do it, though. I just need—" But Mom was already ushering them out the door. Dad was shaking the man's hand again. And I was so enraged at how helpless I felt.

Rennick came and stood close to me, his head bent over mine, an intimate gesture. "You believe it," he whispered.

"I believe it."

11

The tapping on my window woke me in the morning. The new light of the day was just starting to eke into the room, all purple and blue in the slants between the pear tree branches. In my dream, Seth Krane was knocking repeatedly at my front door, but when I woke, I knew the sound immediately. Pebbles at the window.

I patted at my hair as I leaned my forehead onto the cool glass of the window, my hand already opening in a wave. There he was, a duffel bag slung over his shoulder, a box in his hands, his face full of something. Purpose.

I threw my blue fuzzy robe around myself and found Mom and Dad in the kitchen drinking coffee, Dad dressed for work and Mom looking a lot like me.

"He could've just knocked," Dad said with a smirk. "What's all the stuff? Is he planning on moving in?"

"Very funny," I answered. "I don't really know."

I opened the back door and stepped out onto the stoop. The morning was really something, cool for New Orleans, with dew-wet grass and birdsong in the air. I could've just let him into the kitchen, but there was a part of me that wanted him and his visit all to myself.

Even with so much on my plate, and even with my morning breath, my tangled hair, my ratty old bunny slippers, I couldn't help how I reacted to him. But there was something about him this morning, Rennick in all of his glory. Oh God, the shape of his shoulders through his T-shirt, the corners of his mouth as they turned up just as he raised his head to see me, the plane of his jaw. His hair was disheveled and he had on faded jeans, a tattered T-shirt. He was in full science-geek mode.

"Hi," I said.

"We have to figure this thing out. Ourselves. You'll believe it wholeheartedly. You'll own it."

I loved the way that sounded. Own it. "Then I can go find Seth Krane."

"So you're accepting this?" he asked.

"I am," I said, grabbing the box from him. "What are we going to do?"

"Make a Leyden jar, for starters." We moved toward the back door.

"We gotta have some rules," I said. "I call the shots. If it gets too much. If I feel it getting . . . out of control, you have to listen to me and leave." I had my hand on the doorknob and looked back at Rennick.

He nodded. Did some kind of crossing-his-heart, Boy Scout salute. He wanted me to smile, but I couldn't. My mind's eye kept flashing to Sophie's little face. The goggles, the rocks in her hand, the empty look of her death on the Lake Michigan shore.

"'Cause I believe it, but I'm still scared. Of hurting someone," I added, averting my eyes. "Seth Krane. Anyone. *You.*"

"You're scared to move on from this."

I rubbed my knuckles on my lips, opened the back door. I nodded just once. There was some truth in that. I couldn't deny it.

I expected Mom and Dad to be in the kitchen, all greetings and raised eyebrows, but I heard Dad's truck pulling out of the garage, and so I assumed Mom was upstairs. I was getting privacy. They probably had talked about this. What had Mom called my friendship with Rennick, my attempt to help Seth Krane? *Good for the soul.*

I didn't know about that. But I had to do something.

"One more rule," I said, unloading the box onto the kitchen table. I turned to look at Rennick, who was pulling all kinds of stuff out of his gym bag. Lengths of wire. A roll of tinfoil. A small cooler.

He looked up from under the fringe of his lashes. "Anything."

"I can't touch anyone yet. I just can't do that for . . ."

"Got it," he said, and continued to unload stuff onto the kitchen table. I watched him for longer than necessary. Did I imagine that he swallowed hard against that comment? Did he care about this? Me not touching him? What was I to him? Who was he to me?

I pushed these thoughts away.

He pointed to the glass jar on the kitchen table, the roll of tinfoil, a bottle of carpenter's glue. "I already spoke with your parents. I hope that was okay. I just wanted them to know what we were doing."

"What are we doing?" Oh Jesus, this sounded like a loaded question.

And something—embarrassment?—quickly flashed across Rennick's face. "Only changing the world." He gave me his most mischievous smile, and my mouth turned up.

He took this as encouragement. "We are going to plunge into this. Do some real work on this. Scientific stuff. Tests. My kind of thing."

"I'm in, but—"

"You know, we could contact the Tulane lab, include the doctors working on—"

"No!"

Mom came in then to fill her coffee cup. "I can make pancakes?" she offered.

"No thanks," I said.

"Sure," Rennick answered at the same time. The two

of them chuckled. He gave me a wink. "Moms love me," he said.

I rolled my eyes. "Of course they do."

"You need to eat too, Corrine," Mom said as she began to take ingredients out of the cupboard.

"If you say so."

"So what are you going to make here?" she asked, eyeing the glass jar.

"A Leyden jar," Rennick answered. "It's part of our scientific approach." He smiled easily at my mom.

I didn't share in the smile. I did, however, resist—over and over again—the urge to close the space between Rennick and me, to sniff the scent of him, the sheets-dried-outside-on-the-first-day-of-spring smell that seemed to emanate from him. I wanted to kiss him for showing up this morning with all of this. For his plan of action. For his dedication.

And I wanted to kiss him for other reasons too. Just draw him near, run my hands through that ridiculous rock star hair, lick the stubble on his chin.

I absolutely loved him for showing up this morning, for coming back and trying.

I took the scissors from Rennick and began to cut the tinfoil as he instructed. "Just glue it all around the jar," he told me. "It's like an early battery."

It felt right to be doing this in my kitchen, working at something tangible. This was good, productive, and maybe a little dangerous.

* * *

When we were finished with the Leyden jar–and the pancakes–he opened a cooler.

"I don't want to," I said.

"Corrine, they're crawdads. We're not using lab chimps."

I looked up at the ceiling, took a deep breath. "I've read as much as I could online. There isn't much."

"I know." He sat across from me. "But let's get serious. The first step is that you have to control it. Whatever it is, you have to own it. Maybe summon it."

I tried not to balk at this. Summon it. "Can you summon the power to see auras?"

He seemed to consider the idea. "Yeah. I see them always. But sometimes I want to see them more clearly. Focus. Anyway, that's what you are going to do. Try and bring that feeling–whatever it is–back."

"I have always spent so much time and energy praying for that feeling to stay away." My voice sounded puny.

"You are in control," he said, and looked at me sternly. "You gotta believe that, Corrine."

I bit my lip.

"We can stop anytime."

But could I?

He took out a small crayfish. Placed it on the coffee table, atop a paper plate. "He's fresh. Hasn't been dead long. Less than an hour probably. What can you do?"

Rennick sat back in his chair, put his hands behind his head, and smiled, watching me.

I closed my eyes and focused on the symptoms, the things that usually preceded the indigo lens. I thought about the churning in my chest, the engine of power flickering to life under my ribs, and I concentrated.

Nothing.

"It's probably going to take a while," Rennick said.

I tried. I really tried. For the better part of an hour, I tried to get myself into some kind of Zen state, some kind of meditation mode that might bring about the power so that I might possibly dream about harnessing it. But nothing. Zilch.

Truth be told, it was difficult to concentrate with Rennick's eyes on me. It was difficult to do anything except focus on not touching him.

I vowed to myself to try to summon it on my own. Alone. Later.

We played backgammon instead. Rennick won. Of course he won. All three games. When he was packing up his dead bugs and crayfish, he grabbed a sketchbook from his box of goodies and tossed it across the coffee table at me. He made it seem nonchalant, but I caught the look out of the corner of his eye. "For you," he said. "You can look at them later. I have to go help Dodge out at the dock."

"Thanks," I said, knowing that "thanks" didn't really

cover it. He was letting me in, even as I kept my proverbial distance.

"And Mia-Joy is coming with us tomorrow."

"She is?"

"She is. I saw her at the Shack. She wants in."

"Of course she does. God forbid I do anything exciting that Mia-Joy might not be a part of."

Rennick chuckled.

"I'm sorry," I said, and headed for the stairs, because right then, right when I wasn't concentrating on it, it had switched on inside my rib cage. Just a little spark, but it caught me off guard. And I felt open, scared. Not in charge. I balked. I had to get away.

Later that night, I sat on my bed, the Leyden jar on my nightstand. We had painstakingly glued tinfoil all around the inside and the outside of the jar, filled it with water, and then put an electrical charge in it and measured the voltage. It was really nothing, just the first in a long line of ever-improving batteries. A visual for how Rennick liked to think of the physio-electric power that we somehow tapped into. "It's like you hold on to a charge—electricity," he said, "but more than that. You hold the spark. Give it away through the touch."

I looked at the Leyden jar, the flame in my chest now gone, and I tried to summon that flame. To bring it, that power, back to the surface. Conjure it. Own it.

Nothing.

I listed in my mind the reasons why I had to move forward from here, the reasons I knew it was safe to at least try. Number one: I knew when it was coming, i.e., the indigo lens. Number two: Maybe I could learn to control it. Number three: I could heal?

I focused and meditated, tried and tried. Nothing.

I had given up and was playing Angry Chipmunks on my iPad when I heard the pebbles at the window.

I couldn't go down there, because I didn't trust myself. I didn't want to be near him in the dark.

I got up and slid my window open. "Hey," I called quietly, trying to adjust my eyes to the dark, searching the shadows for his form. Rennick stepped into the soft light from the streetlamp.

"Hey, you." He smiled a tender smile. "I didn't say it earlier, and I just have to say it." He rubbed at his chin and looked up at me through his lashes in that flirty way. "You're *so brave*, Corrine."

"Rennick," I said, but that's all I could get out. I had to swallow against the emotion in my throat.

"Good night," he said, and he left through the back hedge.

I stayed awake a long while, trying to summon it, reinvigorated by his visit. And when I finally fell asleep, exhausted from the exertion, I dreamt of Sophie again. And this time, when we were on the beach, she played on the rocks, digging for fossils with Rennick.

"I didn't know there was going to be an entire zoo's worth of dead bugs involved." Mia-Joy turned up her nose at Rennick's collection of roly-polies and other dead insects spread out on the kitchen counter.

"We'll start smaller." Rennick looked serious today. There was an edge to his voice too. Something had changed since yesterday. He showed me the crawdads in his cooler. "I brought minnows too. I don't know." He ran his hand through his hair, then kept bringing out more stuff.

"Corrine, you're going to resurrect an amoeba." Mia-Joy cackled, then started looking in cupboards for something. But I studied Rennick, wondering at the worry line between his eyes.

"Did you make any headway last night, trying to summon it?" he asked.

I shook my head. Even after his impromptu visit, I hadn't had any success. But I had spent a lot of time leafing through his sketches, some watercolors, some pastels. Jesus, they were beautiful. Just colors and colors, prisms of light. And there was one aura, repeated over and over, each one from a different perspective. I wanted to ask him if it was mine. I wanted it to be mine, for him to have thought so much about me, even when we weren't together. But it seemed much too personal a question right now, in front of Mia-Joy, in the daylight.

"I'm making coffee," Mia-Joy announced, pulling the

canister from the cupboard. "Where's the sugar?" I pointed to the cabinet next to the sink.

"Did you check your schedule online?" Rennick asked.

"School?"

"Yes, Corrine," Mia-Joy chimed in. "Three weeks till senior year. And why the hell won't this coffee machine turn on?"

"I haven't even thought about school." The whole concept seemed far away, like it belonged to a different Corrine.

"So are you two going to be all will-they-won't-they, making eyes at each other all school year?" Mia-Joy said, eyeing me. She gave the switch on the coffee machine several last tries and then swore under her breath.

"Try another outlet, farther from Corrine," Rennick said. "Corrine sort of *interferes* with machines."

Mia-Joy laughed. "Okaaaay." She turned her attention to me. "There's also this article I wanted to tell you about."

"The one where they refer to me as the anonymous teenage healer, yet they name my parents one paragraph later? Or how about the one where I'm the Gypsy medicine woman. That was on someone's blog."

"No," Mia-Joy answered. "Something else."

Rennick shook his head and took one of the minnows out of the water, placed it on a paper towel. I watched its eyeball. I didn't want to, but I couldn't look away. Its mouth kept going, kept hoping and trying for that water.

I reached to scoop him up and put him back in Rennick's

cooler, but Rennick gave me a look. "It's a minnow," he said. I stopped myself.

"So tell me," I said.

Mia-Joy was pouring water into the coffeemaker now. She and Rennick were having some sort of conversation with only their eyes. It ended with the haughty look I'd seen Mia-Joy give so many times, to her mom, to me, to everyone. Mia-Joy did what she wanted.

"Mia-Joy, we talked about this." Rennick sat down at the table. "Are we going to start?" he asked me, a last-ditch effort.

"No. Tell me about the article."

"You'll only get upset and—"

"Listen," I said, an edge to my voice, "you may have your opinions. You may think you know what I do or don't need to know. But I am not some delicate flower. And I want to know."

Rennick looked taken aback, Mia-Joy pleased with herself. "Okay," she said. "The boy you spilled coffee all over at Café Du Monde last summer. Remember, Bryant? Apparently, he's some kind of seer or telepath. Whatever." Rennick shook his head, got up from the table, and for a second I thought he was going to leave. But he didn't. He just walked over to the sink, stared out the window for a second.

"What about him?" I said. "Did you know he was . . . ?"

He nodded. "His aura."

"He got beat up, Corrine. Pretty bad," Mia Joy finished.

"Why? I mean, why did they—" I hadn't been expecting this. I balled my hands into fists. I thought of Bryant's smile, the way he always opened the door for Mia-Joy and me before bio. He had the most perfect teeth. Had they punched him in those pretty teeth? "Why?"

"He pissed off the wrong kids," Rennick said. "Who knows? He's different. It's all some people need to know." And when he turned around, I saw that hopeless look on his face, and I absolutely hated it.

And before I realized it, it was there. In my chest. Flaring.

I summoned my courage, visualized harnessing this light in my chest. I made myself stay there in the kitchen and not run away. "I gotta try it," I said, breathless. "Stand back," I ordered them. "Is the minnow dead? Is he really dead?" I was out of breath now, and it was working itself up into a rolling, churning engine of heat and power in my chest. My limbs started to tingle and my vision seemed to focus, clear itself of everything but what was on the kitchen table.

I eyed the dead crayfish already on the paper plate. Several half-squashed roly-polies, a long-dead cricket. It was like I could see everything so clearly. Defined.

Rennick picked up the minnow, shook it. "Dead," he said, and what was there in his face? Did he look a little scared? I looked away. I took a deep breath, and it rolled inside me, growing and blossoming.

"It's tied to your emotions, girl," Mia-Joy said. She took a few steps closer, like she wanted to get a good look at what I was about to do.

"Stand back. I mean it, you two. And no matter what happens, if I pass out, whatever, don't you touch me!" I screamed at them. And then it was there, the indigo lens, and I could feel it charging, pulsing through me, out to my limbs, like a hard, powerful light surging through me, out of my eyes, out of my hands.

I picked up the minnow, and I cupped it between my palms, and at first nothing seemed to happen. Its scales were wet and cold. It was still. I relaxed my muscles, let the surge move through me, reach its fever pitch, work its way into my hands. And then out of my hands.

The current prickled the inside of my palm. And there it was. I felt movement, something whisper-soft against my flesh. I removed one of my hands and looked at the fish. The minnow's eye was *back*, the life behind it was there. The mouth moved, hoping again, its body bucked.

I dropped it back into the water-filled cooler and watched it swim. I was breathing little shallow breaths.

"Jesus, Mary, and Joseph," Mia-Joy said. I looked at her. She was still blue, indigo.

"Sit down, Corrine," Rennick said. "Before–"

"No!" I said. "It's not gone." And I picked up the craw-dad, pressed it between my palms. Pushed the surge through me. Held it there in my hands. Focused it.

The crawdad came alive. That same tickle. The antennae,

the claws. I laughed as I dropped it on the table, and Rennick laughed too.

I picked up those damn roly-polies, and sure enough, in a few seconds all but two came back alive, squirming, rolling themselves into little balls. I placed them on the table, moved to the cricket. I pressed him between my palms. Nothing.

"No, been dead too long," I said. "Too long." And I moved on to another crayfish.

I pressed it between my hands and closed my eyes. My breath came in fits and starts now, and I kind of half sat, half fell into the kitchen chair.

I became aware that Rennick was pleading with me. "No more, Corrine. It's too much." I opened my eyes and placed the newly alive crayfish on the table.

"I did it!" But I saw now that Rennick was right next to me.

"No more, please." He was desperate. I didn't know what was wrong. I was so happy! I couldn't fight this kind of evidence, but Rennick's eyes were pleading.

"Just one more. It's amazing. It's crazy, and the blue isn't gone yet–"

"I'll touch you, Corrine!" he said, low, serious. "No more, please."

Mia-Joy watched us intently, playing with the newest crawdad. She placed it on the table.

"What are you afraid of?" she asked him.

But I was already nodding. The lens had shifted. It was

gone now, and I was exhausted. But I couldn't tear my eyes away from Rennick's. He looked so panicked, wide-eyed and desperate.

"I'm sorry," I said, not knowing exactly what I was apologizing for. The moment passed, and Mia-Joy was jumping around.

"She did it!" Mia-Joy screeched. She gave Rennick a high five that seemed to snap him back from wherever he was.

"Proof! Real live proof!" he said.

He turned to me then, and it's like he forgot himself. He reached to pull me out of the chair, but I recoiled.

"Right," he said. "Sorry."

"I did it!" I said, smiling, trying to gloss over the rebuke. "I can't believe it, but this is really true. This part of it."

"But you can't *hug* us," Mia-Joy said, plopping down in the chair across from us.

"This is *part* of it," Rennick said, sinking into the chair next to me, our victory celebration amazingly short-lived. "But you think there's another part."

I nodded. My body ached, exhausted. And suddenly, I couldn't think anymore. It's like the pathways in my brain were worn and short-circuited, all used up. "I'm just so tired," I said.

"You need to get some rest," Rennick said. "Sleep."

He and Mia-Joy started to pack everything up. But before he left, he said, "Promise me, no more today."

"Okay."

"I mean it, Corrine. If you ever, ever trusted me, like I knew anything, you promise me that."

I knew for whatever reason this meant something to him. "I promise," I said. He watched me carefully for a long moment and then finished putting away the fish, the crawdads.

My nerve endings felt frayed and raw, my head fuzzy and heavy.

"Corrine, we should be celebrating. You gotta give this thing up," Mia-Joy said. I nodded.

But Rennick interrupted. "You're doing great." And I managed to stick out my tongue at Mia-Joy, who only stuck hers back at me.

Part of me wanted to yell after Rennick, *Stay with me! Don't leave me here without . . . what? You.*

Then they were gone, along with my newly alive menagerie. For a second, I kind of wished that they had left the evidence. I wanted it near me, so I would know it was real. I had *healed*.

Mom came in the door just as I was trudging up the stairs, my legs heavy with exhaustion. "Corrine! I just ran into Rennick and Mia-Joy outside!" she yelped. "You did it!"

She ran to me and hugged me. I bristled, but she didn't relinquish her hold on me. And after a few seconds, I kind of collapsed into her. I don't really remember getting to my room. But Mom must have gotten me there, where I fell onto my bed.

* * *

I woke up much, much later, from a deep and dreamless sleep. My room was pitch-dark, with only a slight sliver of a moon visible out my window. But there it was again, the *plink-plunk* of the pebbles.

I lay there for a long time, listening to his persistence.

Then I got up and snuck outside.

He was different at night, alone in the dark. I felt different too.

We seemed like truer versions of ourselves here. In the dark. It was easier to put away all the pretenses without the sunlight glaring off our intimate truths.

"You came," he said, standing up from Sophie's bench. I took a step toward him, shoved my hands into the pockets of my robe. I could barely make out the features of his face, but I knew he was smiling. It was in his voice.

"Hi," I said like a moron.

"Hi, you," he said. We stood there for a long moment. He took a step toward me, and then another. I tipped my face up to him. We were close, so close, and I didn't back away.

"What is it?" I said, breathless.

"I have to tell you what I know. I have to tell you about Dell. How he died. What I think happened, Corrine."

"He died?" I asked, taking a seat on the garden bench. He paced a little bit.

"The whole thing is a little foggy, like memories can

be when you're little, you know. I was only eight. Cale was twelve or thirteen."

"Your brother?"

He nodded. "Dell was his friend. They hung out all the time, started getting into trouble. Anyway, I'm not making sense." He stopped. Ran his hand through his hair. "There's a lot to the story. But the gist is that looking back, I think Dell had the touch."

"His aura was like mine?"

"In a way," Rennick said. "I think maybe when I was about eight, he saved me."

"You're kidding."

Rennick shook his head. "We were fishing, Dell, Cale, and me. I went out too far at the end of the wharf. Fell in. Couldn't swim back then. I had a huge fear of the water. Used to have all these drowning nightmares. Anyway, we were fishing on Algiers Point, and the current swept me along down the shore. By the time Cale got me out, I mean, I don't know. I can't remember it. Not well. But I think I was gone. I was outside myself. Hovering. I think I was dead."

"Jesus, Rennick."

"I watched him save me. He put both his hands on my chest, and something racked through his body. And then it was like I got sucked back into myself. Came back, sputtering water."

"Why didn't you tell me this?"

But Rennick ignored me now. He was remembering. "Dell was a normal kid. He was always around. He and Cale still hung around a little in high school. Dell knew what he was by then, I bet. There was a car crash, some kid trying to outrun a train out in the Marigny one night. Two kids got killed. But Dell was at the party where they were headed. Anyway, I'm not sure, but I've heard kids tell it, and I think . . . I think he saved the girl. April, her name was. And he died."

"How did he die?"

"I think he used himself up."

I processed this. "That's why you were scared today."

"I'm still scared. That you could give away your spark. Use it up. Whatever *it* is." And I thought about those frog legs. Electricity made them move, mimicked life. But what was it that Dell—or I—could also give them? Life?

When you put it that way, the enormity of it squashed me. The pressure that would come with it. The sheer vastness of responsibility. This thing was ginormous. Why me?

Rennick sat down next to me, our legs touching, and I looked into his eyes. There was fear there. What else?

"Rennick . . ."

I watched him searching me with his eyes. I recognized something in him. Something I knew too well, from the mirror. He was telling me about Dell. But . . . Things fit into place then, and I got it. I understood. I realized what was at the heart of all this for Rennick.

Guilt. Overwhelming and inescapable.

Cale's anger. Blame.

"Oh my God, Rennick." I swallowed hard. "She died saving you. You were stillborn. And your mother used herself up to save you?" He hung his head. "This is why you're scared. Oh, Rennick, I'm so sorry." I reached for him but then caught myself.

Rennick stood up, turned away. Then he gave a nearly imperceptible, defeated nod. "Corrine, I–"

"Rennick, you are not responsible for what happened to your mother. Oh, Ren." I stood and moved toward him. I wanted so much to comfort him, to hold him in my arms. But I couldn't. Yet.

"She painted porcelain."

"Your mother?"

"She painted porcelain dishes, teacups, plates. She was an artist." I didn't know what to say to this, so I just let him talk. "She had blond hair like Cale. Dad says she was the worst cook this side of the Mississippi." He laughed.

"I'm so sorry."

"It's not your fault."

"Or yours," I said. He turned back to me, nodded.

"I know that. Usually. Sometimes."

I understood this.

He closed the distance between us. I tipped my face up to his. In the moonlight, his eyes shone, glittered. "I want to kiss you," he whispered, leaning in toward me, his lips an inch from my ear. "I know you aren't ready. But I just wanted you to know." His voice was music, the notes playing down the skin of my neck. I closed my eyes and leaned in, let his breath play over me.

"A lot has changed," I said finally, opening my eyes. "The bugs, the crayfish. I—"

"Between us," he said, and he was looking at me so intently. My eyes had adjusted, and I could see that worry line in his brow. I could see the want in his eyes. "I can keep from touching you," he said. "And I will. Still," he said, swallowing, "I just needed you to know that I don't *want* to stop myself." I watched the silhouette of his Adam's apple in the moonlight, transfixed. "You can't hurt me, Corrine." He tipped my head back up to him, and I let him, met his eyes. "You didn't kill Sophie." I looked away, took a step back. "Don't do that," he said. "Don't leave."

"I was there," I answered. "I know what happened."

"But you tried to help Seth. You must believe it on some level."

I nodded. "It's . . ." I couldn't really explain it. "It's hard to give it up."

He leaned closer again, and I let him. Again. His breath was on my neck, and then his hand was on the small of my back. He pulled me to him, and I let him. I melted into him, my body against his.

The warmth, the comfort of being held. My throat closed against the emotion of it.

"Corrine," he breathed into my hair. "Corrine, please don't push me away."

"Rennick," I began to protest, but I inhaled against his T-shirt, and then I just sighed, let myself relax into him. I let him hold me, his chin resting on top of my head, my hands still balled in my pockets. I listened to the rhythm of his heartbeat. *Da dum. Da dum.* And I thought it would be perfectly okay if I never moved again.

"Corrine," he whispered, his words shivering down my neck, his hands tracing the knobs of my spine. "Corrine, touch me." His voice was low, soothing. "Believe this is okay."

"I can't," I said, and after a long moment I pulled away. He was right. I was on the precipice. I was. But I wasn't ready.

"Why?" he asked. And he looked hurt. "You saw what you did today. You know—"

"I'm scared," I said. And this was the simplest way I could explain it. His eyes were not mad, not angry. But there were other things there. Longing. Frustration. Worry.

I turned and ran back up the porch. Things had changed but not changed. Things were better but not better.

In my room, in the dark hours of the morning, I needed to move forward somehow. I pulled my violin from the dusty hiding spot under my bed. Mia-Joy was right. She had to be. It was tied to my emotions. And this was me, accepting this, coming to terms with what I could do. This was the pendulum of my belief swinging, slowly now, nearly still. Nearly decided. But if I was going to accept it, I had to own it. And part of that was being able to summon it, bring it into being. Otherwise, what was the point?

My mind flashed to Professor Smith. She had faced Katrina and come out the other side of it to wear red high heels. I thought of Bryant. And Rennick. There were others out there with secrets and fears. Just like me. So instead of pushing it back under my bed, I took out my violin.

The scroll was plain yet elegant, so familiar in my hand. The weight, the proportion. I couldn't wait to hear its voice.

I tightened the bow, the smell of rosin sweet with familiarity. I put the violin under my chin delicately, with deference. When I struck the first note, C-sharp, I was shocked at the clarity and the fullness of it. It had been too long. I closed my eyes and played like I had never stopped. Like I had always meant to.

I played Mozart's *Requiem*. But I didn't play the notes. I didn't think of the notes. I played the feelings.

I began slowly, softly. Pianissimo. The beginning of this piece was thoughtful, uncertain. I brought my bow down gently, long, full strokes.

And then the piece picked up. Forte. No longer did it feel like a question was being posed. No longer was the piece unsure of itself. It became forceful. Certain. Challenging. Scary. Crescendo.

My bow worked hard, quickly, my fingers finding the correct positions on the strings. I was not thinking now. I was beyond thinking. Above it. I played in a fugue. This piece was coming from somewhere else. Deeper inside me.

And then it began to burn, the churning, within the heart of me. I had brought it to life. I had summoned it. I just had to know how to get myself to that plane, to that thin place, where the veil between what's real and what seems impossible is so very thin.

The violin had showed me the way.

When I had finished and opened my eyes, tasting sweat on my upper lip, I saw her. Sweet and little and solid and here. My Sophie standing in my room.

Her goggles were pushed up on her head, her curls spiraling out of control. She watched me for a long beat, and then she opened her mouth, let out that lonely whistle through the gap in her front teeth.

"Sophie?" I said, blinking, feeling my insides twist and loosen. I didn't know what to do.

She took one step toward me and said, "It was just a storm." And her little face was so grave.

I set my violin on my bed, still watching her, and she smiled. Tears began to cloud my vision, so I wiped them quickly on the sleeve of my T-shirt, but when I opened my eyes she was gone. I blinked, rubbed my eyes. Nothing.

I looked under my bed like a moron. I looked in my

closet, behind my door, in the hallway. She wasn't anywhere.
Had she been?

The Chicago version of myself tried to blame exhaustion. But the New Orleans part of me knew better.

I looked everywhere again, all through the upstairs. But she wasn't there. I curled up on my bed and hugged myself. It made me miss her more than ever, to see her. Her ghost? My projected, exhausted memory? But there was also something about this Sophie, something in her peaceful little smile. I couldn't really put my finger on it, but it felt like a kind word right in your loneliest hour, or a helping hand when you needed it most.

I chose to take this literally. And I planned out what I would do in the morning. Because Seth Krane needed me. A thousand Seth Kranes were probably out there. And if I could save just some of their parents from experiencing what my parents had, well then, I guess I could accept this gift. The touch.

I stretched out on my bed and let my mind wander. To Sophie. That lonely little whistle. To Seth, the aged empathy in his young, beaten face.

And that's when I thought of it. *My heart knows him.* Sophie. Of course she was the one who had said that. I had been so tired of that smelly kid Mitchy Rogers from down the street. He stuttered so badly I could hardly understand him. He had a perpetual Kool-Aid mustache. And in many ways, he and Sophie drove me nuts, with their potion making and magic shows. But, God, did he and Sophie have fun together. When I asked her why she liked that annoying Mitchy Rogers so much, that's what she had said. "My heart knows him."

Rennick. My heart knew him.

M om left the next morning to register me for classes and buy my books for senior year. It took a little schmoozing, but she gave in. I told her I didn't want to have to face the possible reporters, answer questions, stuff like that.

I was glad she was doing this errand for me, but what I really wanted was to be alone and have the house to myself.

I almost had qualms about it, because she probably wouldn't technically approve of my plans, at least the part about me doing them alone. In fact, she'd probably freak. But I knew what I had to do to make peace with this situation, and I didn't want anyone—Mom or Dad or even Rennick—to try to micromanage it. I had one more experiment, one more test that just had to be done. Logic or no logic.

I took out my old bike from the garden shed and circled around the back alley to avoid the lone news van that wouldn't give up and leave my street. I rode over to Garden

District Pets, which was way too close to Mom's church for my liking, but it was the only pet store anywhere near me. So I just tried to keep a low profile and get the supplies I needed.

I bungee-tied the cooler to the back of my bike and pedaled home, feeling all sorts of scientific.

At home, I got myself set up in the kitchen. I took out the first fish, using Mom's slotted spoon. This made me laugh a little bit. Was there room in the scientific method for slotted spoons? I knew I wasn't trying to publish an article in *Scientific American* or get myself into MIT. I wasn't being very scientific, but that was okay. Because this was for me. For my conscience.

The fish was a dingy white with orange spots.

I laid him on the dish towel, and I thought about things, terrible things—about Sophie dying in my arms, the vacant look in Mom's eyes for so many weeks after, the sound of the handfuls of dirt being thrown onto Sophie's casket. Sophie in the earth. Sophie gone. I thought of my guilt, the excruciating hollow core inside me when I thought of my dear little sister. I thought of all these horrible things, and my face crumpled, but I didn't let myself cry. I watched that fish intently, and I held myself close, arms wrapped around myself, waiting. I watched that damn fish. But what I really saw was myself on those first few nights after Sophie's death, nearly catatonic with what had occurred on the beach. I was back in the hospital, confused, grief-stricken, crazy with guilt. I waited until the fish's mouth quit trying, just until then.

I tried to channel the awfulness in me, the despair. I thought of all the inexplicable, horrible, life-altering moments that we have to bear. All the things that human hearts have to carry, and we just wonder, why? Why? Why can't love be enough?

My senses heightened. The drip-drop of the kitchen faucet, the striations in the fish's scales, the feel of the wood grain underneath my hands as I gripped the table's edge. All of it crystal clear. I decided it was time to summon it, but the heat was already there. Blossoming. An inferno inside me. Stronger than ever before. I closed my eyes, focused on my purpose, and when I opened them the kitchen was blue. I grabbed for the tiny little fish—not quite dead but almost, from what I could tell—and I held it in my palms, pressed it there, feeling the surge blow through my limbs. And I thought: *Kill him. Take his life.*

"Prove it!" I yelled.

He wiggled. I opened my palms, and there he was, that mouth moving again, fins flailing anew. Like he was back, had gotten a breath. Back to life.

I dropped him back into the saucepan full of water. Grabbed another with the slotted spoon. Completely alive this time. I focused my energy. "Take the life out of it," I said to the empty walls of my kitchen.

Nothing happened. I waited. The churning was there,

the flowing, pulsating power of the touch was in me, through me, around me.

"Die, you stupid shit!" I screamed.

I threw him back into the water, disappointed. So disappointed. I had finally gotten the nerve to try this, to prove it to myself. And nothing! I tried again and again, more fish. And nothing. I could not kill.

I grabbed the old fern on the windowsill. From what I could tell, I gave it the shock of its lifetime. The surge ran through me, out my fingertips. If anything, the leaves seemed to perk up, the stems seemed to stand a little taller, happier.

"What in the hell?"

I left the fish in the cooler on the counter, and I got on my bike and pedaled back to the pet shop. I had to do it before I lost my nerve. So I rode as fast as I could. The Garden District passed by me through an indigo lens. I blinked it back and watched the blue disappear gradually as I biked, like it was draining from my vision.

I didn't want to have to do what I had to do, but there was no way out. I could think of nothing better.

The clerk with too many piercings gave me the skunk eye, and I knew that I must look like some kind of wild-eyed freak, but it was what it was.

When I got home, sweaty and crazy-haired, I placed the cardboard box on the table and pulled out the first small white mouse. "Forgive me," I said to his little pink nose. Mia-Joy would argue that I didn't really want to hurt the mouse, so of course it wouldn't work. But I knew that logic didn't matter. I never wanted to hurt Sophie either.

So I summoned it.

It came alive and forceful, from zero to eighty in my chest, out of nowhere. I cupped the mouse in my hands, his fur soft and warm against my palms. I knew now, after so much recent practice, how to help the surge through my body, sort of focus it with my muscles into my hands. I focused, and I pictured myself draining the life from this warm-blooded creature. I pictured Sophie in my arms on that rocky beach, that empty patch of time that I could never quite recall, and I tried to kill that mouse.

For so many reasons, I tried to kill that mouse.

And I fell to my knees with the exertion of it. I tried and tried, pushing and forcing the surge from my core. The mouse bit me then, and I let him go. He scampered away, underneath the table, his beady eyes staring me down. "You're alive, you son of a bitch!" I yelled at him.

But then I thought of the missing variable.

Hadn't it been raining when I hurt Sophie? Water conducted electricity, right? Leyden jars. I pulled myself up from the floor, taking care not to step on the mouse. The blue lens was still in front of my eyes. I walked to the kitchen sink and turned on the faucet. I grabbed the sprayer and just sprayed myself down until I was soaked, until I was standing in the middle of a huge puddle on our kitchen tiles. Then I took the rubber band from my hair and, with a few tries, rigged it onto the sprayer so it would keep spraying on its own. I balanced it against the faucet, backed away, and stood in an arc of kitchen sink rain.

My flip-flops slapped against the water as I went to get another mouse from the box. He looked pretty much the same as the first one, save for a tiny gray spot over his left eye. "Sorry, buddy," I told him, and then I enclosed him in my hands.

I walked to the perfect spot in the kitchen puddle, let the water fall on me, around me.

The power revved like an engine, and I waited. I controlled it somehow, didn't let it course out to my limbs until I thought it had reached its maximum potential. I was getting better at this. I concentrated, let the power work itself into a frenzy, and then I let it go, let it do its work. I focused. "Kill this thing!"

It shuddered through me. Harder, more forcefully than ever, racking my body, clanking my teeth together, making a terrible noise. I waited, let it play itself out.

But when I opened my hands, there was the mouse. Alive. Up on his hind legs, peering at me.

With that, I collapsed onto the kitchen floor, an exhausted heap. When finally I opened my eyes, I saw that the blue was gone. And the next thing I knew, my mother walked into the kitchen and screamed bloody murder. "A mouse!"

I held my head up, followed her gaze. There it was, the gray-spotted one, standing on its hind legs on the kitchen tile just inside the back door, looking as healthy as ever.

"Corrine, are you okay?" Mom bustled toward me, ignoring the spraying water, the mouse forgotten.

I collapsed again, exhausted. "I'm sorry," I said. And I think that's when she called 911.

When I woke up, he was next to me. I looked around. I was in the hospital, the room hushed and quiet, smelling like bleach and old people. It was late and dark, with only the blue-green glow of the monitors lighting up the room.

"Your mom and dad are talking with hospital security. There's a bunch of press, and—"

"Rennick," I said, my throat scratchy. His face looked haggard and worn, deep circles under his eyes, his hair everywhere.

"Corrine, why didn't you ask me to help?" He gripped the handrail on the side of the bed, white-knuckled. "I should've been there. What if you had . . . ?"

I sat up, barely noticing the bandage on my hand from a recent IV. I kept my eyes on him, the concern there. Had I almost used myself up? Was that what he was worried about? I watched the way his whole body arched toward me but also kept its distance. How hard was it for him not to touch mc right now? I thought I kncw.

"We can redo it all as soon as you get out. Set up controls.

I'll videotape it." I was only half hearing him, mentally running my fingers over every plane of his face, the high cheekbones, that worried brow, the scruffy chin. "Will you let me? We can reproduce the results. Your mother is speaking to this university doctor—after the security thing—they want to assist our studies, you know, like—"

"I don't want to," I said, clearing my throat.

"Corrine." He worked his jaw, his nostrils flared. He took a deep breath. "We are so close to . . . everything. And if we keep on it, you will eventually believe."

I sucked in a deep breath and gathered my courage. I tried to become the Corrine that Sophie would want me to be. I tried to be the old Corrine. The one who jumped in. It was hard to believe all of it. My head believed what I saw, knew that the proof had scampered across my kitchen floor. My head knew this.

My heart might never give in.

But it was time to move on.

"I believe it," I said. "Right now anyway, Rennick." I reached my hand out, watching it slowly shake, and I placed it on top of his. He met my eyes—grateful, disbelieving—and he placed his other hand on top of mine. We sat that way for a long time, looking into each other's eyes. And the heat registered, not from my chest, not from my power, but from his hands, and there was a different feeling below in my rib cage, warm in its own way. A different, comforting feeling, like coming home.

"Let's leave," I said finally. "Leave a note for my mom. There's somewhere I gotta go."

"Corrine." Rennick shook his head, cupped my chin with one hand. "The doctors. I don't know."

"I'm fine. You know I'm fine. They didn't find anything wrong with me, did they?"

"Just dehydration." He squinted at me. "Hurry. Before I change my mind."

In the bathroom, I changed into my clothes as quickly as possible, my heart leaping out of my chest. Rennick and I walked past the nurses' station like it was nothing, but the nurses were the least of our problems. When we saw a bunch of reporters and cameras at the front entrance, he turned us the other way, and we went toward the cafeteria. Here, he yelled out that he had seen a cockroach at the salad bar. Pandemonium ensued, attention was diverted, and we snuck through the kitchen, out the back door near a loading dock. We stepped onto a dilapidated asphalt parking lot, the coolness of the night surprising me.

He picked me up then, arms around my waist, twirled me around, his face in my hair. When he put me down, I looked up at him, and the corners of his mouth turned up almost imperceptibly. He leaned in a fraction of an inch closer, and I closed the distance between us and pressed my lips to his. A quick kiss. An answer to a question.

Without saying another word, he led me to his Jeep and

we drove quietly, with his hand in mine, lying there between us on the front seat like a promise.

The Kranes' house was in the Upper Garden District, a really beautiful rehabbed place with a second-story balcony, cornstalk wrought iron along the porch. The cicadas hummed in the background as I listened to the nervous beat of my heart. I stuck one shaking finger out and pressed the doorbell. A light came on somewhere inside the house, and pretty soon I heard the clomp of footsteps on the stairs.

It was late, nearly midnight, but I didn't think I could wait another minute. And Rennick, if he was nervous, if he doubted me, didn't let on. He just kept his hand on the small of my back, a supporting pressure, steady. Constant.

It was Mrs. Krane who answered the door, her eyes going wide when she saw it was us. She didn't even have the door all the way open before she was yelling for Declan, her husband. But he was already there, glasses cocked at a funny angle.

He gave me a skeptical look as Mrs. Krane ushered us into the foyer. "Are you here because you think . . . ?" Clearly, he didn't want to get his hopes up again.

I nodded, and Mrs. Krane fell to her knees, her body racked with sobs. It was too much for me, and I had to look away. I turned and Rennick held me against him, my head pressed into the hollow of his collarbone.

"You can do this," he whispered.

I turned toward the couple. Mr. Krane was helping his wife up from the floor. She was gasping out a litany of thanks. "I'm sorry," Mr. Krane said. "This is just more than . . ."

"I can't make any promises," I told them, my fists balled at my sides. I could already feel it inside me, awakening, coming to life, at the ready. The scene with the Kranes, the room thick with emotion, it was enough to get me where I needed to be.

"I'll go wake him," Mrs. Krane said, drying her eyes with a handkerchief from the pocket of her robe.

"Actually," I said, "I could try it while he's asleep." I hadn't even really known that I was going to say this, but there it was. And it made sense to me. So I decided to go with it.

The Kranes consulted each other with a look, and then Mrs. Krane nodded.

As we followed them up the stairs, I cleared my throat. "I have to remind you of what happened to my sister, to Sophie," I said. "I can't explain that. There's a chance . . ." I let my words hang there, the implication plain and unyielding.

If I was going to do this, even though I now believed, I had to be sure they understood the risks. When you were dealing with this gift, this crazy, unexplainable thing, I couldn't pretend to myself or to these poor tragedy-stricken parents that I knew all the ins and outs.

Mr. Krane turned around on the stairs then, leveled me with a look. I felt Rennick's hand on my back again, that reassuring presence. "Corrine," Mr. Krane said, "forgive my bluntness, but the doctors have given Seth *days*. Only days."

I nodded. The horrible words echoed around us, and the flame flickered higher inside me.

Seth's room was decorated in an outer space theme. With only the dim light from the hallway, I could see the glow-in-the-dark stars on the ceiling mimicking constellations. He had several NASA posters, hand-drawn rocket ship schematics, real or imaginary I had no idea. But there were also more ominous placeholders in his room, starting with the hospital-grade bed, the stainless-steel IV stand, the nightstand filled with medications.

I realized then that I was holding my breath and wringing my hands. The Kranes and Rennick were silent, watching me. Waiting. I didn't quite know how long I had been standing there.

He looked so small in that big bed, his face pressed into a sleepy grimace. Was he in pain? I shook the thought away. It was time.

I closed my eyes and let the flame unfurl in my chest, fanned it with my will. When I couldn't stand it anymore, when the buildup inside me was nearly more than I could bear, I opened my eyes, and I could see the blue, even in the dim-lit shadows. The indigo-blue lens.

I stepped forward, and the energy pulsated in me, around me, shooting through my limbs, out my pores. I reached for his hand. It was small and featherlight in my grip. And it was so cold.

His skin was like paper against mine, and that's when I let it go. I let the power do what it was meant to do. It surged, blossomed wider, grew in waves, plunging out of me into Seth.

I was semi-aware of falling to my knees, but I paid no mind. I just held on. Whatever it was that I had, he needed it, as much as I could give him. I couldn't back away.

The more it conducted into Seth, the more I felt his body actually pulling it from me. It was an odd feeling, like the pulling of a tooth, both right and wrong at the same time.

At some point, I opened my eyes, and the current waned. His eyes popped open. A smile replaced the grimace.

If he was surprised to see me, surprised to know I was holding his hand in his bedroom in the middle of the night, or if the physio-electric force falling silent between our hands seemed out of the ordinary, he did not let on.

He simply let out a great sigh. "Thank you, Corrine," he said. And then he asked for a Popsicle.

We rode with the windows down in the Jeep, the wind tangling my hair. It was still and hot outside. I felt exhilarated and alive, so very alive. I talked on and on. And Rennick watched me, a little smile curling up the corners of his mouth. What was he? Proud?

"I mean, do you realize what this means I could do?" I

said. "There are so many people. So many opportunities. I could really make a difference." Already my mind was getting six steps ahead. "But how will I choose who to help? Will I just stay local? How many people do you think I could help, like, in one day, without ... you know."

Rennick's face hardened, and I plunged ahead. "I mean, I'll be careful. Very careful. I'll never let it get so that I—"

"You know, my mother couldn't help everyone."

"I know," I said, tipping my face into the wind out the window. But did I really know this? I mean, what if I had had to accept defeat with Seth? What if this had all turned out differently and I'd had to read his obituary in the paper in a few days? Could I handle the emotions that came with that? The guilt?

I thought of Sophie. I would have to handle it. For Sophie. I had to keep going. To make it all up to her somehow. I mean, I owed her that.

"Thank you, Rennick," I told him. "I wouldn't have been able to help Seth without you."

He nodded, and for a second he looked like he was going to say something. But he didn't. Then he slowed down, driving even slower than usual, and pulled us into the parking lot of the Upper Garden District's community pool. The pool was dark and surely locked up tight at one in the morning, but his tires slowed against the gravel, and when he shifted into park he gave me a smile with that glint in his eye. "Let's celebrate," he said.

"Celebrate?" I asked, getting out of the Jeep and following him to the fence.

"Can you climb?"

"Of course. But why?"

"I'm hot."

"Me too," I said, and suddenly the idea of hopping over this fence and illegally cooling myself off in the water seemed like just the perfect ending to the night. Not only did I want to feel that cool water on my skin, I needed it. Ever since the Kranes', my skin was tight on my body, hot and prickly.

I climbed carefully and tried not to seem like a clumsy moron. Rennick beat me over the side, and he was already pulling his shirt over his head when I hopped down. I kicked off my flip-flops. We both stopped, frozen for a second. Surely, he was thinking the same thing as me. What was I going to swim in?

I answered the question by taking a running start and diving right into the deep end, fully clothed. I gave a little war cry, and then I was in, the water hugging my tank top and jean shorts to my body. But oh it felt good, cool and calming. Rennick jumped in after me, but I was already swimming. The butterfly. He called after me, but I was in a groove, the water slicing around me, my body falling into the familiar pattern, my lungs burning. A relief to be so right here, so normal.

On the return lap, I switched to freestyle. As happy as

I was, I was aware that my episode with Seth had taken a toll on me, my nerve endings on fire and frayed. But with each stroke in the water, that feeling disappeared a little bit more.

A few more laps, and then I stopped and scanned the darkness for Rennick, and he was there, at the shallow end. I caught sight of his lanky form, the silhouette of his torso against the far reaches of a blue security spotlight shining on the pool. My breath caught in my throat. He was beautiful, the ropy lines of his shoulders, the V of his torso, the tilt of his head as he watched me swim toward him.

"It's amazing what you can do." His voice was quiet. Legato.

I sat on the step beside him, aware of his body next to me, aware of how my body responded to the proximity. I swallowed hard, wondered if it showed on my face. Because surely it did. This was a moment, one of those moments you think happens only in movies or only to girls like Mia-Joy. My stomach dropped in that oh-so-good roller-coaster way as he turned to me. And before I knew it, his hand had found my knee under the water. And his touch was hot, a question. Something inside me swelled and sang, a feeling like I'd never had before.

When he dipped his head forward, his eyes watching me, going slowly, so slowly, I held his gaze. My eyes gave him permission. His eyes closed, and then so did mine.

When his lips brushed mine, I was surprised by the softness. The gentleness. He pulled back, but I didn't let him. I leaned into him.

I kissed him back, tasting the chlorine, his sweat, and before I knew it, my hands were in his hair, that gorgeous hair, and it was surprisingly soft, wiry silk. His hands were on my face, a palm against each cheek, and he stroked my cheeks with his thumbs. His lips were so soft and full, questioning and greedy, and I kissed him back hard, hungrily.

I had kissed three boys in my life, one being Cody back in Chicago, but none of those kisses had anything on this moment.

He broke from the kiss then, and he smiled, leaned his head on my forehead, his eyes still closed, the fringe of his eyelashes on his cheek. And he said my name, *Corrine.* Just my name over and over as his fingers traced the knobs of my spine. It became a song, my name, the rhythm like his laugh.

His lips found mine again, then the point of my chin, my neck, that spot right under my ear. He pulled me close to him, pulled me onto his lap. And I ceased thinking. It was just Rennick and me, his tongue in my mouth, his hands on my body. It was at once more than I could take and not enough. A hunger deeper and stronger than I'd ever known had woken inside me, and it was singular, only for Rennick, for his touch, for his taste, for his body next to me, the feel of his fingertips tracing my collarbone.

When I didn't think I could take it anymore, when I

thought I would explode from the pleasure, I pulled him under the water. I opened my eyes and looked at him. He had done the same. I pulled away and just looked at him, letting my eyes soak up every inch of his face, his body. His eyes moved on me as well, and it made my skin prickle with life.

It was every bit as sensual as the kissing from a few seconds ago. But there was something else I wanted to do. Something he was waiting for. And so I did it. I reached out my hand and traced the beautiful structure that was his face, his jaw, down to his Adam's apple. Then my fingers found his shoulders, and I flattened my hands, pressed them over his chest, moved them down over his stomach. I stopped there, my fingers running across the skin above his shorts.

My hands on Rennick. My *hands*.

He grabbed my hands then, and he held his hands up, in an obvious gesture. I placed my palms flat on his. A seal. A trust. All that I wanted to say to him was right there in that gesture.

We stayed that way until we had to break the surface. Annoyed that we had to give it up for something as mundane as breathing.

A flashlight shone on us, bright and unforgiving. "Get out of the water, kids." The guard's voice was bored and annoyed.

I heard Rennick suppress a chuckle behind me as I

pulled myself up the aluminum ladder, but I couldn't help it, I laughed. And then Rennick couldn't stop himself. We didn't win ourselves any points with the crabby guard. He gave us both a squinty-eyed shake of his head, but then he threw us each a worn white towel. "Just get yourselves home."

I couldn't be sure, but I think I heard him chuckle too.

I woke up with a start, knotted and tangled in my sheets. I could feel the tension in my throat, the one-note sound of it echoing in my ears. I must've just screamed.

I rubbed at the back of my neck, where there were new balls of stress in my muscles. Every part of me seemed to be sweating. I threw the sheets off, just as Dad knocked on the door. He came in, a look of concern knitting his brow.

They hadn't been mad about my sneaking out of the hospital or my trip to the Kranes', and I had sort of left out the detail about the pool, but still, I had thought they would be ecstatic, knowing I had saved Seth, knowing what I could now do.

I mean, their words were the right ones. It wasn't that. But the worry lines on Mom's forehead, the way she rubbed her knuckles across her lips, said otherwise. But I had been exhausted and had excused myself to bed. I hadn't been up to hashing it out.

Dad settled his large frame into my desk chair, the back of his bed head standing up straight like a silver cock's comb.

"So this touch is real, huh?" He scratched at his stubble and looked toward me with a mix of emotions on his face. Concern? Fear? For me or *of* me? Both?

I just nodded. I really wanted to take a cold shower, I was so hot. And drink a huge glass of water. Ice water.

"Corrine, we're with you on this. It's going to get huge, though, I think." He held my gaze for a long moment. "Are you prepared for that?"

"No," I said. "But I still have to do it."

"You don't have to," he answered, and his voice was serious. He leaned forward. "We can leave, just disappear, if you need to, Corrine. If you don't want this . . . if you want another choice."

I nodded. I tried to picture that. It seemed an over-reaction, a parent's worry. For me, I finally felt like I was on the right track, finally getting somewhere, moving forward, and I could've explained all this, but my throat was sandpaper. I had to get a drink, so when Dad got up and ruffled my hair awkwardly, I didn't stop him. I didn't explain that I had high hopes for my touch, that I thought Sophie would want me to make up for her death, to help others, to reach out. I just let him leave, and I quickly went into my bathroom, started the shower on cold, and drank for a long time, straight out of the showerhead.

Mom was jittery and talking constantly as I sat down with coffee. "Dad left already to check on the Kranes, see if he could get them to downplay what happened. Keep it quieter.

"I have to go to Chartrain today," she said, tossing me a granola bar from the cupboard. "You look flushed."

I shrugged. "Who do you think I should help first?"

Mom stopped washing her mug in the sink, turned slowly. "I don't think we can do it that way, can we?" There was a little sense of panic in her voice. "I mean, we can't seek people out, babe. If they seek you out, okay. But I just don't know..."

"Okay," I said. I had been thinking about this, and it did seem to make sense. "We don't want anyone suing us or anything," I chuckled. But Mom's back straightened, and she stood very still for a moment.

She turned to me. "Dad is checking with his lawyers today. I mean, I don't know, Corrine. Who do we talk to about this? Especially if we don't want your life to, well..." She shook the thought away with a wave of her hand. "I would feel better if you would let me know when and where you were going to do this, so that I don't have to worry that you're off somewhere, needing me, or needing...I don't know. Is there anything you need when it happens?"

"Water. I get hot." I stood up, walked to where my mom was standing. She looked older to me, so scared. I hugged her. It had been a long time. Such a very long time. I just hugged her close. She grabbed my hand between hers, held it there. "Corrine," she said, and she smiled. Then her expression changed.

"Do you have a fever?" She pressed her hand to my forehead. I shook my head. Mom held my gaze. "You feel all right?"

"Yeah."

"And what are you doing today?"

"Hanging out with Rennick and Mia-Joy. We might go to the carnival over in Woodmere. Might be far enough away that people don't know me."

"Be careful." Mom cupped my face in her hands. "I've missed you." And she pulled me to her again. "Take your phone."

And then she left for work, and I felt so very normal, so very seventeen again. I swallowed back the lump in my throat, pushed back the urge to pore over the pictures of Sophie upstairs. This was me. The new me.

If the past few days had been a new beginning for me, a new window back into life, arriving at the carnival with Mia-Joy, Jules, and Rennick was like baptism by fire—all the sights and sounds and smells. The Mardi Gras paper lanterns strung around the park, the sweet aroma of funnel cakes and cotton candy, the zoom of the salt-and-pepper-shaker rides, the ringing bells of the carnival games. The music was loud with a *boom-boom-thwack* bass beat that I could feel in my teeth.

And the people.

So many people, their shoulders brushing mine, their laughter a little too loud, but everyone was so happy, so in the moment. Mezzo forte. I had missed being in a crowd like this.

Being so very alive.

From the second they picked me up, I could tell that Rennick had pulled out all the stops for me. His hair had a new, combed look about it, and he smelled fresh and clean, a soapy scent mixed in with the smell that was just him, his skin, his sweat. The confident smile, the easy way he laughed with Mia-Joy; he reminded me of my old black-and-white movie heroes. And I had dressed up too, my favorite summer dress, white, short, and flirty. I had knotted my hair at the nape of my neck, stuck a daisy from Mom's garden in it on a last-minute whim.

But I knew I was hanging back a little. It was one thing to act boldly in the dark of the night. Everything seemed a little more possible then. But now, here, in the stark sunlight of the carnival, I didn't know how to act. It felt a little like last night hadn't counted. It had been such a crazy time, with saving Seth and jumping into the pool.

Mia-Joy and Jules rode in the back of the Jeep. Jules's arm swung around Mia-Joy, their heads together, talking, giggling. Jules was a big guy. I knew him from school, a little too popular. But Mia-Joy seemed to think he was better than all right. He paid me no attention, but that was fine with me.

As we walked into the carnival, Rennick saw me watching them ahead of us. They had skedaddled right for the Tunnel of Love.

"You don't mind if we disappear, do you, Corrine?" Mia-Joy had asked. I shook my head.

"Jules is all right," Rennick said, motioning ahead.

"Yeah?" I said, watching them, wishing I didn't think that Mia-Joy only went for the lookers.

"Isn't that what you're worrying about? He's got an ego, this whole cool thing going on, but he's okay."

"It's not just that," I said as we stood in line to buy some tickets for rides. "I just keep wondering when she's going to have a . . . problem. The rip in her aura."

"So you believe me," he said with a grin. "Twenty bucks' worth," he told the ticket taker.

"I can pay too—"

Rennick shook his head, one curt little shake. I watched that gravity-defying lock of hair move back and forth.

A group of teenagers came at us then, laughing, sharing popcorn, and they weren't looking where they were going. A short kid with a ring in his nose came stumbling right at me, and I tried to get out of his way but he ran square into mc.

"Whoa!" he said, spilling his popcorn.

"Sorry." I backed away from him, hands up in surrender.

"Sorry, dude!" he apologized, but the unwanted physical contact unnerved me.

"No problem," Rennick said, but he was eyeing the kid.

Rennick grabbed my hand then, held it for a second, pulled me closer to him. "Okay?" he asked as he pressed his palm into mine. It was much rougher than mine. I let my palm press against his. My hand fit so perfectly in his, and my stomach flipped when he squeezed.

"Yes," I answered, looking up at him.

"You sure? We don't have to."

I nodded.

We walked around the carnival for a while, slowly. We got ice cream cones. Pistachio for him, strawberry for me. And we talked about other things. I never let go of his hand—the connection there, it was something. Physio-electric. Both calm and alive. Reassuring.

He asked me about Chicago, about Sophie. My drawings. He told me how he wanted to travel out West before he went to college, maybe even med school after, if he could stomach school that long. It made me think of college again. I hadn't for so long. And now I could hope and plan and do . . . *anything*.

I learned he hated pizza (*Tomatoes, blech!* he said), and he loved to golf. But his first love was definitely science. That's what he had been doing all those years on the lake, on that Fourth of July when I met him. He had been collecting rocks.

Just like Sophie.

"So that's gotta be weird, to love science and have this unexplainable power," I said as we sat on a bench near the Ferris wheel.

"Nah," he said. "It *is* science. We just haven't figured out the equations behind it all, the figures. Not yet. I reckon soon.

"You want to ride this?" he said, gesturing to the Ferris wheel.

"Sure." We stood up. I was taking a few last licks of my ice cream cone when that same bunch of teenagers came up out of nowhere, and one of the bigger ones–he had a spider tattoo on his neck–said, "That's the girl from the news, from over in the French Quarter."

"The freak show," one of the girls cackled.

"Hey," Rennick said. His voice was new, a warning.

"Why don't you take your voodoo ass back to your own neighborhood," the big guy said, and then the girl on his arm reached out and pushed my ice cream cone right into my chest, into my eyelet sundress. I stood openmouthed, unable to believe that somebody could be so brazen.

I didn't have time to process it. In a flash, Rennick was in the guy's face. His voice was a growl. I realized how deceiving his looks were–tall, sinewy, unassuming–but now, in the thick of it, the square of his shoulders, the clamp of his jaw looked so different and threatening. "You will step away right now. Or you will be sorry." His fists were balled at his sides, and I saw the other guy's reaction, how taken aback he was. How he hadn't been expecting this from a skinny guy like Rennick–the fierce reaction, the fiery look in his eyes.

Rennick took one step closer, jabbed the guy in the chest with two fingers. "Now." The guy stepped back. "Get out of here," Rennick snarled, waiting for anyone to advance, cocking his fist. I found myself thinking, *Rennick's a lefty.* "Get the fuck out of here," he said to the whole group. They were all backing away. There was just something about this new version of Rennick.

You didn't want to mess with him.

Rennick relaxed his shoulders. The group was going, gone.

"I'm sorry," he said to me. He took my hand back, and I could feel that he was shaking. His breathing was quick, shallow.

"You said you didn't fight at Penton or–" I didn't know what to make of this scene.

"I don't *like* fighting." He gave me a look. "But I never said I couldn't do it. Especially when some asshole is going to hurt someone I..." He let his voice trail off. He took his hand away from mine then, lifted his T-shirt to wipe his sweaty brow. But I caught it, the flush in his cheeks, however momentary. What had he almost said?

Mia-Joy and Jules came running up. She took the ruined ice cream cone from my hand, threw it in the garbage, fussed over me. "What happened? Are you okay?"

"Rennick just nearly punched somebody for me."

"Rennick Lane? Jesus, Mary, and Joseph. Could you guys get any more romantic over here? OMG!" Mia-Joy squealed as she hooked her arm through mine and led me toward the House of Mirrors. "Omigod!"

"Mia-Joy! Shhh!" I said, but I was smiling. Even though in my head, I saw Rennick's face and heard the kid's words—*voodoo freak*. Too much was happening. I couldn't process everything. I needed things to slow down.

But Mia-Joy was already pushing me toward the House of Mirrors. "You okay? You look freaked."

"Yeah," I said.

"Yeah?" she asked, eyeing me. Jules met up with us then, with Rennick hanging back.

"I'm fine," I reassured her.

Mia-Joy gave me a look, hooked her arm through Jules's, and made for the House of Mirrors. I waited for Rennick.

"Thank you," I said as he walked up to me. I could see in his posture that he wasn't sure about what had just happened.

We walked into the House of Mirrors. Pop music was blaring and lights switched from flashing disco bulbs to complete darkness to white Christmas lights. It was a little overwhelming. Rennick's presence reassured me, but our unlinked hands were like a question between us. Our reflections kept time on either side of us in the funny mirrors, shorter, squatter versions of us. I stole a glance at Rennick's face in the mirror. He looked embarrassed.

"Corrine," he said. The disco lights switched to twinkling

white. He stopped, faced me, and let a pair of little kids move ahead of us.

Complete darkness.

I felt it then, this physio-electric warmth between us, and I loved how unknown and exciting everything was in that moment, how it was all in front of us. I realized right then that this was *life*. And I hadn't been living *life* for so many months, since Sophie. I had shut myself off, and that had taken away all the interactions, all the uncertainty, all the difficult decisions and judgment calls.

I had given up.

But here I was. Although I knew that I had a lot going on—I had some pretty spectacular things happening with the touch, with Rennick, with life—I also knew that I was jumping in headfirst. Like the old me. Decisive? Reckless abandon? Somewhere in between. Choosing Faulkner. Choosing the butterfly. In life. Not just with the touch.

I had to. Wouldn't Sophie want me to really live? And help others to do it too?

The decision, of course, had already been made. But it was right then that I acknowledged it.

And darkness or daylight, I knew what I wanted with Rennick too.

I reached in the dark for his face. I stood on my tiptoes and placed my hands on his cheeks. I pressed my palm against his stubbly chin and felt him exhale, his body lean into mine. I leaned in too, and my lips found his in the dark, so lightly, just brushing. I took a deep breath, savoring the roller-coaster-drop feeling in my stomach. But just as I was about to lean in again, kiss him for real, he pushed me away gently. "Corrine," he said.

And the lights flashed on. He took a step back. I dropped my arms, looked up at him. I was confused by what I saw in his eyes—the tenderness, the brashness, the protectiveness, the hesitation. I let the charge between us, the electricity, sweep through me, flip my stomach, make my head woozy. Then I stepped back. "I'm sorry. I thought you wanted—"

"Corrine," he said again, as the lights switched back to Christmas twinkles. "I wanted. I *want*. It's just that I . . ." He ran his hand through his hair. "Is it because you need somebody, anybody, right now, or is it that you need *me*?" But then, before I knew what was happening, he had pulled me back to him. He put his arms around me, one on the small of my back, one higher around my shoulders, and he kissed me.

This time, it was a real kiss. I wrapped my arms around his neck, and I pulled myself to him. I pressed my body to his, he sighed behind the kiss, and my body shivered—seriously shivered—with excitement.

We ignored a group of tweens who giggled as they made their way past us. The lights went out, and in the darkness Rennick kissed my mouth earnestly, my neck, my jaw, behind my ear, and his hands pressed me into him. After a long moment, he broke from me. I opened my eyes and saw that his were still closed, and he was smiling. He wrapped his arms tighter around me, brought his lips to my ear. "Wow. And I thought nothing could top last night."

My body prickled with energy, with life, with happiness at the sound and feel of his voice against my neck.

I stood on my tiptoes. I whispered in his ear, "You. Rennick. Not anyone else. Only you."

I felt his eyes close against my cheek, the fringe of his eyelashes tickling my skin. And he sighed, this wonderful little sigh. Had he really been so nervous?

The hairs on the back of my neck stood up. "Do you feel it too? The charge? The energy between us? Is that because of our . . . powers?" I whispered.

"I feel it," he said. "I think it's just *us*."

He leaned down, kissed my neck lightly, and a new shiver went down my spine. The disco lights came on, twinkling and colorful, and Mia-Joy came rambling back, calling out our names. I knew she was hoping to catch us in the act.

She and Jules turned the corner in front of us, and she did catch us. We were still wrapped around each other. Rennick gave me a quick peck on the lips and we pulled apart. He grabbed my hand, and we followed after them.

"Oh, caught red-handed!" Mia-Joy was so happy with herself. "Or should I say red-lipped!" She laughed so hard at her own joke. Even Jules cracked a smile at that one. I held on to Rennick's hand and we exited the House of Mirrors.

I brought a hand to my eyes to shield my face from the sun. And for some reason my skin shifted and tightened on my body, and suddenly Rennick stood ramrod-straight. It registered with him too.

And then we heard it.

"You're the girl!" someone squealed. "The miracle lady!" A tiny girl with this screechy voice screamed at me from across the carnival walkway. Her matted and sweaty pigtails swung behind her as she came running our way. An exhausted-looking mother, pushing a stroller, followed a ways behind her, but the girl kept yelling at me, and a small crowd gathered loosely around the edges of us. She was right in front of me then, and I kneeled down, said hello.

"You can fix her."

"Who is it that needs fixing?" I was powerful, not scared at all, and I liked the way it felt. So much the opposite of how I'd lived for so long after Sophie, like a ghost. This was a different kind of existence for sure.

What I didn't like was the crowd, the knot of people around us thickening by the moment.

"My mommy has cancer. You can tell, that's why she doesn't wear her real hair anymore. She's wearing a wig. I combed it." The little girl was proud of herself, smiling, putting her hands on her hips. But I could see there was a bit of panic behind her little eyes, a wisdom too large for them to hold. It made me sad. Crazy sad.

The mom had worked her way up to us by then, and she apologized breathlessly. I noticed that, yes, her dark pixie hairdo was a wig, and what at first had looked like young-mommy exhaustion now registered with me as worse. Much worse. The swollen face. The blue-gray shadows underneath her eyes.

"I told her not to, but she watches the news with her nana, and I tried . . ." I let the mom keep talking. Her voice was musical, small, with a touch of the Cajun drawl.

I waited politely. And then I said, "Do you want me to try?" And there was Rennick's hand on my shoulder, a squeeze, reassuring. He was there. We were in this together.

The young mom just gasped, hung her head. "Yes," she whispered, tears falling down her cheeks. "I can't pay you. I have nothing to—"

"Shhh," I said. And I led her over to a nearby bench.

I gave Rennick a look, but he had already bent down and was joking with the little girl. She didn't need much encouragement. She was describing in ridiculous detail the amount of spaghetti she had thrown up last week at preschool.

I briefly thought about asking this woman to come with me to a different location, but then it was there, and it was surging, working, igniting.

I just grabbed her hand, sat on the bench next to her. This thing was bigger than me. I was its servant. I told myself not to ask too many questions or try to micromanage it.

Let the people in this little crowd see it. Let the word spread if it had to. I needed to help this poor woman.

I concentrated. The woman's worry weighed down on me, her concern for her child, to be brought up without a mother. This was what I focused on, and this brought it to life. It sparked within me and grew quickly. I let it rise, flame into an inferno. It grew and blossomed, swelled. And I let go. I opened my eyes, and there it was, the indigo lens.

I pushed the power, the heat, through me, out of me, into this poor mother. The woman's face, covered in tears, crumpled into itself and she fell backward, but Rennick was there. He caught her before she tumbled off the bench, and I didn't let go. I gave it all to her, focused the current into her.

And when it waned, I let go, and I fell to my knees.

Her little girl was hugging her around her neck, pecking her with these little kisses, sloppy and desperate. "Wake up, Mommy. She fixed you!"

She woke up, looked momentarily dazed. But she took a few deep breaths and immediately got to her feet, swinging her little girl up onto her hip. For a moment I was terribly nervous, my stomach lurching up into my throat, but the woman had this unfathomable color in her cheeks. Healthy spots of peachy color right on the apples of her cheeks.

The knot of people around us had gotten so quiet, so reverent, but they clapped now, and I felt so . . . exposed. I caught Mia-Joy's and Jules's eyes in the crowd.

Mia-Joy mouthed the word "Wow" to me, but the woman was there, thanking me, shaking my hand, and I went wobbly-kneed. There were suddenly several people in my face. Questions. Did I always know I could? What was my phone number? Could I help someone's aunt? Could I fix birth defects? What didn't it work on? People were flashing their camera phones at me.

I swayed on my feet. And Rennick was there, leading me away quickly.

"I need a minute," I told him. And Mia-Joy was suddenly at my elbow. "I think I might be sick." She pulled me toward the washrooms.

"Girl, it's like I believed it, but now I *believe* it!"

I bent my head over the disgusting carnival toilet, and Mia-Joy held my hair back. I wretched once, twice, three times. But nothing came out. The smell of the citrus disinfectant in the tiny cinder-block bathroom was overpowering. And the lights in the place were these weird rose-colored fixtures. They were blindingly bright.

I stood, moved to the sink, and splashed some water on my face, rinsed my mouth. After a few deep breaths, I was myself again. I stared in the mirror, and there I was, red-cheeked and wide-eyed.

Mia-Joy held on to my elbow as we left the washroom. "Think if you charged for this, Corrine. We could shop at goddamn Prada." She was babbling. I laughed loudly, and I was happy to see there was no crowd waiting for us outside the bathroom.

I smiled, and then something—someone—caught my eye. I saw a little girl through the crowd, near the merry-go-round.

She was wearing goggles, and her curls stuck out in all directions.

"What is it?" Mia-Joy asked, looking toward the merry-go-round.

"Wait here," I said, and pushed past kids and teenagers, a man selling balloons. The girl stood near the entrance, next to the ticket taker. My heart thumped and I blinked a few times.

I was about twenty feet away from her. The girl saw me then, waved. It was her. A large group of mothers with their toddlers and several strollers cut in front of me.

I called her name. "Sophie?" My blood ran cold. The edges of my vision faded to dark. I took a few deep breaths and pushed forward.

I lost sight of her as the mothers passed. I ran over to the ticket taker. Sophie was nowhere. I circled the merry-go-round.

"Have you seen a girl? With goggles? About this high?" I asked the ticket taker, motioning with my hand to the height of my chest. I could hear the panic in my voice.

He shook his head, disinterested. I walked around the carousel several times, scanned the crowd on my tiptoes. I stood up on a nearby bench and tried to find her.

Mia-Joy and Rennick caught up with me. "What is it?" Mia-Joy asked. "Who did you see?"

"It was nothing," I said, shaking my head, still scanning the crowd. I jumped down from the bench. *I'm crazy*, I told myself. *I'm just seeing things.* I swallowed hard and balled my fists at my sides. *It's just been too much to take in.*

"We're going to catch up with Clayton and Laura," Mia-Joy told Rennick. Jules joined us now. He hung his arm around Mia-Joy. She smiled approvingly.

"You sure you don't need a ride?" Rennick asked.

"No, you guys go be aloooone," Mia-Joy said. "Privately." She winked at me and I smiled back, but my mind was on the girl, the goggles. Rennick offered his hand to me and we headed for the parking lot. I scanned the crowds as we left, but I shook my head against it. It hadn't been Sophie. Of course it hadn't been Sophie. It was just like the other morning in my room. A new species of crazy.

"You okay?" he said.

"What does your aura look like?" I said to distract myself. "Is there a lot of red?"

"There is."

Our feet crunching on the gravel parking lot made a ridiculously loud sound. I winced as the noise ground against my eardrums.

"You okay?"

I nodded. "So what does red mean again?"

"Passion. Creativity. You look flushed."

"I think that might happen after . . . you know. I don't know. I need a drink of water, that's all."

"You sure we shouldn't go get you checked out or call your mother or just find a–"

"No!" I snapped, glad to be at the car now so I didn't have to hear the grind of the rocks against my feet. Like nails on a chalkboard. Everything was magnified, the sounds, the heat, the brightness.

Rennick opened the door of the Jeep for me, and I sat down. He handed me a bottle of water out of the back, and I drained it quickly.

I rested my head on the window and asked him to crank the air conditioner.

I could feel his eyes on me, but by the time we were nearing the Garden District, I felt well enough to be myself, and I saw Rennick relax next to me. His posture changed, his gaze less questioning, more calming.

"I'm so proud of you," he said, grabbing my hand across the seat.

"I'm proud of me too," I answered.

I was okay now. At least well enough to ignore it.

But there was something nagging at the back of my mind for some reason, a diagram from one of Sophie's favorite books. *Do-It-Yourself Inventions,* or something like that. It looked like one of those crazy setups from an old cartoon—all these little devices and intricate mechanisms, like where you drop a marble into a tube and then it goes through a bunch of machine parts in order to do something mundane like flip on a light switch. There was a name for these inventions. And it hit me, while I had my forehead leaning on the glass: Rube Goldberg. That's what those things were called.

And I had a sinking feeling in my stomach, in my nerves, that the display at the carnival was the first domino falling in my very own life-size Rube Goldberg contraption. Something had just been set in motion.

When we arrived home that afternoon, Mom explained with a shocked look on her face that our voice mail was filled to capacity. Her work email had 672 messages asking about me. Asking for her help. Media outlets: newspapers, morning shows, from everywhere from Baton Rouge to Mobile. And Dad said the calls to Harlowe Construction were nonstop. That's the word he kept repeating: *nonstop*. Nonstop requests. Nonstop calls. Nonstop texts, emails, people.

I listened groggily on the couch while Dad and Mom and Rennick brainstormed how best to stay ahead of all this. Apparently, the Kranes had immediately contacted their doctor this morning. The doctors took scans, blood samples, and several other kinds of tests, all of which showed that Seth was completely healthy. All traces of his leukemia were gone.

Between that, the carnival, and Chartrain, I knew I should be more concerned. But all I wanted to do was stick my head under a tap and drink. Water and more water. Either that or sleep. Exhaustion won as I drifted off. The last thing I heard was Dad say that a man from Tallahassee had contacted Suzy, the head of his legal department, and offered a check for one million dollars, no questions asked, if I would come and just try to heal his teenage son, who had lived with muscular dystrophy his whole life.

I pictured Tallahassee—a swamp? Alligators? Orange groves? And then I was out.

Mom shook me awake in the early morning. "Let's get you out of here." I didn't know exactly why she wanted us to leave, but it wasn't too hard to deduce. She smiled at me while I threw on some clothes, but it was painted on. Obviously, people were done with just leaving messages. People were showing up on the doorstep.

As we drove into the French Quarter, I told myself to stay calm and plead my case logically. "You know, Mom, I want to help these people. It's okay."

"Our home," Mom said in a dark tone, "needs to be a safe place for you. For us. We will not let you think that every time the doorbell rings someone is going to be begging you, pleading with you. You have to have some say in this, Corrine."

"But, Mom–" I began to argue. She cut me off.

"You may not think so right now, but twelve hours from now. Twelve days. You'll be glad we set some parameters."

I pulled down the sun visor and looked at myself in the mirror. My face surprised me. I looked healthy, pink-cheeked; my unwashed hair even had a sheen to it. I raked a brush through it and tied it back at the nape of my neck. I considered what Mom was saying.

"I can see your point," I said. "Where are we going, though?"

"The Shack. Sarah said we could hide out upstairs."

We rode in silence for a few moments, then Mom continued. "Dad's lawyers are putting together kind of a contract, something people will need to sign. To cover us. Also, his legal team has contracted someone to make a website, an eight-hundred number." Mom glanced at me, her mouth a hard line. "I want you to help these people too, Corrine. I just want you to be at the helm, okay?"

I nodded and thought about yesterday at the carnival. Mom hadn't been there. She couldn't know how some things, especially this particular thing, were not going to be orderly, controlled, or even logical. I knew that somewhere deep down. This was who I was now, and although it seemed scary and a little bit out of control, I welcomed it. It was better to step into this life than to keep going with my old one.

If nothing else, it gave me something to do, something beyond good. It gave me something to occupy my thoughts other than the way the air had smelled charged and alive on those rocks with my little sister. If it kept me from picturing her eyes rolling back in her head, well, then it was a good thing.

"What's up?" Mia-Joy greeted me. She handed me a café au lait, just the way I liked it, but not before she took a sip for herself. Mia-Joy was still in a lacy pink nightgown, a do-rag covering up her hair.

Mrs. Rawlings pulled me into her arms, so tight it hurt a little. "God bless ya, Corrine. God bless you." I nodded at her when she pulled away and stared at me level in the eyes. "You doin' right." She moved on to my mom then, and they chattered away. They moved toward the far end of the counter, and I could hear their voices above the din of the breakfast rush, Mrs. Rawlings's all smooth with comfort, Mom's all staccato with worry.

The Shack was really hopping, with the smell of Mrs. Rawlings's famous beignets in the air. Clouds of powdered sugar puffed from customers' mouths as they took that first heavenly bite.

"I need me one of those," I said, scooting toward the kitchen just as Mrs. Rawlings yelled at Mia-Joy to go get some clothes on already. I grabbed a beignet off the cooling rack in the back, took a bite, and Mia-Joy pulled me up the stairs to their apartment before I had a chance to argue.

"So give up the goods already. Tell me about this boy." I settled onto her patchwork comforter, made by Granny

Lucy, and realized that Mia-Joy didn't even know that the rumors about Rennick weren't true. "He was about to just clock that guy for you yesterday. Are you okay with him? I mean, has he changed, or is he—"

I licked the powdered sugar from my lips, swallowed. "None of it was true, Mia-Joy. Really. He's not like that." But I couldn't keep explaining, because she had her back to me and was changing out of her nightgown. And when I saw her bare back, I could hardly believe how thin she was, her ribs jutting. She had always been thin, always willowy, moved like a gazelle. But this, *this* was something new. Her ribs were too prominent, her shoulder blades sharp and protruding.

"So why did Rennick end up here?"

I shook my head and explained how we had both actually met him years ago on that Fourth of July at Lake Pontchartrain. But all the while, I was studying her face. Did she look unhealthy? I cursed myself for forgetting about what Rennick had said, about the rip in her aura. I should've been more in tune with Mia-Joy. What was going on?

"So we know him from what-in-the-what-what now?" She was fully dressed in capri pants and a hippie-looking tunic. She began combing out her gorgeous mane of hair, working product through it, and I tried to find a way to ask her about her health, her diabetes. But it just sat there on my tongue.

"So was Rennick always so *fine*? Even back then?"

"You should know. You were there." I took another bite of my beignet.

"Was his ass just so *pow* even then?" She gestured with her hands like she was grabbing his butt, and I laughed.

"Mia-Joy!" I threw a pillow at her, and she flopped on the bed next to me.

"Girl, you look good. Rennick must be doing something right." And she elbowed me in the ribs.

"It's not like that," I said, but did I want it to be like that? I swallowed hard. So much was happening.

"I like this."

"What do you like?" I said. "Embarrassing me at every opportunity?"

"I like hanging with you. You really being *here*."

"I like it too," I told her. "Like old times." I finished my beignet, licked my fingers.

"It's like you're coming alive again along with the people you're saving, Corrine."

She grabbed my hand and held it between hers for just a beat, such a very un-Mia-Joy-like action, it made my eyes tear up.

"Mia-Joy, are you feeling okay?"

She waved my question away with her hand. "Corrine, you playing the violin these days?"

"Yeah," I said, but I realized that, curiously, no, I wasn't. Just that one time.

Raised voices wafted up from the restaurant below. You couldn't tell what was being said, but one voice was definitely Mrs. Rawlings's booming tone.

"He looks at you, ya know," Mia-Joy said.

"Rennick?" I asked. She nodded. "How?"

"It's like you're the only person in the room. No, that's not it. It's like you're the only person anywhere. In the whole freaking galaxy. The only one who matters."

I smiled, felt the blush rise in my neck. "He does?"

"You deserve that, Corrine."

I smiled. "Thank you, Mia-Joy."

"Seriously, you deserve it. I wish I had that. I think every girl does."

"How can you say that? Half the guys at Liberty look at you that way!"

"No," Mia-Joy said, suddenly so serious. "They ogle. That is different. Rennick looks at you differently."

"Mia-Joy!" Mrs. Rawlings's voice bellowed up the stairs.

"I'm coming!" Mia-Joy yelped. And I let it go. I didn't ask her any more about her health. For better or worse, I let it go.

I quickly followed her down the stairs. But when we emerged into the back section of the kitchen, Casey, one of the bakers, did not look up at us, and I could tell by the way she hid behind the wall of her blond bangs that it was on purpose. Something was up.

And then we could hear them. Many voices. People were

here. They had to be looking for me. Mia-Joy had my arm, tried to pull me back, but I yanked it away. I appeared behind the counter, and the whole place went quiet. The patrons were all looking up from their Saturday-morning coffees; the knot of people around Mom and Mrs. Rawlings turned, and I saw then what was going on. There was an older gentleman with silver hair, and with him were a younger man and woman, and then there was this young thing. This tiny girl, her legs in braces, her arms leaning on a walker, her limbs awkward and underdeveloped, the victim of some kind of disease. Maybe multiple sclerosis? I didn't know. But her eyes found me. And they were bright and shiny, her smile radiant. "You don't have to," she said into the silence. "I'm okay with it, but Papa wants you to try."

I took a big breath. I was going to help her, of course, but what to do about Mrs. Rawlings and Mom, I didn't know. So I just ignored them. And I didn't know if it was that they expected some kind of warning, some kind of preliminary setup or what, but they didn't have a chance to intervene. Or maybe, maybe it was just that they knew, deep down, that this was bigger than me. Bigger than their worries about keeping a little slice of normal life for me.

I walked toward the little girl. "What is your name?"

"Amelia." And in a moment, I had a whole narrative in my mind of Amelia's life, the things she struggled to do like a normal child, how she wanted so badly to learn ballet, how

237

second grade had been a tough year when so many kids ridiculed her condition. She loved farm animals, drew them on everything.

I didn't know if any of this was true, probably not. But it made me see her in a deeper manner. It made the pilot light of my power switch on, fan and flame. I took some deep breaths, and before I knew it she had slid her hand in mine. I gripped it and let the current grow and shift until it became enormous, so powerful I could feel my body shaking, and then it plateaued. And I let it go. It surged out of me. I opened my eyes to see the restaurant flooded with the strange indigo light.

Little Amelia smiled through the entire exchange, although I shuddered with the power of it all. And when it had run its course, when I knew I had given all I could to her, I let go. And I sat down, my body feeling spent but more than that, fiery hot.

"Thank you," Amelia said, and she brushed a strand of hair from my face. I laughed this little laugh. And then she turned toward her papa, her parents, and she very purposefully kicked off her leg braces, set her walker to the side, and took one, two, three unsteady steps.

The place buzzed and hummed in disbelief as her family enveloped Amelia in tears and hugs. But quickly, the crowd grew boisterous. People had their cell phones out, they were calling others, snapping pictures of Amelia and me.

And then Phillip Bullhouse, a kid at Liberty, came right

up to me. "My father, he just had a stroke. He's only fifty-three years old. Can I bring him here?"

I heard Mom's voice behind me, but I nodded, and Phillip was off.

I stayed at the Shack the rest of the morning. Word spread quickly. Mrs. Rawlings sold more crawfish jambalaya than probably any other day of the year. Mom eventually settled into a quiet, somber watchfulness. Mia-Joy started passing around a wicker basket for donations, which I made her announce would go to the DayBreak Center in the French Quarter, helping the homeless and the needy. I didn't want money for this.

In short, I healed thirteen people at the Shack that day. It made me ashamed about the kind of person I used to be, back in Chicago before Sophie, so oblivious to people's suffering. Because didn't we all suffer? In one way or another?

Several of the people had cancer, one of the pancreas, one with no voice—esophageal cancer. Some of them, I didn't even know their exact ailments. One woman had such gnarled, arthritic limbs, I could hardly believe my eyes when her hands just straightened out, her joints moving backward in time in front of my eyes. One man was so thin he reminded me of pictures from the Holocaust in history class. He had cirrhosis of the liver, his skin a jaundiced yellow, but when he left he looked as healthy as anyone else.

And there were two more children. The Florida man with the son who had muscular dystrophy. He had found me in less than a day. "The power of the Internet and GPS," the dad kept saying. His son, his body so atrophied from the disease, didn't want to be here. The son scowled at me, crabbed about the whole ordeal, but in the end he let me grab his hand. I doubted my ability to help him, because the disease had so emaciated him, but he walked out of the Shack. On his own two legs, his eyes wide with disbelief.

It was after him—he was maybe the eighth person—that I began to feel the throbbing ache around my rib cage, and I knew that I should stop. But I couldn't. I didn't even really consider it.

There were so many intricate and horrifying ways for a person to suffer, and I was only able to help the physical. What I was doing seemed small, too small. How could I stop?

And they brought me things, odd little things. Heirloom jewelry. Pictures of what they looked like before they got sick. Pictures of loved ones who had passed on. Prayers written on napkins. They each wanted me to know their story. And it broke my heart in so many ways, like they had come armed with all of these things to show that they were worthy, loved, and I should choose them to be healed.

As if I could turn them away.

The kids brought drawings and thank-you cards. Stuffed animals. Their favorite Legos. And not just sick kids, but kids who had sick parents or sick relatives. These kids looked the worst. Worn out with worry. Lost little shells of the children I usually saw popping crawdads into their mouths during the lunch rush at the Shack.

People tried to give me money. Loads of it. Checks, coins, their credit cards. I pushed them off to Mia-Joy, who made bug eyes at the amounts these people dropped into our donation basket.

By two o'clock, I thought I spied Rennick's face in the far reaches of the crowd, but I couldn't focus on him. I needed water. I couldn't wait any longer. So while the fourteenth person, a ninety-two-year-old man who had been blind since the '40s, waited patiently for me to take a little break, I went into the back to get a drink. I felt a little woozy now too, along with this brittle, hollow feeling in my ribs, a deep muscle soreness around my midsection.

Mia-Joy went about scrambling some eggs for me. I was exhausted physically. Spent but invigorated too. My limbs, my hands, seemed to vibrate even as I shoveled the scrambled eggs into my mouth. And I drank glass after glass of water.

"What did you put in these? They are so good," I said, talking around another bite of eggs. They tasted so hearty.

"Nothing, not even salt." Mia-Joy filled my glass again from the tap. "Aren't you a little bit freaked? I mean, come on. Aren't you sort of all what-in-the-hell-am-I?"

I shook my head, then tilted it back to drink the water

in one big gulp. The swinging door to the kitchen flew open and I spilled the water all over myself. It was Rennick. A crazy-looking, hair-in-all directions, wild-eyed Rennick.

"We had a deal. I've been watching." He crossed the space between us in a few long steps, and then he was kneeling in front of me. "You promised me. You promised you wouldn't use yourself up."

My eyes shot over to Mia-Joy, and she looked at me with raised eyebrows. "Can you give us a minute?" I asked her.

"Nope. No way," she snapped. "I want to hear this."

I shook my head, didn't like the idea of them ganging up on me. Knowing they would easily get Mom on their side too. "Rennick thinks I can use up my power, give it all away, and then give away my spark too ... or whatever."

"I don't think anything, Corrine. I *know*." He gave me a look, and I lowered my eyes. I knew he was right in a way. But I didn't feel ... close to being used up. Did I? I didn't want to think about that.

"Is this still about Sophie?" Rennick said, placing his hand on mine.

I shook my head. Was it?

He placed a hand on my forehead. "You're burning up, Corrine."

Mom came into the kitchen then, and I stood up. "I'm coming," I said quickly, before we could have this conversation with her.

"Let's make this the last one today," she said.

I nodded.

"I don't even think she should do that," Rennick added. I waited, but neither he nor Mia-Joy explained the used-up problem to her.

"Last one," I said. I made this crazy cross-your-heart motion, and then I shoved my hands into my pockets so they wouldn't see them shaking.

Mr. Vickers waited patiently at the small bistro table in the front, his cane leaning against the table, his dark glasses over his eyes. I asked him quietly if he would take the glasses off. He did, and then I saw the damage there. He was not only blind but truly ravaged.

"I was hit with a mortar shell in the Second World War."

My mind flashed to the horrors of war, the things I couldn't even really comprehend. But it was enough for the spark to ignite. It was enough to feel it come alive.

I held on to his wizened and pale hand, sandwiched it between my own. His skin was coarse and wrinkled, his hand cool and still.

The heat inside my ribs churned and rose but died. Again and again. I couldn't get it going. I concentrated, tried to put myself into the heart of the pain of this man. I imagined living inside his loss, never seeing a Monet painting, never seeing the worry line between Rennick's eyes, the overlap of his front teeth.

The depth of this man's loss registered, and the spark returned, grew quickly, exponentially, and my body was racked with the force of the current moving from my hands to his.

After a long moment, I pulled my hands from his, hopeful but curious. It had moved differently. Faster, more violent.

Mr. Vickers only sighed, gave me a small smile. "It's not what we don't have that defines us, young lady," he whispered, "but how we use what we do have."

He opened his scarred eyelids for the first time, and I saw the milky and violent remains of his eyes.

He wasn't seeing me out of those eyes. I placed my hands on his again. We both waited.

"I'm sorry," I told him, thinking about what he lived without. What he would probably live without forever.

I reminded myself that Ruth Twopenny couldn't fix everyone. I reminded myself that I was prepared for this outcome. I reminded myself, but it didn't matter. I couldn't help him. He was the cricket. Too far gone.

"Thank you for trying, young lady." His smile wasn't sad or regretful. It was only kind.

"I'm sorry too," I said, and when he stood up he put his glasses on. He picked up his cane, and the crowd in the Shack let out an audible sigh. At a respectful distance while it was going on, they now milled closer to me, started murmuring words of supposed comfort to me. Again with the cell phone pictures.

I stood up and turned, Rennick and Mom right behind me. I nearly smacked into them. I pushed through them and went into the kitchen, the swinging door making a big *slap* as I hit it with my still-vibrating palm. I walked to the sink, splashed some water on my overheated face, and then began drinking from the tap.

"You'll get more familiar with the limitations, I'm sure," Mom's soothing voice said from behind me.

"Too much in one day," Rennick added.

I didn't know why, but I wanted to yell at them. Both of them. Everyone.

"Honey, I know you don't want to hear this, but maybe we just have to do this more in moderation." Mom was trying to sound even-keeled. I knew this tone in her voice.

"Leave me alone," I whispered, and plopped into Granny Lucy's old rocker near the screen door.

Mia-Joy bustled in. "Here," she said, handing me my cell phone.

"Why do I want this?" I asked.

"You told me to get it for you," Mia-Joy said incredulously. She blinked at me. "Right after the blind guy."

"No I didn't." I had no memory of this.

I watched Rennick and Mom give each other a look. "You asked Mia-Joy to get it just a few minutes ago," Mom said.

I looked at them, confused. I had no idea who I wanted to call. I stared down at the blank screen so I didn't have to meet anyone's eyes.

"Corrine, are you okay?" Rennick asked.

I leaned my head back on the cool wood of the rocker and closed my eyes. "There are a few still waiting out there."

"You can't be serious," he said. I tried to nod. But no, no, I wasn't okay.

I got home somehow, because I woke up in my room, in the thick of the night, the crickets working their way into a frenzy, my window cracked open and that singular New Orleans breeze wafting into my room. My lacy white curtains responded to the breeze. And I heard their voices downstairs, the singular timbre of strained, angry voices trying to stay under the radar.

When I reached the kitchen, I saw Mom and Dad, still fully clothed, an empty pot of coffee between them, Dad's favorite crackers and a tin of sardines smelling up the whole kitchen. Only Dad ate these things, and only when he was stressed. I could remember the funny way Mom used to tease him about it, before Sophie died, before we knew what real stress was, when he would have a big project on deadline. "Paul, you need me to pick you up some sardines?" she'd joke in that cutesy way she had with him when he was spending too much time in his home office on a Saturday, or if he'd been glued to his cell phone. I'd roll my eyes at Sophie, and Dad would answer, "Only if the girls will eat 'em with me."

There were no cutesy looks, no jokes when I sat down at

the table with them now. I tried not to wince as the muscles in my rib cage spasmed.

Dad spoke first. "We have to control this, babe."

Mom's eyes and nose were raw and red from crying. "I think it's already beyond that, honey. I think we just go back to Chicago for a while. Let this cool off. Return when people have forgotten."

"No!" I objected.

"Just hear us out," Dad countered. "Not leaving forever. Just a break from the craziness. Then we can come back, if we choose, and then you can do this . . . healing quietly. It is imperative that we work harder to keep it quiet."

"Why?" I said, and I hadn't meant to sound so snarky, but there it was.

"You're not thinking clearly," Mom said.

"Right," I snapped. "I want to help people. Of course that's not thinking clearly."

Mom brought her fist down on the table hard. I don't know who jumped more, me or my father. But she pointed at me, and she hissed, "Rennick told us both what happened to his mother, what happened to this Dell he knew. What do you have to say about that, Corrine Marie?" My eyes dropped to the table. They had me there. "What are you doing to prevent that? Can't we go in the shallow end, Corrine? Or do we have to just jump right in, let this thing swallow you whole? I'm not going to let that happen."

I answered with silence, and Dad reached over and put his hand on Mom's arm. She was crying now, dabbing at her eyes with a tissue. She whispered, "Not you too, Corrine. I can't lose you too."

"Corrine, your mother and I are going to think this over. And you have a right to know that. But if we decide it's best to leave, we're all leaving."

I thought of Mia-Joy, of Mrs. Rawlings, but mostly of Rennick. I didn't want to leave. Because of them. But it was more than that. I didn't want to go back to a life of silence and inaction. A life of all the things that could've been for Sophie. I needed a different focus, and the touch gave me that. I didn't know exactly how these things were so tightly and intricately wound up inside of me, but I knew, I *knew,* that if we went back to Chicago, I would suffer, my power would suffer.

I quietly pushed my chair back and worked my way up to my room. What in the world could I do?

I lay awake on my bed, feeling too warm, relishing the open-window breeze, thinking about my options. I was nearly eighteen. I would only have to be in Chicago for a year. Even if they never decided to come back, I could come back.

I could try to reel myself in. Keep things going, but in moderation.

All of this seemed impossible to me. It was like the touch was the only thing keeping me from going back to my guilt-ridden world, and I had to use it, keep it in motion and alive. I knew it didn't make a lot of sense, but there it was.

I must've dozed off eventually because I awoke to a one-note whistle, the gray-yellow light of an overcast sunrise filling my room. I got up and looked out the window, and sure enough he was there. When I went down to greet him, I knew I looked like a hot mess.

But I didn't care. He opened his arms to me, and I was in them, folded into him, resting my head on his chest, his chin on the top of my head. "Corrine," he said. He kissed the top of my head.

I could smell the leaves of the banana trees out in the wet dew of the morning. And I could smell the scent of Rennick, his laundry-fresh skin.

"You told my parents," I said into his chest.

"I had to."

"I'm trying not to be mad at you."

"And I'm trying not to lay you down on this grass and get us both into more trouble than we need."

This made me chuckle. I lifted my face to him, and he kissed me, slow and soft. "Mmm," I said. "Good morning."

"What do you say we go to Jackson Square today, maybe ride the ferry? We only have so many free days till school."

I shook my head. "I'm going back to the Shack. Come with me?" I readied myself for an argument.

He sighed deeply, and I braced myself. "Corrine, I think

your parents are right when they say that you have to walk a thin line here."

"They are talking about moving."

I watched him closely, to see if he knew this, but when this registered, his face blanched and he had difficulty recovering. "We gotta play by their rules. I want you here."

I nodded. But I knew I had to do what I had to do. "Let me shower, and meet me in the kitchen in ten." I pulled myself away from him, but he held on to my hand.

He shook his head at me. "Corrine, I told myself I wasn't going to come here and give you ultimatums. I wasn't going to try to pressure you. I figure you got enough of that on all sides. But going right back there this morning?"

I nodded, jutted my chin out in defiance.

"Do you still have a fever?" he challenged.

"No."

"Are you still shaking?"

I held my hands out in front of me and, thank God, they were steady. He rubbed at his jaw, pulled me over to Sophie's garden, and sat us down on the little cement bench. "Why can't you let it go?"

"What are you talking about?"

"You didn't kill your sister."

"I know."

"Do you?"

I couldn't hold his gaze. He continued, "Is that what this is about? Trying to make up for allegedly killing Sophie?"

"No." But it felt like a lie, and the heat kicked on under my sternum.

"Because I think that's what this is about. I watched you yesterday, and it was like you didn't give a shit about what happened to you. You just kept going and going. It's like you didn't even want to have time to think. You just wanted to *do*." His eyes pierced me.

I rubbed my knuckles against my lips. I knew there was some truth in this. I hadn't really been able or willing to put words to it, but I knew there was a part of me, a huge, self-destructive guilty part that knew there was truth right there. A seed of it in everything Rennick was suggesting.

"I can't say no to anyone." My voice sounded small.

"How many will it take to make up for Sophie?"

I shrugged and fought against the tears in my eyes.

"A hundred? A thousand?"

I said nothing.

"Or will it only be even when you use yourself up and kill yourself in the process?"

It fired up, roared, and I swallowed it back down. Rennick reached for me, just a tiny gesture, a hand to tip my face up, but I pushed him away. Pushed him hard. I got up and walked back into the house.

I hated him. Because of what he'd said.

Because it was true. Every word.

The Crawdaddy Shack opened at seven, but there were already a few people out front when I came biking up. "Morning," I greeted them.

"Good morning, Corrine," one middle-aged man answered. The rest sort of chimed in.

None of these patrons had any requests for me, so I went into the kitchen when Mrs. Rawlings opened up, and she was all up in my business from the get-go. "You are not going to make me a party to this when you know good and well your parents are taking issue with you setting up shop here."

I ignored her as much as I could. I greeted Casey and grabbed a deep-fried donut from the cooling tray, poured myself some coffee. But Sarah Rawlings did not suffer being ignored.

"Girl, you better look at me when I'm talking to you."

I turned around, looked into her face. "I have to do this," I answered.

To my surprise, Mrs. Rawlings looked more empathetic than I had expected. "You got till noon. Then I am kicking you out."

"Thank you," I said.

"Granny Lucy used to help a lot of folks. You girls, you laugh at the old tinctures she used to put together. The spells. But there was something to them. She had herself a way, Corrine. She kept it on the down low." She eyed me. "You'll learn."

I heard Mia-Joy's barking laughter from out front, and then she was calling for me.

The little restaurant was filled again, and there was already a small crowd around the bistro table from yesterday, front and center. "This woman here, she's got lupus and lymphoma," Mia-Joy whispered to me.

"Ma'am," I said in greeting, sitting down at the table. One look at this poor woman's face and I knew I was right to come back here this morning. She still had all her hair, but her cheeks were sunken, her skin sallow, her fingernails yellow. She looked seventy-five if a day, so when she began speaking, no wonder the flames erupted inside me.

"I'm only forty-four," she began, and I fought against a gasp. "I don't have insurance. I didn't get any treatment, and I know I'm almost at the end of it here. My children don't know that, but I know it," she said. And the matter-of-factness in her voice leveled me.

I gripped her skeletal hands and let it rise, brewing and growing, swelling into one powerful wave. The woman's eyes, they had a flat look to them, of things borne, endured. I wanted to help her. I let the current reach its frenzied peak. And when I focused the flame, when I directed it into this woman, something happened. It left me in a different way, not in a smooth current but in jolts. I couldn't see anything different. It was all still indigo blue, but it felt different, spastic and uneven.

The woman jerked, fell to the ground, and seized with ugly convulsions. Like she was being electrocuted. Just like in the movies. Horrible jerky movements.

I broke the connection, let her hand go. I held my hands out in front of me, watched them for a moment before I bent down next to the poor woman at my feet. Was it my imagination, or could I see little sparks of something crackling off the tips of my fingers, flaming indigo?

I heard the gasps from the other customers. I saw Mia-Joy running toward her, and I heard Mrs. Rawlings screaming for 911, but none of this really registered. It was like it was all happening far away from me.

"What was wrong with her again?" This was a paramedic in his blue uniform. He was right next to me, kneeling. How he got there so quick, I didn't know.

"I have the touch?" I told him.

"We know about you," he said. "But what is her ailment?" He was listening for breaths as he spoke to me.

I racked my brain. I could sense that I should know this, that I *did* know this less than five minutes ago. It was there, on the very edge of my brain, but I couldn't grasp it. What was wrong with her? What was I fixing?

"She has lymphoma and systemic lupus," Mia-Joy answered, eyeballing me and pushing me down into my chair. I sat there, watching the events unfold around me. The saving of this woman's life. The sideways glances from the other patrons. The clucking of Sarah's tongue as she brought me a glass of ice water.

Then all of a sudden it was like I lost some time, because Rennick was next to me but I didn't know when or how he had gotten there. I looked around and saw that the woman and the paramedics were gone.

"It was akin to a mild electric shock. She just passed out," he was saying in a soothing voice, over and over. Like a repeat sign at the end of a measure.

He reached for my hand. I yanked it back.

"You should be glad about this," I snapped. "Now it's all gone to shit. They can just move me back to Chicago. Everyone can forget about it all." I got up so quickly that I knocked my chair backward.

"Corrine!"

I didn't turn around. I stalked out to my bike and rode home. Confused. Hot. Frayed. Guilty.

I retreated to my room. It was like I didn't know anything anymore. I played Angry Chipmunks on my iPad and listened to music through my earbuds as loud as I could stand it, and I forced myself, tried desperately at least, not to think.

Mom and Dad tried to talk to me. Mrs. Abernathy was fine. Rennick had been right, it was only a moderate electric shock. She had not been cured, but she was getting treatment, thanks to the donations Mia-Joy had been collecting. And thanks to a handful of generous doctors on her case. But I hadn't saved her.

I had expected a quiet relief on Mom's face or in Dad's demeanor, because maybe people would leave me alone now after such a public failure. But no, there was none of that. They were my parents, after all. It made me feel guilty for thinking that they could so easily be appeased by the situation when they knew it made me miserable.

The next morning was Sunday. Dad went with Mom to her church, and I stayed holed up in my room. When the doorbell rang, I looked out my window and saw Rennick's Jeep.

I waffled for a long minute, but eventually I let him in, and we stood in the foyer awkwardly. He looked at me with those eyes, those eyelashes, and I wanted to cross the distance between us. I wanted to throw my arms around his neck. But I didn't trust myself. My hands. My body. What lived underneath my ribs? I didn't want to hurt him.

Was I back here? Really? Had I ever left?

"How are you?" he said as he moved into the living room. I backed away from him, but still he stood only a foot away from me.

I shifted from one foot to the other. I tried to hold it together, I really did. But a couple of tears slipped down my cheeks. I wiped them away quickly with the back of my hand. I looked up at him, shook my head. My lip trembled.

"Baby," he said. He moved forward to pull me toward him, but I backed away.

"I can't."

"Corrine." And when I looked back up at him, I saw there were tears in his eyes too, his face, his beautiful face, a study in pain. "Baby, let me hold you."

I shook my head.

"Okay," he said, and settled on the couch. I sat down across from him on the loveseat. "You didn't hurt Mrs. Abernathy."

"It's too risky. All of it."

"Corrine, how can I make you see it like I see it?" He leaned forward, his elbows on his knees. "Listen, you know with auras? We're not all one color, right?"

I nodded.

"There're all kinds of colors in there. Some traits are positive, some negative. Some a mixture. But the overall auras themselves, they are just—"

"Beautiful."

"No." He shook his head. "No, they are *real*. They are life. Us. It's all we got."

"I don't know," I said.

"None of us have total control of anything. Not you, not

257

me, not anybody. And we're all taking risks, every day. Nothing's promised."

He came over to the loveseat then, sat down next to me. I let the tears fall down my cheeks, and I thought about what he said. He brushed his hand through my hair, and the hairs on the nape of my neck rose. It was like the first touch ever, so real to me, exaggerated for some reason.

"I'm taking a risk right now," he said. "But it's worth it."

"The risk of being electrocuted?" I said.

"No, Corrine, the risk that you won't love me back."

My heart swelled at the word, and I turned to him, my eyes meeting his. His beautiful face, his gorgeous eyes, watching me, seeing me, only me, the real me, searching me for what? An answer to the unasked question?

I swallowed against the dryness in my throat. And then I answered him. "I will." I wanted to sound brave, but it came out small.

He leaned forward, kissed my eyebrow, kissed away my tears, and then his lips were on mine, and we were kissing. His mouth against mine, our connection. Soft, gentle. Questioning. And I let it happen, and I wanted it, I wanted him.

"Touch me," he whispered. "Put your hands on me, Corrine."

"I can't," I said. And I pulled away, a promise unfulfilled. He sighed, raking his hand through his hair. After a few moments, he stood up; he left me something, a piece of paper, on the coffee table, but he left wordlessly.

It was more than just my heart knowing him. My heart loved him.

I took the paper upstairs to my room, unfolded it. It was a beautiful chalk drawing: an aura, a version of the one aura that had most populated his garage. His favorite subject. The colors were rich and jewel-toned, like the leaves of a Chicago autumn, maroon and orange, purple and gold, bright red and indigo. I flipped it over and he had signed it in bright blue ink.

My name and the date. I had been right. This was me.

My heart ached because I couldn't agree with this rendering, this beauty. I felt weak and paralyzed with the complications of this touch. I was not worthy of this power. Of Rennick's attention, his admiration. His love. He had used that word. *Love.*

I caught a glimpse of myself in the mirror. I made myself really look. When would I quit hating myself?

When would it be enough?

I thought of Paganini's *La Campanella*. The power of it. The strong start. Right from the first measure. So sure of itself. I thought of how Mrs. Smelser had first assigned me this piece on the violin back in sixth grade. As I had been waiting for the student ahead of me to finish, I sat down at the piano in the school hallway and began to play it, but different. Not allegro. I slowed it down. Ritard. Gave it more of a nocturne flair. Just playing around with it.

I had really lost myself in the playing of it. Transforming

it. And when I finally opened my eyes, I flushed at seeing Mrs. Smelser and her other student standing beside the piano. I had apologized, explaining to her that I knew that wasn't how it went, that I was just messing around. I insisted on playing it for her on my violin. The correct way.

"Corrine, don't forget this, though," she told me afterward, sticking her pencil into her messy silver curls. "Music isn't static. Don't ever apologize for making something beautiful. Don't be scared of what you alone can add."

I left Rennick's drawing on my desk and knelt down, looked under my bed, and took out my violin. I tuned each string, turning the knobs at the scroll just enough. I applied the rosin to my bow, tightened it to exactly the right amount of tension. I brought the violin to my chin, rested it in the familiar little nook of my collarbone.

I played *Canon in D*. My fingers remembered the notes, and my soul remembered the music. I played for a long time. Sousa. Mozart. Piece after piece. Not for any reason other than I needed to play. I needed to remember what it was like to be my real self.

I was still playing when I heard my cell phone ring for the fifth time in a row. I gave up, put my violin down on the bed, and reached for the phone. Mrs. Rawlings's phone number.

"Hello?"

"I'm at the hospital with Mia-Joy," Sarah said calmly. "It is not an emergency, but please come. We will explain."

She hung up. Obviously her phone call had been planned specifically so that I would not freak out, but what I was actually doing was freaking out. "Oh shit, oh shit, oh shit," I repeated, pacing around my bedroom before I could make a cohesive plan. And, of course, in the back of my head I had more guilt. Hadn't Rennick predicted this? The rip in her aura? And hadn't I just let it all go?

I didn't have a car. Mom and Dad turned off their cells at church. Biking out to the hospital would take at least an hour.

Rennick.

I called his cell and he answered on the first ring. He was in my driveway within ten minutes, and I was in his car, trying to explain the situation.

He clenched his jaw. "We'll get there in time," he said, driving faster than I'd ever seen. I knew what he meant. No matter what was going on, I could fix her. I could heal Mia-Joy.

My stomach clenched. How was I supposed to use this thing when I didn't have control, really?

I tried to remind myself of the mouse, of how sure I had seemed after that. It didn't help.

As soon as we walked into Mia-Joy's hospital room, I knew that this was a different kind of situation than I had expected. Tenuous in a different way. She sat in her hospital bed, and her face was pinched and angry, defiant. That famous Mia-Joy scowl. But if she looked scary, Mr. and Mrs. Rawlings looked downright terrifying.

"You want to tell your friend here? Or shall I?" Sarah barked at Mia-Joy.

Mia-Joy broke then. She looked out the window, and I saw the cover, the mask, dissolve for a second; I moved to go to her, but Mrs. Rawlings was already there, holding her in her arms. She pressed Mia-Joy to her ample bosom, rocked her back and forth. She whispered things to Mia-Joy, and I fought the tears back too. I had to look away because of what this did to me. It undid me. This show of kindness.

So powerful.

Mr. Rawlings got up and motioned for Rennick to leave with him. Rennick looked at me for the okay, and I nodded. Mrs. Rawlings finished comforting her daughter and turned toward me. "She wants to tell you about it herself."

Was she pregnant? Oh Jesus. What could it be?

"Sit down, Corrine."

"What is it, Mia-Joy?" I sat down in the chair across from the bed. She composed herself, applying some lip gloss and fixing her curls in her compact mirror before she began, all the while my heart thudding in my eardrums.

"I knew something was up," I told her. "I knew I should've—"

"Shut up, Corrine," she said. "This isn't about you. And you don't know anything. You're not the only one who can have a crisis in this world."

I sat back, wounded. But I deserved that, didn't I?

"Oh, stop it," Mia-Joy teased. "Just let me get it out, okay? It's embarrassing. It's . . . shitty, ya know?" She bit her lip for a second. "I work at it—seeming like I got my shit together. For you. For the kids at school. For everybody. But mostly for my own sorry self."

I waited.

"I like seeming like I'm in control, working it, ya know?"

"You do have it all together, Mia-Joy," I said. "I don't understand."

She took a deep breath. "Okay. Summer of seventh grade. It started then."

I made a face at her. "Seventh grade?"

"Yep. Puberty."

What did she mean? The year she got boobs? The year she became beautiful? "You handled that like nobody's business, Mia-Joy. Ugly duckling to a swan. Although I don't know if I'd go so far as ugly duck—"

"I spent half the year throwing up every meal I ate."

"You did?" I was flabbergasted. Mia-Joy? Bulimic?

"You didn't know about that, Corrine?"

"No. Jesus." I was speechless. Dumbfounded. "So since then . . . *now*?"

Mia-Joy blanched. "On and off." She was embarrassed, wouldn't meet my eyes. She knotted and unknotted a stray string from a curl of a blanket in her lap. She looked so small there, sitting in her mint-green hospital gown. It hurt her to tell me this, to show me this weakness. "With my diabetes, it makes things worse. Messes with my pump, the insulin, if I'm screwing up like that. Mom caught me. That's why I'm here. Last time, she told me she'd give me one more chance."

I couldn't believe what I was hearing. "Mia-Joy, you're too smart to—"

"Spare me the speech, Corrine, okay? I get it. I know. I know it doesn't make sense. I know that. But I know I need help. People aren't perfect."

"But you have to know how beautiful you are. Guys are like drooling—"

"I think . . ." Mia-Joy licked her lips and closed her eyes. This was hard for her to talk about. "I think I've learned that it's how I keep control. I feel things getting crazy and I—"

"But you're the one who always handles things so—"

"No. You can't put me up on that pedestal, Corrine. Not me." Then she eyed me, looked a little bit more like herself. "You can't put anybody on that pedestal, yourself included."

I nodded and stopped myself, realizing I was only going to sermonize. "So you're staying here?"

"For a while. Then outpatient therapy."

"You don't think I could help with the touch or anything?" I was surprised when the offer came tumbling out of my mouth.

But Mia-Joy just gave me a look. "Girl."

"I just thought maybe I could get you back to normal, back—"

"There is no normal!" she snapped.

"I'm sorry," I said.

"Corrine, if I've learned one thing about trying to be perfect, it's that it's not attainable. Nobody's normal. Nobody's perfect. Not you, not me. And none of us has it all worked out. We don't *get to perfect* and then that's it, ya know? It's about waking up each day and trying. Making better decisions."

I sat in silence with her then, trying to digest this. How did I never know this about Mia-Joy? How had I been so oblivious? She had needed me, and I had never even known.

"Mia-Joy, you're beautiful. Everyone thinks so. You can't seriously think you are too—"

"Sometimes ... sometimes ..." I saw the mask lift from her face again. I got up, sat on the edge of her bed. I hugged her. "Sometimes I know," she said quietly.

"Can I help?" I said. "Let me help somehow."

But Mia-Joy had her own agenda. "Yes, you can. Let's talk about you."

"Mia-Joy, no, I didn't come here to—"

"Corrine, you're lost right now."

"Gee, thanks."

"No, listen. I know you. You miss how you used to be in Chicago. Confident. Things were all black-and-white, cut-and-dry."

She was right. How could she know this? And why were we talking about me? "How do you—"

"You weren't perfect there either, Corrine. You just like to think you were."

"Mia-Joy, I–"

"That asshole, what was his name? The rich kid you brought down for Mardi Gras last year?"

"Cody?"

"Cody. Arrogant rich kid. What had he said about your violin playing? *Cute.*" She made a gagging sound at the thought.

"I can't believe you are going to–"

"Believe it. I'm just trying to snap you back into reality, Corrine."

"Consider myself snapped," I retorted.

"He might hurt you," she said.

"Cody?"

"No. Rennick." She gave me her know-it-all look again, and I liked it, even though what she was saying was hitting a little too close to home. "He might hurt you. You might hurt him. But you have to let somebody in finally, don't ya, Corrine? I mean, you need to live. Sophie would want that."

"I am living."

"No. Not really." Mia-Joy rolled her eyes. "You hold everything and everyone at arm's length if you can't completely control it. People. The touch. Definitely that boy."

Was I doing that? "Mia-Joy, I'm not–"

But she was still going. Really going now. "Truthfully, you are worse off than me. You should be sitting in this bed, having all these old bald men asking you, 'And how does that make you feeeeeel?'"

"Mia-Joy!"

"Just listen, Corrine. Life is messy. If it's good, it's really messy. I think you sometimes forget that. Life before Sophie. After Sophie. You idealize it all. And this touch, this blessing you have, it's just making it worse. Nothing's easy. Clean. Black-and-white. It doesn't work that way."

I pursed my lips, tried to blurt out some zingy comeback. But nothing came. Because she was right.

"Just give in to the flucking chaos that is life, Corrine," Mia-Joy told me. She was really on her high horse. But I could see it there in her face that she was sincere too. "Have some fun." She smirked now.

"Jesus, you've been spending too much time with the shrinks already." I gave her a smirk right back.

And I hugged her, hugged her close to me, and she shuddered and let out a few tears, and it seemed so out of place, so un-Mia-Joy-like. I promised myself that I would be more present for her. I had been so stupid for never once thinking *she* might need *me*.

16

I called my mom and checked in, and Rennick said that he wanted to take me home for lunch. Lila and Dodge were antiquing up north, and Rennick turned a little flushed when he said we could be alone.

We talked about Mia-Joy on the way over to his house. He explained how Mr. and Mrs. Rawlings blamed themselves, how he blamed himself for not speaking up about the rip in the aura. I took my part of the blame too.

"I think she's going to be fine now, though," I told him.

"Yeah? And what if she hadn't been?" He eyed me from the driver's side.

"I don't know," I told him. "I don't know yet."

"I don't think you need to be afraid of it." He said this quietly, and he reached his hand over toward me, laid it on the seat between us. An invitation. "Either way, Corrine, I am here."

I thought about all the advice and expounding Mia-Joy had just given me in her hospital room, and I realized that it had affected me.

I didn't know exactly why or how, but it had me thinking. And, yes, I was scared. But I could move on, push forward. Rennick and me. The touch. They were both scary. They were both out of my control, but they were not tied to each other. They didn't have to be.

I had no warning signs now.

I reached across the seat of the Jeep and grabbed Rennick's hand. He clasped onto mine tightly and let out a sigh, as if he had been waiting for this. Just this. Only this. Could he really want me, just me? With or without the indigo touch? And if so, did I deserve it? After everything? After Sophie?

"Thank you," I said, and leaned my head on his shoulder.

"For what?"

"Kindness."

We pulled into the driveway, and he steered us back toward his garage. His hand never left mine, and I trailed behind him. He opened the old sliding barnlike doors, and there they were. His paintings. Auras, dozens of them. Beautiful combinations of colors, a kaleidoscope of stripes melting into hazy fogs, pastel clouds meeting a storm of jewel tones. There were many auras here, all beautiful in their own way, but I saw the one everywhere—mine—repeated in many different perspectives.

As I spun around, Rennick let my hand go finally, and there was one painting my eyes were repeatedly drawn to, the only one of its kind. It was a dark and haunting mixture of blues and reds. And even as I was asking the question, I knew the answer. "Whose?"

"Mine. Before I met you."

I processed this. "So auras are in flux." I realized that this only made sense, but I had never really thought about it.

"Don't sound so surprised. Life is flux. Life is change."

"And whose aura is the one?" I asked. "Painted and repainted?"

"You know it's yours," he said, and wrapped his arms around my waist.

"Exactly what changed in your aura when you met me?" I asked, except his lips were on my shoulder now, running up and down my neck, his hands pressing on the small of my back. "Mmmm," I moaned.

"Hope is in there now. Pink," he murmured. "Purple," he added, and he picked me up then, just swept me up with one arm under my legs and walked us toward the sofa in the back corner. He gently laid me down.

"Purple," I repeated, my whole body nearly about to explode. Purple. Love. Did Rennick really love me? Hadn't he just about said as much? Why did my mind act so surprised? My heart already knew this. My heart had known it for a long time.

Rennick braced himself above me, and he hovered there, kissing my collarbone, his lips brushing that spot under my ear. "Corrine," he murmured, his eyelashes tickling my earlobe.

"Purple?" I asked again, teasing.

"Listen." He smiled. "I wouldn't be too cocky here. Your aura has purple in it as well." The flush rose in my cheeks. Rennick sat up and pulled his T-shirt over his head. I sat up, breathless, my heart pounding.

I kissed him, and he kissed me back deeply. I tasted his lips, his stubbly chin, his jaw, his ear. "I want to put my hands on you," I whispered.

And he shivered against me. "Corrine, I–" He pulled away a little bit. But I wouldn't let him. I pushed him back onto the sofa and lay on top of him, pressing my body into him, kissing him, letting him know I wanted this.

I sat up and picked up his left hand. I kissed his roughened palm. I placed his hand over my heart, and then I used my fingers to trace every muscle on his torso, his ribs, his abs, his delicious abs. Our eyes locked. I pressed my palms flat on his chest and kissed his neck, his Adam's apple, ran my hands through that hair. Kissed those ridiculous eyelashes. He pulled me to him and sat up. He repositioned me in his lap, and I crossed my legs around him.

His hands were on my back, under my tank top, palms flat to my body, and we were so close, so close, and he pulled me to him, closer, closer, and it felt so good, I could hardly contain myself. I threw my head back, sighed, and his lips were on my neck again.

I reached down to pull off my tank, and Rennick froze. "Corrine," he said, "we don't have–"

"I want to," I said, and I meant it. "I trust you. Us. This moment."

His face twisted up, like he was going to protest. He raked a hand through his hair. He pulled me close, kissed me hard. But then he pushed me away. "Corrine, wait."

"Rennick, I want to–"

He traced his fingers over my lips then, onto my cheek, my chin. "I love your chin. That little point." He kissed me again softly. Sighed. Pulled away.

"What is it?" I asked.

"It's just everything. Us. It doesn't have to be such a grand gesture. Huge decision. It's not like either we can't touch at all or we completely *do it*. I mean, don't get me wrong, I want...I would *love* to ..." He raked his hand through his hair again.

And I resisted the urge to be hurt by this, to slink inward. I tried to really hear him.

"I mean, it doesn't have to be all or nothing. I want you, Corrine. But I want you *always*...a million yeses, every day. Forever." He swallowed hard, and I could see that he was scared of how honest he was being. "It doesn't have to be one huge yes. It can be us. Together. Over and over. Every day. I want that. Not just one big decision to prove something."

I thought I understood what he was saying.

I nodded, tried to internalize this. I kind of got it. And I thought of Mia-Joy. It's not like we *get to perfect* and then we're done. Isn't that what she had said?

I could do this. I believed in the power of decision. And I could decide yes to Rennick, over and over. Again and again. *A million yeses.* I liked that. My heart swelled and floated when I stepped out of my own insecurities enough to really hear what he was professing to me.

Him and me. Every day. Forever.

Inside my head I was listening to Beethoven's *Romance in F Major.* The flurry of crescendoing excitement. I looked at the guy in front of me. The well of emotion in his eyes. The sweet, heartbreaking wrinkle of concern between them. "Thank you," I said, wanting to kiss that sweet, beautiful spot on Rennick's front teeth, right where they overlapped. My Rennick. We held each other's gaze then for a long moment and he changed then. Became gentler, slower, more in charge, made us savor it. Poco a poco.

And later when he held me close to him, his arms wrapped around me, I pressed my palms to his face, brought his lips to mine. It was still Beethoven in my head, but now *Ode to Joy.*

"I love you, Rennick."

His eyes softened then. He buried his face in my neck, and he whispered it. Dolce. "I love you too, Corrine."

That night, as I lay in my own bed, I was back in that place, where I felt so open to possibility. To everything. To meanings.

Nobody tells you that this is what growing up is.

I mean, Rennick was right in everything he had to say to me, and Mia-Joy was right too. But they both were still only circling the target.

Nobody tells you that this is what growing up is, learning that you actually control very little in your life. Learning that you can't force your hand. Learning that you are not in charge. Learning that you have to risk, take chances, walk that thin, thin line. Moderation. Faith.

These are difficult things for a person like me. It goes hand in hand with humility.

When I came home from Rennick's, Mom and I had talked about Mia-Joy, and she asked me if I had tried to heal her at all. If I thought that was possible.

"I think," I told her, "that sometimes there are things, certain important things, that you can only fix by digging down deep into yourself, finding that faith. Nobody can give you that. You have to find that on your own."

Mom had nodded, and the way she sucked in breath and absolutely forced herself not to relate everything back to my situation, well, it was written all over her minister's face. And there was something else written there. Pride. Love.

Now, watching the shadows of the pear tree dance on my bedroom wall, listening to the cicadas sing their nightly song, I let myself consider that there was nobody to blame for Sophie's death. I considered that I might never know the whys of it. The hows. And I had to make my peace with that, inside. This is what growing up was. Understanding that nothing real has a glossy, shiny sheen to it. Nothing perfect lasts. And we are all left with this reality eventually.

I had to give it up and move forward. This seemed scary and exhilarating. And I felt naked going out into the world without that insulation. Because although Rennick was close to understanding how I was using Sophie's death to push others away, he didn't understand one part of it. Giving up that insulation, that cushion of guilt, meant facing there was no more Sophie. Letting her go.

No Sophie graduating from high school. No Sophie learning to put on makeup. No Sophie at my wedding. No letters from Sophie when I went away to college. No more ridiculous pantomime shows performed by Sophie and her buddy Mitchy. No more checking under her bed for spiders while she played with seventeen earthworms housed in a jam jar by her bed.

No more Sophie. Whether I saved others with the touch or not.

No more Sophie. And that insulation had been a barrier,

something to focus on rather than staring that fact in the face.

I tiptoed out of my bedroom into Sophie's old room. I wanted to look at her pictures. I wanted to think of her, just how she was. But when I got there, I saw that Mom was already sitting on the floor, the album in her lap, a glass of wine in her hand. I settled down next to her, folded my feet under me.

"I miss her," I said.

Mom nodded, sniffled, took a sip of her wine. I slipped my hand into hers and tried to ignore her tears. I let her have this moment. I heard Dad clear his throat from the doorway. I got up and hugged my father. My mother joined in the fold, and the three of us held on to each other. Broken, imperfect. But ours. Dear. Irreplaceable. Real.

I eyed Sophie's second-grade photograph, the open album on the floor. Her gap-toothed smile. I felt her there, right then, with us.

Dad pulled away first. "So are you going to move forward with this thing?"

"I think so. Maybe," I told him. "I might want to interview a few of the scientists. See about some help. Take it slower." *A million little yeses,* I reminded myself.

17

I was listening to Beethoven cranked up high on my iPad, and I knew that I was sketching Rennick's face, I knew that. But I was in that zone. I wasn't really thinking about it. The square jaw, the little scar in his eyebrow, the lashes over those dark blue eyes.

It took me a while to get the *fwoof* of his hair lifting off of his forehead, but I did it, and then I was finished with the pencil sketch. I began to add some color. My mind was back at Rennick's garage, though: the feel of his skin beneath my hands, his lips on my collarbone.

At the same moment that Mom came bursting into my bedroom, I realized what I was doing and dropped my pastel.

"What in the world?" I said, yanking the earbuds out of my ears. I could see in Mom's face that something was very wrong.

"It's Rennick!" I screamed, taking one last look at my sketch. His eyes were not right; they were flat, unseeing, but it wasn't just that. I had colored his face, shadowed it, with white and with blue. He looked ... gone.

Lifeless.

"Tell me in the car."

Mom flew, going well above the speed limit, out to the wharf, to Crescent Charters. As soon as we pulled into the gravel parking lot, I jumped out of the car before it had even stopped. I could see the knot of people standing on the small dock, their heads bent in reverence, their shoulders slumped, their voices silent.

I ran. I had to get there. I had that feeling again that I could see these things, and they registered, yet they were so very far away. I heard the slapping of my running feet against the wet boards of the dock, and that brought me back into myself a little, but when I saw his face, ashen white, with blue eyelids, his chest not rising or falling, that shocked me back into myself in a moment, in a flash. In that second, my world focused into a pinpoint on those beautiful eyelashes, holding drops of seawater.

My mother had explained it on the way to the wharf. He had been fishing. Dodge had been short of breath, but they had become stuck in the weeds, the cattails, out near the swampy edge of Egret Inlet. Rennick got nervous, surely thinking of another heart attack for Dodge. He dove in to dig out the propeller from the seaweed or whatever, instead of just rowing. Dodge didn't know how it happened. But Bouncer began acting weird, whining as they waited in the boat, his tail between his legs.

And Rennick never came back up.

He had drowned. My Rennick. He was gone. How long had he been without a breath? He would not be that fucking cricket. Never.

I watched the paramedics do their rescue breathing, the pressure on his chest. How long had they been at it? Were they still hopeful? I gave them five seconds. Six.

The sharp jut of his Adam's apple. The black-oil color of his hair. The unseeing eyes. I couldn't wait any longer.

I pushed through them. Risks. Guilt. Perfection. Control. None of it mattered. Only he mattered. Some things had to be charged at, saved, worked for, again and again, if need be.

All this talk, all these issues, none of it really mattered. Because Rennick was gone, and I had this power. A=B.

I knelt down next to his body, spied Dodge's face above me filled with panic. Bouncer was at my heels, nudging me closer to Rennick with his snout. Mom had joined us, but these things didn't matter. I only had to think his name, all he had come to mean to me, all that he was, and there it was. The indigo lens in front of my vision. The crackling spark of life inside my ribs. Like an explosion of heat from the heart of me.

I held on to his hands, both of them in mine. They were

cold, so cold. I placed them over my heart, held them against me with my palms. And I couldn't help it, I was bawling.

He had believed in me when I hadn't even believed in myself. He had saved me.

"Please, please. Rennick, please," I said between gasps.

And then it was there at its height, plateaued and waiting for direction. And I let it go, I let it move freely, surging and charging into my beloved Rennick.

And in that moment, time stopped. It's like I was there, but I wasn't.

I hold Sophie's body in my lap, cupping her face in my hands, the blue surges through me, in her. It brings her back. I saved her, I think. Here it is. I remember it now. The part I could never quite account for. The lost time. "I got you, Sophie. I got you."

She smiles at me, shivers. "You saved me," she says, lisping her s *through that gap in her teeth.*

"Did I?" I say, flummoxed, holding on to her face. I am exhausted, and we lie back on the rocks. Her eyes close as she lays her head on my chest.

I awake to her teeth chattering along with mine. It's darker, colder. And I see that Sophie is pale again. Why had we not left? Walked back? I remember the surge of electricity through me, the exhaustion.

Sophie's eyes roll back in her head then, her body jerks. Not again! But then things change, the power pricks back up inside me, and I reach for her, to cup her face again, to fix her.

But the wrong thing happens. The white light explodes around me, in me.

The lightning.

One lone bolt of lightning emerges from the atmosphere around us, blinding us, a terrifying and powerful glow around us, bathing us in current, jolting us, electrifying us. I absorb it and I don't. Not enough. Sophie doesn't recover.

I smell the ozone in the air. The crisp Lake Michigan air. It is just a storm.

I saved her. Lightning killed her.

I woke back up to where I was now. Here in my life without Sophie. Holding Rennick's hands to my heart. The physio-electric life churned through me, out of me, into Rennick. I shuddered with exhaustion.

For all my power: I could heal, I could fix Lila Twopenny, I could maybe save Rennick, but I still wasn't *all-powerful*. I still was not in charge. I couldn't fix Mia-Joy. I couldn't control lightning. I couldn't do a lot of things.

It was good and it was bad. I was just a human Leyden jar.

"Please," I said out loud, and I could feel the surges rack my shoulders, press against my ribs, exit my hands.

And then I snapped my eyes open because I could feel the current change, plunge from deeper inside of me. This was when I would normally stop, what I had come to recognize as the time to let go. But Rennick was not back yet. I couldn't give up.

It pulled from inside me, deeper in my core, and I pushed it, willed it out of me.

Rennick coughed once. And then he was still. I wanted to pull back, but I couldn't. Rennick needed me. Needed the blue.

I had it. He needed it. I gave it all.

And then it went black.

18

I watched Rennick gasp, cough, and wretch. Beautiful, gorgeous, life-affirming coughs. He vomited water and green stuff. He doubled over and coughed some more, and my heart swelled. Rennick. Alive. He turned on his side and curled his knees to his chest, coughed again.

By now I realized that I was watching this from an odd angle. I was above him, far above him. I could see him, but I couldn't hear the noise that his coughs made. I reached out to him, but I could not see my own arm. I was air. I was wind. I was space. I was nothing and everything. I somehow hovered above it all, outside of myself.

This alarmed me, but not much, because Rennick was okay. He sat up now, the scary pallor of his face only a memory.

He turned his attention to the small knot of people to his left. They were surrounding someone. Rennick got to his feet quickly, swayed, then pushed his way into the center.

It was me. *I* was down there, lying on the dock, and it was my turn to be ashen. Empty. I had used myself up. Just as I had promised not to do. And if I had been careless before with my power—arrogant, even—well, I was so sorry now. I struggled against nothing and everything trying to get myself back into my body, back down there, back with Rennick.

When I had so much and so many had so little, I should be hanging on to my life, tooth and nail. I realized this now.

One of the paramedics performed rescue breathing on my body, but Rennick pushed him aside, and the medic let him. Did the medic think it was useless? I watched Rennick in a panicked state. He cleared my airway. He pressed on my lifeless body. It was so white. And it looked so small from up here. Again I tried to push myself nearer, but... nothing. If anything, I floated farther away, up higher.

I struggled more from my vantage point to move, to get there. But it was all in vain, because I was nothing. I was gone from myself.

Rennick pinched my nose, breathed into my mouth. A sad and desperate last kiss. I struggled, but it was useless. Then he began to press on my chest, three even compressions just like they teach you in CPR class. But something changed. I could feel them, the pressure on my sternum, on my rib cage, right there, right at the source of all of this. And with the pressure came the spark.

My vision tunneled and it all turned indigo, a blinding indigo flash, and then all was silent. For what seemed like a very long time. All I knew was the indigo. I was surrounded by it, bathing in it, tasting it, hearing only it.

Then it was his face, just his face so close to mine. And I wondered, was this heaven? But then, no, I saw salt water dripping from his hair, like it was happening in slow motion. A bead dropped from his forelock onto his eyelashes, then onto my face.

The first breath burned hot in my throat. He moved his mouth, but I couldn't hear him yet. He smiled that smile. I reached up a shaking hand, and with one finger I touched that spot, those teeth, that overlap, and he was saying something over and over. And gradually a din, a little rustle of sound, then his voice. And it was in my ear. "Don't leave me. Don't leave me."

I threw my arms around his neck, pulled myself up to him, and he held me against him, cradled me in his arms, in his lap.

After a long time, I opened my eyes, and he pulled back to look at me, the sun glinting off of his hair. A crash of thunder jarred me back into myself.

"I used myself up," I said.

"I know." He didn't seem mad, didn't seem anything but

relieved. He kissed the tip of my chin, each of my eyelids, my nose.

"Guess I'll have to keep you around." My voice was a scratchy whisper. "You're getting good at this lifesaving thing," I said.

He laughed then, a glorious, booming sound. And when he kissed me, the sky broke into another boom of thunder, and rain began to sheet down on us, the sun still high in the sky.

"Thank you," I whispered.

19

"I have a present for you," Rennick said, holding out his hand as we stood by Sophie's headstone. In his palm was a delicate silver chain, but instead of a charm there was the most magnificent rock, a tiny polished yet uncarved blue stone, sparkling in the September Chicago sun.

"Rennick–" I said, my heart fluttering in my chest.

"I found it on the shore of Pontchartrain. That Fourth of July. It's quartz." He smiled. I picked it up and admired the way the sunlight hit the surface of the rock.

"It's the most perfect color." It was just this side of purple, just that side of blue. Indigo. I rolled it around in my fingers. "Thank you." And I thought about something. "What does indigo in an aura mean?"

"We don't want to inflate your ego or anything," Rennick joked. "Wisdom," he said, eyeing me. "Bravery."

I flushed. I couldn't hear this about myself. "Could you

put it on me?" His fingers graced that spot on the back of my neck and I shivered. "When we first met, you said you knew I was stubborn and generous . . . kind. Which color of the aura goes with those?"

"I didn't know any of that from your aura," Rennick said, finishing with the necklace.

"No?"

"That's just from watching you, seeing how you operate." He smiled, squinted at me playfully. I thought of that first day I met him, that first time I looked in those eyes. The day at the Crawdaddy Shack, the sun shining along with the rain. And then again that day on the dock, when we saved each other.

I saw now that this was what life was. I looked down at Sophie's granite headstone. And I looked up again at Rennick. The sun along with the rain.

And it made me think of what Mom had said when I told her and Dad about the lightning.

"It's the price we pay for love, honey. It hurts this much because we love so much," she had told me, holding on to my hand. "We are not in control of things. Ever. We only have that illusion. The death of a loved one shatters that."

The lightning had killed Sophie, stopped her heart, and shattered me. There had been no other signs, no burns, nothing on Sophie's body, but that was how lightning worked. It was haphazard. Random. Messy. Like so many things in life.

In a way, it seemed worse, not better, to know that I had had nothing to do with it. Worse because it was just so arbitrary. Unpredictable.

But I had nodded at Mom. "The thing we learn, though, is that we still have to keep going. Even though it could happen again. To me. To someone else."

Mom added, "We love anyway. Even with death around every corner. That's hope. That's faith."

And wasn't that the biggest decision of them all? Behind everything in life? Wrapped up in every step of our journey? Every chance we took? Faith. The question and the answer.

A million yeses.

I fingered the blue stone. "Thank you," I told Rennick, feeling the blush rise in my neck. "For the necklace, for visiting Sophie's grave with me, for so many things."

"You're welcome," he said, and he tipped my chin toward him.

I stood on my tiptoes, kissed him on the lips. He smiled. And the look on his face, it was . . . something. The tender, hopeful gaze of his eyes. What was it? Pride?

And in that instant, I knew. It was love.

I pressed my face into the hollow of his collarbone and inhaled his laundry-fresh scent. *So this is what it feels like.*

I bent down on my knees then, did what I came here to do. I said a prayer for Sophie, for her soul, for where she was; to God, or to that power greater than us, than me, than the touch, greater even than lightning. "I love you, Sophie," I said.

I opened my case, withdrew my violin in the chilly September sun. I stood up and played for Sophie, Mozart's *Laudate Dominum*, which I couldn't bring myself to play at her funeral. It spoke of love and loss, sadness and grief, but also hope and remembrance. Tranquillo. I played it all, my eyes closed. And I felt it all, with every note, with every push and pull of my bow, the symphony of emotions I held so close for Sophie, for all she meant to me, for all I wanted to tell her.

And when I finished, I opened my eyes, and I saw Rennick, his eyes closed too. He was feeling too. He knew what it all meant. He didn't live only on the surface.

"It's your voice," he said. "That violin is your voice."

I nodded. Because for so long, I had been silent. And I had so much to say. To everyone. To Sophie.

I sat on the grass, tracing Sophie's name on her simple marble headstone. I spoke to her in my mind, told her I was sorry, told her I loved her, told her goodbye. I pictured her then, not on the rocks of that beach, but on Christmas morning, her curls a mess. Learning to ride her bike without training wheels. The elation on her face when she succeeded. Sophie living. Sophie jumping in. Sophie being happy.

This was what I held on to. *It was just a storm.*

And when I was ready, Rennick stuck out his hand to help me up from the ground, and I grabbed it, my palm thrust against his. And there it was again, that human touch, that spark, that simple kindness, a helping hand when you really needed one.

Just like I had needed it so long ago, when Rennick first placed the crawdad in my palm. He didn't have to care. He could have ignored my colors. He could have ignored me. He could have given up on hope. Given up on faith in the face of so many everyday deaths: apathy, fear, pride.

Sometimes that touch, that squeeze of a hand, that arm around the shoulders, it tells us that we are not in this alone. And for me, Rennick made all the difference.

We were in this together. I knew that.

We'd figure out what to do with the burning coil beneath my ribs, that power, always ready, always there. I would use it, I knew that, to help others. One day at a time. There was no big master plan that needed to be made. Not just one decision. But rather a million little decisions made each day, over and over. A million yeses.

This was my life. In flux. Always. The aura of my life being painted and repainted daily, unfolding itself as a thing of beauty in the process. With me working and learning and hoping, so that each stroke, each color, each decision might add a little more beauty, a little more peace, a little more hope. Adding up to a piece of wonder.

I took in a deep breath of the cool autumn air and held it there in my lungs.

The possibilities now seemed endless.

And I was caught off guard by my optimism, here, in the

moment. How impossible it had seemed such a short time ago, to be on the other side of the paralyzing grief of losing my sister.

But here I was. Here *we* were. It wasn't the size of the circle; it was who was in it.

And that made all the difference.

ACKNOWLEDGMENTS

So many thanks to those who've made such a big difference to me as a writer and to this story: Chuck and Judy Simonich, Caryn Wiseman, Chelsea Eberly, Suzy Capozzi, and the entire team at Random House Books for Young Readers.

To my circle–my colorful, lively, brilliant circle–I love you all so dearly. Thank you for your constant humor and inspiration: Cooper, Clarke, Maddie, Alex, Rebecca, Hannah, Jonah, Jacob, Henry, and, of course, Jack, Maia, and Zoe.

Last but not least, for Greg, a million yeses.

ABOUT THE AUTHOR

GINA LINKO has a graduate degree in creative writing from DePaul University and lives outside Chicago with her husband and three children. She teaches college English part-time, but her real passion is sitting down to an empty screen and asking herself, "What if...?"